"Please! Help me!"

Miranda couldn't tell if it was a man, woman or child. The voice sounded less than human, almost animal. She strained her ears to filter the sounds of the nighttime wilderness. Unzipping her sleeping bag, she slowly got to her feet. In the darkness, the long-remembered contours of the trail came back to her, and she stepped forward, half-crouched, the hatchet ready.

On the third step, something slid beneath her foot. There was the sound of metal on stone, and she felt herself tumbling. The river was below her. She could hear it, almost taste the spray of water. Her hands grasped a tree limb and she clung until she heard the sickening sound of the limb tearing. She felt her body spin into the darkness.

ABOUT THE AUTHOR

Caroline Burnes visited the North Carolina mountains as a young girl with her family. She has returned often, and she harbors the dream of one day walking the entire Appalachian Trail. The inspiration for *Deadly Currents* came from her work as a journalist and her interest in preserving and protecting the environment. When she isn't at the computer hatching a new plot, she likes to hike in the Alabama woods with her three dogs, Ouzo, Corky and Giblet.

Books by Caroline Burnes

HARLEQUIN INTRIGUE

86–A DEADLY BREED
100–MEASURE OF DECEIT
115–PHANTOM FILLY
134–FEAR FAMILIAR
154–THE JAGUAR'S EYE

Deadly Currents

Caroline Burnes

DEADLY CURRENTS

Harlequin Books

TORONTO • NEW YORK • LONDON
AMSTERDAM • PARIS • SYDNEY • HAMBURG

For Debby Porter Pruett, who never lost faith

Harlequin Intrigue edition published May 1992

ISBN 0-373-22186-X

DEADLY CURRENTS

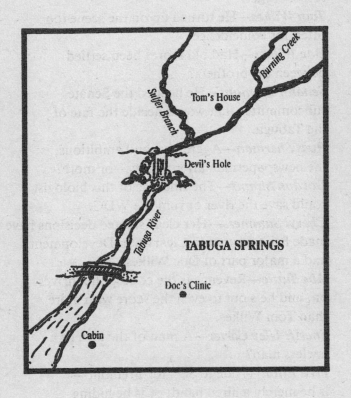

Burning Creek

Sulfer Branch

Tom's House

Devil's Hole

Tabuga River

TABUGA SPRINGS

Doc's Clinic

Cabin

CAST OF CHARACTERS

Miranda Conner—She had a past she'd rather forget.

Tom Wilkes—He turned up on the scene too often for coincidence.

Doc Wilkes—Had old scores been settled between the brothers?

Senator Fremont—He headed the Senate subcommittee that would decide the fate of the Tabuga.

Russ Sherman—Aggressive and ambitious, is the newspaperman after a story—or more?

Gordon Simms—The findings of this biologist could save the river or ruin the WDC.

Cheryl Summers—Her clear-sighted decisions have made her a partner in Clearwater Development and a major part of Doc Wilkes's life.

Abe Tuttle—Revenge is the concept he thrives on, and he's out to even the score with more than Tom Wilkes.

Sheriff Uley Carter—A man of the law, or a lawless man?

Fred Elton—Aide to Senator Fremont—is he merely a hired hand, or is he hiding a deeper involvement?

Prologue

The sound of the typewriter split the early-morning quiet. Each letter was pecked out with care. At times, when his fingers hunted futilely on the unfamiliar board, the writer swore silently.

Please accept these funds to outfit an expedition in the Wilderness Defense Fund's fight against development of the Tabuga River. The express intent of this donation is to fund a fact-finding/public-relations trip that will shed new light on the proposed dam project. The money is given with stipulations. Miranda Conner, whose work I greatly admire, will head the expedition. Fred Elton, aide to Sen. Harry Fremont, and two journalists, Russ Sherman and Cynthia Wickham, will also be included, along with a biologist who will study the river. I am certain the WDC will make the most of this opportunity to inform the public about the Tabuga. Although I prefer to remain anonymous, I am a concerned citizen.

The note was pulled from the typewriter and wrapped around a neat stack of hundred-dollar bills. The package was inserted into an envelope with the address of the Wilderness Defense Center typed on a label on the front.

Staples secured the package, and the man who'd written the note hurried out into the warm sunshine to the nearest mail drop. The thud of the package hitting the bottom of the mailbox brought a smile to the man's face. He crossed the busy street and went straight to a pay telephone.

"It's done," he said as soon as someone answered.

"Yes, I'm certain that it can't be traced back to Clearwater Development. I've been waiting years for this, do you think I'm foolish enough to risk it all with a careless mistake?"

His hands rubbed the stubble along his chin. "Yes, I'm in Washington, but I'll be leaving soon. I can't take much more of this city. Okay. I'll see you then."

He hung up, looked around, then darted down the street and flagged a cab.

"THE WDC SHOULD RECEIVE the funds soon," Tom Wilkes said as his dark eyes swept the small room. "I'm glad you both agreed with me that it was the right thing to do. I can see the benefits of development, but personally I hate the idea of damming the river."

"We can't let personal feelings hold back an entire community," Doc Wilkes noted. There was a spark of sadness in brown eyes that were almost identical to his brother's.

"We'll keep Clearwater Development's name a secret until the WDC report is in, and I think it's important not to have any association between Wild Horse Designs and the development company. They are, after all, completely separate entities." Tom looked at the other two people in the room. "You both know the proposal to dam the Tabuga is going to stir up volatile emotions."

"Calling in the WDC to explore the matter was a great idea," Cheryl Summers said as she stood and brushed her red curls off her hot forehead. "Just remember, though, some people might interpret this 'environmental' concern as a way to salve your conscience. There's also the fact that by stalling development today, you can make a slaughter instead of a mere killing when the resort is finally developed." She arched her eyebrows, daring his answer.

Tom's dark eyes flashed, but his mouth turned up in a grin. "People do have a way of interpreting things, don't they? Let them think the worst. The money has already been sent to the WDC, and we're committed to this course of action."

"Yes, everything depends on how well the WDC does its job," Cheryl said.

Chapter One

Dusk was falling softly over the mountains as Miranda Conner slowed her long strides and finally stopped. Before her the mighty Tabuga River roared through a narrow pass. The sound was almost deafening. She shifted her heavy backpack slightly to relieve the pressure, but she didn't turn away from the sight of the swirling white water that foamed and leapt almost at her feet.

She wiped a single drop of moisture from her face. That it came from her eye and not the river didn't matter. No one was within miles. She could cry if she wished. She could yell and scream and rage, and no one would ever hear her.

She could also turn back.

She'd thought of that option often as she'd hiked deeper and deeper into the North Carolina Tabuga wilderness of the Appalachian Mountains. She could turn back and send someone else to scout and prepare the trail. She could justify such a retreat by saying her work in Washington would suffer from her absence. There were a million good reasons to turn away from the icy waters of the river and the mountain range that spawned them.

Instead, she sat down on a flat rock beside the water. The Tabuga was a living presence as it spun before her, spiraling down to the foothills, meadows and, finally, the cities. The mountain water was pure, untainted by pollution. In many ways she'd been like the Tabuga when she had come to the river nearly fifteen years before. But the river remained innocent. She had not.

She scooped a handful of the crystal water and drank. Cold trickles teased the corners of her mouth and fell on her T-shirt. On the banks of the river, she'd tested her courage and her integrity. She'd also learned the art of wilderness survival—in preparation for "a better world." The familiar phrase brought a bitter smile to her face. How could she have failed to realize what it meant to her friends? The past was a minefield of dangerous memories and easy slogans. She had held it at bay for a long time. It could wait a little longer—until the Tabuga was safe.

It was the present that mattered. With that thought firmly in mind she hefted her backpack. She'd come back to the Tabuga to plan a rafting expedition for the Wilderness Defense Center. The WDC had received an anonymous gift, a generous cash gift in fact, to fund the expedition. A tingle of unease made her shiver, suddenly aware that the sun's warmth had abandoned the day. She buttoned her flannel shirt against a few wild drops of spray thrown by the river. A crackle in the underbrush made her jump. She froze instinctively, only her eyes searching the surrounding woods. The uneasy sensation that she was being followed had dogged her since she'd entered the wilderness.

She brought her hand to her side, feeling for the handle of her camp knife. A poor weapon to be sure, but when had she ever needed a weapon on the Tabuga? Maybe a shield for her heart, but not a knife.

At last her eyes picked up movement behind a copse of yellow beeches. She met the bold gaze of a red squirrel eye to eye. With an angry bark the squirrel flicked his tail and vanished. Miranda's grip on the knife loosened and she smiled. So, her nerves were shot by past history and an anonymous donor. It was a fine state of events. And like all good daughters, she could blame her mother for part of it, she thought wryly.

Her mother had taught her that there was no such thing as a free lunch. Anonymous donors made her uneasy. The trouble was that she wasn't in a position to ask too many questions about the gift horse that had made the upcoming tour-de-force public-relations trip possible.

Instead of asking questions, she had to learn to think more positively—i.e., her misgivings were sheer fancy, a sort of silly superstitious belief that good things didn't come wrapped in a secret.

Anticipation for the rapidly approaching trip brought a smile to her face, and the dimple in her left cheek winked. In two weeks she'd be back on the river with a couple of news reporters, a scientist and a federal employee. Her job, and she'd accepted it with eagerness, was to show the river as the last existing branch of the once-wild-and-scenic river system. Her assignment was to help thwart plans to dam and develop the river. With her knowledge of the Tabuga's history, she could make them see how vital the natural waterway was! She had to!

Gauging the sky, she knew she had to hurry if she was to get to Three Rock Split before dark. That would be the first campsite for her expedition, and she wanted to be certain that it was secure. Years ago the rocks had combined to form a natural shelter from the wind. An extra bonus was the spectacular view. The trail was steep, shooting up from the river at nearly a seventy-degree angle. The hike would make her guests appreciate camp all the more, she thought with a chuckle. She only had to check the campsite and make sure it was as perfect as she remembered.

She stepped back onto the trail and set off. The heavy foliage seemed to drink the sunlight. She was left with only a dim, murky illumination that was eroding with each passing moment. Dusk in the mountains was a time when a camper recognized what it meant to be completely alone. The darkness came fringed with a ruffle of melancholy, but Miranda knew it was just the whispers of the past teasing her. The night was special, a time for appreciating the nocturnal side of nature. A time for...

Beneath the roar of the water she heard another sound. Her heart drummed inside her chest, and she stopped to listen. There was nothing but the water, a symphony of river music.

She started forward again. The sound had come from the river. Or from her own head. At that thought the dimple came briefly into play. She knew the tricks her own guilty conscience could play. The summoning up of an old tune was certainly possible. But the whistle had been clear and true. She'd *heard* the nine distinct notes of "Bad Moon Rising," an old Creedence Clearwater Revival song. She had heard it, hadn't she? Or was it just a memory trapped inside her head, the song she'd first learned to play on the guitar while sitting right on the banks of this very river? She didn't have time to ponder the quirks of her own mind. Darkness was falling fast, and she had work to do.

As she left the river behind, the sounds of the wilderness reasserted themselves. The trail swept up into the denser black of the mountains. It was a difficult climb, but one that a tenderfoot could manage with a little effort. She'd give the reporters their money's worth. Once they came out of the Tabuga, they'd feel as if they'd actually survived in the wilderness. She couldn't *tell* them what a sense of pride that would give them. No, she couldn't tell them, but she could show them.

The three large rocks that marked her campsite appeared in the gloom, and she hurried toward them. In a few moments she had her tent up and a small fire going. The night turned chilly, and she wanted the fire's warmth. She needed the comfort of the small, cheerful blaze for reasons that were not only physical. She was alone, totally and completely, in a place she thought she'd left behind forever. "A victim of my own thoughts," she said aloud as she prodded the fire into higher flames.

Glancing around in the dancing light of the fire, she felt a chill. The hair along her neck tingled. She felt as if hungry eyes watched her from behind the dark wall of trees. The thought that she'd become a city girl who was spooked by nature made her unconsciously lift her chin. She'd never been afraid of the dark, especially not the starry nights along the river. Had she gone soft? There was no cause to be afraid in the forest. She was far safer in these mountains than she'd ever be walking the streets of Washington, D.C.

The fire burned low, and she spread her sleeping bag close beside the glowing embers. It was too beautiful to stay inside the tent. Stars winked through the boughs of the trees, a vast universe undimmed by city lights. She snuggled into the warmth of her bag.

"Help me!"

Weak and panicky, the voice drifted through the clear air to her.

Miranda sat up slowly, her hand inching toward the hatchet she carried to chop firewood.

"Please! Help me!"

She couldn't tell if it was a man, woman or child. In fact, the voice sounded less than human, almost animal. The words were blurred, and she couldn't be certain she'd heard them clearly. Some birds could sound almost human. Some wildcats could perfectly imitate the cry of a baby. Hatchet clutched tightly in her hand, she strained her ears to filter the sounds of the night.

"He-l-l-p meeee!"

The cry wavered on the darkness. Miranda unzipped her bag and slowly got to her feet. The plea sounded as if it came from the south, back toward the river. She had to check it out. She'd never rest easy if she didn't. She started down the trail that led to her river, every sense alert.

"Ple-a-s-e!"

She froze, listening to her lungs and heart work, listening to the pleading cry of someone in trouble. Her mind registered the fact that whoever was speaking sounded as if they were begging. For his or her life? She moved forward again, her body half-crouched, the hatchet ready. In the darkness the long-remembered contours of the trail came back to her. She knew it well, and her feet stepped easily among the stones and roots. When she'd gone fifty yards, she stopped. She'd lost the direction of the voice and she had to wait. It was only a few seconds before she heard it again, distinctly closer now.

"Oh, please!"

Still the age and gender escaped her. It didn't matter, though. Someone was in terrible trouble. She suppressed the urge to rush forward. Never rush. Never.

She steadied herself on the trunk of a hickory, then stepped forward. On the third step something slid beneath her foot. There was the sound of metal on stone, and she felt herself tumbling. To save her balance she jerked back, tottering on the narrow, steep path. The river was below her. She could hear it, almost taste the spray of water. Her hands grasped a tree limb, and she clung until she heard the sickening sound of the limb tearing. She felt her body spin into the darkness. Instinctively she curled into a tight ball and forced her body to relax as her back struck the stone path. The snap beside her ear was loud, the sound of metal meeting metal with a great deal of force. She tumbled down the path until she smacked into a large tree.

Stunned, she waited for the roaring in her head to abate before she sat up. In the darkness she couldn't tell exactly how far she'd fallen. She moved her arms and legs, making certain there were no broken bones. When her heart had calmed, she sat very still and listened. There was only the roar of the river somewhere below her.

She started the long climb up the path on her hands and knees. Her balance was unsteady, and she wanted to take no risks. She also wanted to find whatever had tripped her. The sound of metal on metal had been undeniable. She intended to find out what had caused it.

Halfway up the path her fingers found what she sought. The trap was twenty-four inches wide. A perfect size for a human foot. The force of its jaws would have snapped her ankle with a viciousness that might have crushed the bone. The damn thing had missed the side of her face by only a few inches. The trap fell from her nerveless fingers as she realized how close to mutilation and death she'd just come.

What idiot put a leg trap in the middle of a path? Before she had a chance to consider that question, another one popped into her mind. She found her legs and arms shaking. At first it was a small chill, then a slightly deeper shudder. At last it was an all-out quake. Slowly, carefully she started to crawl backward into the brush beside the trail. In the dense foliage she curled as tightly as she could while her mind went over again and again the three-hundred-yard stretch of path that led from the river to her camp.

Not three hours before, she'd climbed that path. There had been no leg trap. None.

She thought of the voice. In an instant she was straining to catch even the faintest trace of someone in trouble. Only the river sang to her; there was no other sound.

"WHO FUNDED the trip?" Russ Sherman's hands didn't hold a pad and pencil, but the reporter for the Washington daily newspaper wasn't off duty.

"I wish I knew," Miranda answered honestly. "The main office has been digging around since the money came in. They insist they can't trace it."

"Cash?"

Miranda glanced over her shoulder. The rest of the group were fast approaching, and she didn't want her conversation with Russ overheard. She didn't like the idea that Russ had somehow found out that the WDC expedition on the Tabuga was operating on funds from a secret donor. Secret donors made juicy headlines, and the WDC didn't need that type of press. Russ, though, was willing to play a hand of cards to the end. Instead of jumping for the easy headline, he'd wait to see what else he could glean.

"I think the payment was cash, but I didn't see it."

"Instructions?" Russ asked, his voice betraying his eagerness.

Miranda hesitated. In for a penny in for a pound, she thought. "Yes. The dates were given, and the makeup of the group. It was as if the package had been designed by a WDC public-relations staffer." She paused.

Russ gave her a level, searching look. "Did you donate the money? I mean, your love for this river isn't exactly a secret."

Miranda's laughter was light and easy. "I wish. I'm afraid WDC staffers don't earn the kind of salary where they can stockpile funds for secret missions." She held up a warning finger. "And the answer to your next question is no. Not a single one of my relatives has died and left me an inheritance."

Russ chuckled with her. "That was my next question."

"We're unofficially checking the other members of the staff, but I don't think that's going to be very productive. The money may be a mystery that's never resolved."

"The cloak of anonymity can hide a lot of motives."

Russ's statement was lighthearted, but Miranda felt a stab of deep anxiety. Her right fist clenched, and she felt the muscles in her forearm protest. She was still a little stiff from her tumble down the mountain path two weeks before. It was only a miracle that she hadn't been hurt worse. In her mind she heard the snap of the leg trap once again.

"Hey, are you okay?" Russ touched her elbow. "You're shaking."

A flush tinted her cheeks. "Perfectly fine. I may be a little hungry." She knew the excuse was flat, but she had enough to handle without Russ getting onto the leg-trap angle. In fact, she'd told no one about the incident. The trip she was leading was too important. The future of the Tabuga depended upon it. Russ's insightful remark about anonymous benefactors had tapped directly into the nerve of her worst anxieties. Why had someone contributed such a large sum, with such specific instructions? Why had she been singled out to lead the expedition? She wanted to believe it was her expertise. She had to believe that. Why else?

Her thoughts were interrupted by the sound of Cynthia Wickham's petite body breaking through the underbrush. "Miranda, how much farther to the river? We've heard it for the last twenty minutes." Cynthia wiped her forehead with a kerchief. "I like hiking, but I can't wait for the raft ride you promised. White water! I never thought I'd be doing this."

"I promised you experiences you'd never had before," Miranda said. "Just remember, the guides I've hired are experienced. Don't panic, and everything will be fine."

"The truth is that Cynthia, a member of the electronic media, can't take the heat of a little hike." Russ gave Cynthia Wickham a devilish grin.

"Yeah, I forgot how macho you print types claim to be," Cynthia shot back. "You try lugging around as much equipment as I have to carry, and we'll see who can hike the farthest."

"No, thanks. I rely on the power of the printed word, not my pretty face," Russ said, but he was unable to hide his smile.

"Ignore him," Cynthia cautioned Miranda. "First he asks me out. Then he horns in on my river assignment, and now he's insulting me."

"Maybe you should have accepted his date," Miranda said. She liked both Russ and Cynthia. They were bright, ambitious journalists with a sense of right and wrong. They were exactly the reporters she would have picked for her trip if she'd been given the choice.

"I did accept," Cynthia said in a stage whisper. "He wanted to know if I could give him a few tips on professionalism." She shot him a challenge with her eyes. "I told him to start with a new wardrobe."

"You two are perfectly matched," Miranda said. "Your wit won't ever grow blunt because you sharpen it on each other constantly."

"Would you mind if we walked on ahead?" Russ asked Miranda.

"Help yourself. We'll be at the river shortly. I'll wait here for Gordon and Fred."

"That's something I wanted to ask you," Russ said quickly. "Why did you bring a scientist along? Are you hoping to find something of value in the Tabuga?"

"There's always a chance." Miranda tried to keep her voice upbeat. A biologist had been part of the package, and when Gordon Simms heard about the trip, he'd volunteered. "It's a slim chance, but you never know. Mr.

Simms is technically along because he believes strongly
that the river should not be dammed. He's a volunteer.''

"And Fred Elton?"

"Senator Fremont's aide also... volunteered."

"Judging by Fred's enthusiasm, it was at gunpoint,"
Russ commented.

"Fred isn't exactly the outdoors type, you're right about
that," Miranda said. "Still, we're grateful that someone
on the Hill cares enough to send an aide. Senator Fremont will play a crucial role in what happens to this river.
He's in charge of the joint Senate-House subcommittee
that will hold hearings on Tabuga development, you know.
Fred may not be the happiest camper alive, but he's here
and he's hanging in."

"Are you always so diplomatic?" Cynthia asked.

"Always."

"Ever been tempted to resort to violence, like some of
the other groups who want to protect the environment?"

Russ's question made Miranda stop. Could she answer
truthfully? "Let me say that I understand the frustration
of watching helplessly when something is devastated. I can
see where a person might be driven to violence." The idea
of the Tabuga dammed, turned into a placid, swollen river
with resorts and tourist attractions, made her stomach
churn.

"Then you condone acts of violence when the situation
is crucial?" Cynthia followed up on Russ's question.

"I didn't say that," Miranda answered quickly. "In all
honesty, I can't say yes or no. Let me put it to you this way.
I don't believe in violence. I've never believed in even the
death penalty. But if I had a child and someone tried to
hurt my child, then I do believe I could do whatever is
necessary to protect my child."

"And is this river like a child to you?" Russ asked.

"Well, you might say she's like family. Maybe a
cousin." Miranda tried to turn the conversation to a lighter
plane. The combination of ideals and violence was disturbing. "You two run along. Remember the water is
swift. Stay away from the edge of the bank."

Watching Russ and Cynthia strike off down the path, Miranda had another severe twinge of nerves. Why was it that the things she believed in caused so much controversy and anger? Peace. Conservation. Protection of natural wilderness. How could anyone argue against such things? She knew the answer, and it all boiled down to profit. When a person became greedy, then he or she would do whatever was necessary to make a profit. That's how developers justified raping an entire wilderness. That's exactly what unspecified developers planned on doing to the Tabuga wilderness, unless she could prevent it.

"Hello! Anybody around?"

Fred Elton's unhappy voice reawakened her sense of duty, and she started down the path to find the two stragglers. They'd been in the wilderness for five days, and Fred had endured every moment. He wasn't a camper and had no desire to learn, but he'd toughed it out, complaining a lot less than his expression said he wanted to.

"The river's close now, Fred," she said as she approached him. A few yards behind him Gordon Simms, the biologist, was stooping over a small plant hidden beneath a rotted tree trunk. "Find anything interesting, Gordon?"

"Yes, this little plant was used extensively by native Indian tribes as an anthelmintic," Gordon said softly. "It's rare to find it."

"Rare!" Miranda felt a sudden surge of hope. "How rare?" She hurried over to him.

"Not rare enough," Gordon said, pushing his glasses higher his nose as he looked at her. "Not rare enough for what you're thinking. Pink Root certainly isn't endangered."

"Too bad," Miranda said. She bent down to touch the smooth, purplish stem. "I would love to find a rare plant."

"I know." Gordon rose, offering her a hand. "I'd love to find one for you." He took off his wire-rimmed glasses and cleaned them on the front of his shirt.

"Well, let's get on the river," Miranda said. "At least Russ and Cynthia have enjoyed the expedition. The WDC will get some great press coverage."

"That's really all you should have hoped for," Gordon said.

"Maybe, maybe not. A miracle would have been nice." Miranda gave him a wry grin, and they started down the path where Fred rested on a fallen tree.

THE WHITE WATER SURGED around the raft, and Miranda gave Cynthia a comforting pat on the arm. "It's okay," she mouthed, knowing that the roar of the water would drown out her voice.

Cynthia nodded, then shut her eyes. Miranda looked across the raft at Russ. He was having the time of his life, like a dog hanging out of a car window, she thought. Russ's profile cut the wind, and he was enjoying every second of the wild and turbulent ride.

Miranda cast a quick look behind her. Fred Elton was clinging to the side of the second raft, but Gordon Simms looked fine. She signaled a thumbs-up sign to Kurt and Betty Murray, the husband-and-wife team who'd brought the rafts downriver to the pickup point for the final leg of the adventure. The Murrays were longtime acquaintances who lived off the summer rafting business they'd built. For them the Tabuga was their livelihood. They'd been more than happy to assist in the WDC expedition.

Catching sight of Cynthia's face, Miranda decided to let the other raft go first. It was a tricky maneuver in the frothing waters, but she angled into a slower eddy and signaled the Murrays past.

"Will there be a, uh, calmer place downstream where we might take a swim?" Cynthia yelled. She tried for a smile and missed by several degrees.

"Yes, we'll make camp soon. There's a small pool that's perfect for a swim. It's only about an hour downriver," Miranda added, knowing that Cynthia's primary concern was docking, not swimming. "Are you ready?"

Cynthia nodded and Russ signaled that he had a firm grip on the straps of the raft. The Murray raft was well clear, and Miranda steered the raft into the full current. The river took them with a fury that was exhilarating.

Twenty yards ahead the first raft rose and fell on the white water. Betty and Kurt deftly navigated past boulders, trees and treacherous shallows. Miranda gave herself to the tempestuous ride, savoring each second as white spray stung her face and dampened her hair. It seemed only a few moments before she pulled over beside the other raft in a clear, calm pool of water beneath a small waterfall.

"I've never had a ride like that," Cynthia said as she clambered out of the raft. She was shaken but glowing with excitement.

"That's the wildest part of the trip," Miranda said loudly enough for the others standing on the bank to hear. Fred Elton looked visibly shaken, and she wanted to reassure him. "The river widens and slows. There are still some fast places," she said, dispelling Russ's disappointed look, "but I wanted to give you a *taste* of the wild Tabuga, not a full-course meal. There are other tours upriver with companies such as the Murrays. They'll be more than glad to give you the full treatment."

"How did you come to know the river so well?" Fred asked, breaking the silence that usually marked his character. "I couldn't help but notice the way you handled the raft, as if you'd been born to it."

There was something other than a compliment in Fred's voice, but Miranda didn't know how to interpret it. "When I was a child I rafted a good bit with my parents and brothers. Then I spent a summer and fall on the Tabuga when I learned this river inside and out. At twenty there's little fear of mortality."

"You camped here alone?" Fred looked around at the thick wilderness.

Miranda saw that her split-second hesitation had attracted Russ Sherman's attention. Great. That was all she needed, Russ Sherman probing around in her past. "Not alone. The Tabuga was popular with many young people as a summer retreat. We came to the mountains and the river to experience nature, to learn about ourselves and our world."

"It's very isolated. Those mountain communities you were telling us about don't sound all that hospitable." Fred didn't try to hide his anxiety. The raft ride had exhausted him.

"You've been watching too many movies." Miranda took his arm and began to maneuver him toward the campsite. The trip was almost over, and she would be more than glad to be free of the responsibility. Fred's behavior only underscored how completely the members of the party were dependent upon her.

"That's a point," Cynthia said, obvious reluctance in her voice. "I hadn't thought of it before, but if someone were injured, how would we get help?"

"Chances of injury are very slight," Miranda said. She had to get a grip on the situation. "Besides, I'm not going to let anything happen to my charges. The WDC would never forgive me if I got bad press."

"What if you get hurt?" Fred asked.

The hammer of anxiety tapped her spine once again. In her mind she heard the sound of the leg trap snapping. All eyes were watching her, waiting. "WDC staffers have survived the slings and arrows from Capitol Hill for too many years to let a little river slow them down. Now let's get off this morbid subject and make camp. I'm hungry."

"Not only beautiful, but tough and very skilled at dodging touchy issues," Russ Sherman whispered in her ear as he passed her. "I'm going to find the softest piece of dirt for my tent and bag," he called as he hurried by.

The rest of the party followed, and in less than half an hour Miranda and the Murrays had established camp and started a small fire for dinner. As she watched the blaze, she thought of the fresh fish they would pan broil. How could anyone resist fish cooked by the banks of a river? That alone was reason enough to save the Tabuga.

"I'll take care of this," Betty said, taking the skillet from Miranda's hand. You've had five days of tenderfoots. Go take a swim and relax." She grinned.

"Thanks." Miranda didn't wait for any urging. Farther upriver was an almost-hidden crystal pool that she remembered well. It would be heaven to swim, alone, for a few minutes. She picked up a towel and ducked into the woods.

The water in the secluded pool was so clear it skimmed the boulders like liquid silver. Miranda unbuttoned the big safari shirt and carefully hung it on a nearby bush to dry. She knew only too well how important dry clothes would be when she exited the water. Something in her peripheral vision moved, and she paused in the act of unhooking her bra. After searching the edge of the woods in all directions, she chided herself for bad nerves. There was no one else on the river. She slipped out of her underwear and without further hesitation dived into the pool. Her slender body arced in a curve before it slipped beneath the crystal depths.

WITH THE LATE-AFTERNOON sun in his eyes, Tom Wilkes wasn't certain that he'd seen what he thought he'd seen. He moved from the cover of thick undergrowth at the edge of the river and scanned the glittering surface. His amber eyes, searching along the far bank, found and identified the silken white panties and bra. Yes, it had been a female body arcing over the water in a dive that exemplified the word *graceful*. He watched the water, making sure the woman surfaced. When her blond head emerged in the middle of the river, he slipped back into the thick underbrush. The momentary vision of her body against the sun made him smile. The woman was no stranger to the river; that much he could assume by her fearless entrance into the water.

Hidden once more, he watched her apparent enjoyment of the river. The flash of her feet broke the surface as she porpoised and played. A smile of appreciation for her gracefulness and spirit touched his face, highlighting a small scar that angled down to touch a strong, firm jaw. Without a word Tom Wilkes gave the woman a silent salute and turned away. He wouldn't mind waiting for a full view, but surprising skinny-dippers wasn't his style. He'd taken a few swims in the Tabuga and knew the delicious feel of stolen moments with nature. Turning downriver, he headed toward her camp. He knew who she was: the WDC staffer, Miranda Conner.

He'd been tailing her for five days, always far in the distance, always out of sight. Now that her journey was almost over, he wanted to see what results the money from his company had bought. He also wanted to learn more about Ms. Miranda Conner. Clark Presley, whose family owned land on and around the Tabuga River for well over two hundred years, had implied that the WDC staffer was little more than a wild radical.

"She's one of those hippie people," Clark had said. "Used to camp out on the river . . . until they got in some big trouble. Protesting the war, they decided to blow up a federal building, I believe."

Knowing Clark's mountain-man flair for embellishments, Tom had decided to check it out for himself. His one glimpse of Miranda Conner certainly did not fit the bill for a saboteur. No, she might be deadly, but he suspected it did not have anything to do with bombs and bullets. Still, it never hurt to check.

As far as he knew, the WDC was a reputable agency, but he didn't want to take any chances with a group that might plan and promote some disaster just to stop a building project. It had happened in the past.

Clark had made another comment that deepened Tom's concern about the WDC's mode of operation. He'd said that Miranda Conner's boyfriend was "rotting in prison." Miranda had allegedly turned him in to save her own neck.

There was the possibility that the woman was willing to do anything to get her way. And he intended to find out how far she'd go.

Chapter Two

Miranda retrieved the tube of shampoo from her shorts, lathered herself quickly and rinsed. Scampering onto the bank, she dried briskly before taking a seat on one of the flat rocks to soak up the July sun. When she closed her eyes, she could imagine that she was eighteen again, camping on the Tabuga for the first time. The sting of unshed tears burned against her closed lids. Those days were ones she didn't want to remember, but she had to face them. She had to confront the memory of a tall, charismatic young man who'd introduced her to the Tabuga and a new way of life.

Gregory Henson had changed her life. He'd given her purpose, shown her that her beliefs—and passions—were important. And she'd loved him with all the innocence of youth. She'd followed him down a political path, never realizing how treacherous her footing had become until too late. She'd been willing to sacrifice everything for a better world. She'd come very close to that.

She looked around at the beauty of the pool. Gregory had introduced her to the Tabuga, and to adulthood. He had been a daring man with deep convictions. And he had gone to prison because of her. She could almost see the whole group of young people who had camped for a summer along the river, talking of peace and the need for commitment to ideals. She'd sometimes daydreamed about calling some of those old friends, but they wouldn't want to hear from her. Fifteen years may have passed, but no one would forgive her for what she'd done. She opened her eyes and worked her fingers through the tangle of her hair.

The sun warmed her skin, and she spread her hair along the hot, dry rock, letting the rays bake it dry. Downriver the members of her group were waiting for her, eager for an early supper and bed. By tomorrow she would deliver them safely to civilization. The trip had been as successful as she could possibly have hoped. Visions of Cynthia's television report and Russ's story gave her a momentary tingle of pleasure. One more night, and then the final portion of the raft trip downriver to Tabuga Springs. She still had time to give the reporters even more reasons to keep the Tabuga wild. She dressed quickly and started back to camp.

Everyone was busy when she arrived, and she took a moment of satisfaction in watching Fred Elton chop wood while Russ and Cynthia efficiently erected the final tent. Only Gordon Simms was unaccounted for. Scanning the area, she stopped abruptly as she focused on a tall, unfamiliar figure that stood off to one side of the camp. His stance said he was at ease, with himself and his surroundings. His dark eyes watched her with bold intelligence. She stepped forward.

"I'm Miranda Conner," she said, keeping her hand at her side. She'd learned to wait before making any overtures toward friendliness. "Is there something we could do for you?"

For a split second Tom Wilkes rued his decision not to wait for a fuller view of the swimmer. The woman who stood before him was tall, slender and composed. Her dark blond hair hung well below her waist in a wild tumble of curls that reminded him of the tempestuous Tabuga behind her. And the light in her green-flecked eyes was just as beautiful, and dangerous, as any hidden facet of the Tabuga. He was both interested and wary, a strange reaction to a beautiful woman.

"Tom Wilkes," he said, carefully extending his hand and waiting until she held out her own. It was a subtle play of power, and Tom smiled slightly. So, whoever Miranda Conner was, she'd been brought up not to be rude. She couldn't refuse a proffered hand. It was a telling characteristic.

Miranda felt his strength surround her fingers, the power of muscle, and something else. She couldn't stop the smile that accented the laugh lines in the corners of her eyes. Tom Wilkes had given only his name, and a callused handshake. In Washington men were always forgetting their own names in an effort to drop someone else's.

"Mr. Wilkes is from Tabuga Springs," Betty explained, rising from her position near the campfire. "He was hiking and wandered across our campsite."

Wandered up to their campsite. Miranda filed that tidbit for further evaluation. There were thousands of acres of wilderness, a lot of room for "wandering."

"Are you a native of Tabuga Springs?" she asked. Looking into his amber eyes, she thought not. There was something about Tom Wilkes that denied a simple village life, no matter how creased and worn his jeans and flannel shirt were.

"In a manner of speaking."

His voice was softened by the last remnants of a Southern drawl. He stared straight at her, as if he were assessing her for some reason.

"Mr. Wilkes owns some property near the town. He farms some acreage and has a bit in wilderness," Betty said. "He was explaining it to me when you came up."

"I see." Miranda dropped her gaze. Tom Wilkes was an easy man to look at, but when he looked back he ruffled her composure. She noticed the scar by his jaw, and it was on the tip of her tongue to ask him about it. Instead, she turned to assist Russ with the tent.

"Mrs. Murray said you hired her and her husband to raft your party down to the town," Tom Wilkes said just behind her ear.

His voice, so unexpected and so close, sent a whisper of goose bumps down one side of her body. The man could move like a cat, and he had the same lean musculature.

"That's right," Miranda said, tugging at the tent.

"They've never seen the river before, but you have." He made a statement, and the certainty of his words brought her around to face him, the tent stake still in her hand.

"You're very observant, Mr. Wilkes," she said slowly. "Are you writing a book?" She was definitely wary. For the second time the idea crossed her mind that Tom Wilkes's appearance in her camp was not a matter of coincidence.

Tom stepped back and laughed. "Not exactly. Where I come from, this is called making neighborly conversation." He liked her spirit, in and out of the water. He couldn't speak to the accusations Clark Presley had made, but he could say that if he'd had to pick someone to lead a rafting expedition, Miranda Conner would have been a top contender. The woman obviously knew the river and was nobody's fool.

"I'm sorry," she said, her expression easing slightly. "I suppose that wasn't a friendly reply." She was edgy, and she didn't like showing it. Whenever anything out of the ordinary happened, she heard the unforgettable sound of the leg trap snapping shut. "The trip is almost over, and everything has gone perfectly." She paused. "I don't need trouble on the last night."

"Are you expecting some?" He drawled the question slowly.

"No, but I wasn't expecting a stranger to appear out of the woods, either." She matched his look. He didn't flinch or shy away. Probably she was too jumpy. "If you'll excuse me, Mr. Wilkes, I have a camp to set up."

"I could give you a hand, if you'd invite me to stay for some of that trout Betty is cooking," he said. "It's a long walk back to my truck."

There was a hint of mischief in Tom's voice, and Miranda couldn't completely stifle a responding smile. So, he'd play on her sympathies. Well, if he was a Tabuga Springs property owner, he might prove useful to the WDC. "Earn your supper, and you're welcome to stay." She tossed the stake to him. As he deftly caught it, her smile widened to reveal a dimple on her left cheek. Walking away, she sensed his eyes following her and she forced herself to keep a steady pace as she circled the camp. Everything was moving smoothly, except that Gordon Simms was still missing.

"Have you seen Simms?" she softly asked Kurt Murray, hoping the guide had some idea where the biologist might have gone.

"He went downriver to collect some samples. He was mumbling something about mosses or algae or something." Kurt's cheerful tone held a slight tolerance for eccentric scientists. "He said he'd be back in plenty of time for supper. Want me to take a look?"

"I'd appreciate it. We're almost ready to eat."

"I'll be back before the fish have a chance to cool," he said as he moved toward the river. "I think he was headed toward the water."

Miranda helped Betty with the last of the golden hush puppies, feeling the pangs of a healthy appetite as the delicious aroma filled the camp area. Russ and Cynthia came up with John not far behind. Miranda delayed the meal as long as possible, waiting for Kurt and Gordon. When further delay would only attract attention to the absence of the two men, she served the food.

"Anything wrong?" Tom asked as he settled beside her on a fallen tree. Miranda held her plate in her hands, her fish untouched.

"Not really," she said. "A member of my party is a little late coming in. I think my mother programmed me to be a worrywart."

Before he spoke, Tom eyed the darkening sky. His mouth tightened slightly, then relaxed. "Probably just wandered farther away than he thought. He'll be back."

"I hope," Miranda said. "It would be rather difficult to explain how I lost a biologist in the Tabuga wilderness." She spoke with a wry note that didn't completely hide her worry.

"Scientist, eh?" Tom said, carefully looking down at his food.

"Biologist," she corrected.

"I guess you meet all types on the river." He bit into a tender fillet.

"Even strangers who wander in out of the woods," Miranda said. "How did you get to our campsite?" She watched him closely.

"I smelled this fish, and I followed my nose," he replied, his amber eyes dancing.

"The truth," Miranda pushed.

"I followed a mermaid," he said, leaning over to whisper.

"A mermaid? In the Tabuga?"

"A beautiful golden-haired mermaid who shed her clothes on the bank."

As the anger started to color Miranda's cheeks, Tom held up a hand.

"You were watching me," she accused, starting to rise. His firm hand settled on her thigh and pressed her back to her seat.

"I could have watched you, but I didn't," he said, all humor gone from his voice. "I did see your clothes, and I wandered downstream to wait for you to get out. I just wanted to be sure you were okay, with a place to go. Then I stumbled onto the camp and waited here." He'd mentally rehearsed his story, and even to him it sounded plausible.

Miranda stared at her plate as she recovered her temper. "That's a good way to get shot, you know." She was still angry, but her fury was softening. Tom Wilkes had done the honorable thing, and he'd done one better by hanging around long enough to make sure she didn't drown.

"Sometimes I go up to that very hole to swim," he said softly. "I didn't invade your privacy because I respect that need to be with nature. So don't get mad. I share your appreciation for this river."

She met his gaze, examining the ruggedness of his face. His skin, bronzed from the sun, glowed beneath black hair shot with silver at the temples. The same dark hair formed distinct brows over brown eyes that were golden, alert.

"Ms. Conner!"

The sound of her name called in panic made her jump up, almost upsetting her plate. Tom caught it just in time, pulling it to the safety of his lap.

"Over here," she answered. "What is it, Fred?"

Fred Elton rushed to her, his face tense with worry. He threw a frantic glance at Tom Wilkes. "It's Gordon. He's been hurt."

"How?" The dread she'd buried for the past week leapt into her throat. The snap of the leg trap echoed sharply in her mind.

"Kurt found him. He's knocked cold. And he may have a concussion. Ms. Conner, it looks like he was struck from behind!"

The fear unfurled in one corner of her mind. Who would want to hurt Gordon Simms, a quiet, retiring man whose interest was in small creatures and reclusive plants?

"How badly is he hurt?" She pushed back the fear.

"Kurt was afraid to move him, so he came back to camp for help. We need to build a litter to put him on so we can bring him back."

Miranda's heart sank. It was serious then. "We'll use my sleeping bag, and we need some poles," she said.

In five minutes they'd fashioned a crude litter and headed on the rescue mission with Kurt in the lead. Cynthia and Fred elected to remain behind, concerned that they might slow the rescue party. Betty stayed with them.

"Keep the fire going and put some water on," Miranda instructed as she hefted the medical kit onto her back.

Betty nodded, for one brief moment connecting with Miranda's gaze. They did not speak of the dangers of a raft ride at night. They didn't have to. Both knew the risks, and they also knew that if the biologist was seriously injured, he would have to be taken to town.

Kurt led them unerringly to the prone form of the biologist, almost hidden in the undergrowth several yards from the path. Gordon was beginning to come to when Miranda knelt at his side, gently pushing him back to the ground.

With careful fingers she probed his skull, checking to make sure there were no deep wounds. There were bits of bark in the blond curls at the back of his head, and a small cut on his forehead where several streaks of blood had dried. "Gordon, you must remain still until we're certain you aren't seriously hurt," she cautioned him.

"I've had a little medical training," Tom offered, kneeling at her side. "Let me take a look."

Miranda eased back, casting a furtive look at the last shreds of sunlight dying in the western sky. In another twenty minutes it would be completely dark. Luckily they were only a half a mile from camp.

She watched Tom's hands skillfully examine Gordon's skull. The biologist acted as if he were groggy. He kept his eyes tightly closed. She could barely restrain the questions that stormed around in her brain. Had Gordon seen his assailant?

Her gaze swept over the ground near the fallen biologist, uncovering a small, glittering object near a bush. Walking over, she retrieved his wire-rimmed glasses. They were crushed beyond repair, as if they'd been stomped. Deeper in the brush she saw his sample equipment, wrecked and useless. In the dim light there was no sign of any fish samples, but there was no doubt the attack had been deliberate. The small cloud of fear expanded, making her fingers close tightly around the glasses.

"Something wrong?" Russ Sherman's intelligent gray eyes flicked from the glasses to her face.

"I can't believe Mr. Simms has been injured," she said, trying to cover her agitation. An anonymous donor; a vicious attack; a well-planted leg trap. Her heart pulsed but she controlled her expression. "I studied maps of the region, but there is a possibility that we might have stumbled on private property. It's hard to tell with the vague property markings, especially in such mountainous terrain."

"You believe this is a trespassing incident?"

She heard the doubt in his voice. "The mountain people are very peculiar about their property, it's possible."

"Maybe Gordon tripped and fell into a tree."

The sarcasm in Russ's voice was unmistakable. She tucked the glasses into her pocket. "Maybe," she said.

"Kurt Murray said it looked like he was attacked." Russ waited for her reply.

"Well, only Gordon knows for sure, and we'll ask him as soon as he's able to talk." Miranda sensed that she'd better drop the matter. Russ could be a tremendous ally, or if he thought she was lying, a serious enemy. "There *are* old-timers in this area, people who might not understand what a biologist was doing."

"The people of Tabuga Springs wouldn't hurt a stranger." Tom Wilkes was suddenly at her side again. His ability to move without sound or detection was slightly annoying.

"I didn't mean to imply that—"

He didn't let her finish. "City people have this incredible misconception of mountain folk. They watch a movie and then think that everyone living outside the city limits is violent. It isn't true, and I don't like the implication."

"That wasn't what I meant," Miranda responded, her own anger rising. She wasn't trying to convict the local residents. She was just trying to halt the panic that she knew would come if the members of her party began to think someone was trying to hurt them because of the WDC. She bit her lip and turned her attention back to Gordon. "This is a stupid argument when someone is lying on the ground injured," she said, summoning all of her control.

"You're right," Wilkes agreed, joining her at Gordon's side. "I apologize," he added softly. "It's just that so many people come here wanting to take advantage of the people, stereotyping them as ignorant, uncivilized barbarians."

"I know," she said, touched at the tone of genuine concern in his voice. "Now, what about Simms?"

"His injuries don't appear serious, but he's going to have a whopping headache."

"Does he need to go to a hospital?"

"He was struck from behind, and the blow was hard, but I don't think he'll have any problems," Tom said. Night had almost fallen, and he couldn't completely hide the worry in his voice. "If they meant to kill him, they didn't try very hard. There were bits of bark in his hair, so he was struck with a limb. Let's get him back to camp and decide what to do."

Miranda nodded, leaning down to take Gordon's hand. "We've brought a litter to carry you," she offered. His eyes looked too pale and unfocused. Dread almost made her shiver, but she managed a smile.

"No, just give me another minute and I think I can walk," Simms said, reaching instinctively for his glasses.

"They were broken in the fall," Miranda said reluctantly.

"I can't see anything without them. And my samples! Where are they?" Excitement rose in Gordon's voice.

"I'm afraid they were damaged, too," Miranda said.

"But you don't understand. You don't understand at all!" Gordon said, his voice growing more and more agitated. "I found it! No one thought it was still here, but it was. And I had one captured! It took me hours to finally trap one, and—" he pushed himself up on his elbows "—I have to get another before we leave here. The river can't be dammed. We have to stop it!"

Looking around the cluster of faces, Miranda saw that Russ was hovering over Gordon's every word. Tom had retreated to the perimeter of the small circle. He watched Gordon Simms with a strange calculation. Miranda's train of thought made a sudden leap. Tom had stumbled into their camp from nowhere. Was it merely a coincidence? He must have felt her gaze riveted upon him, because he turned to confront her stare. Hurriedly she bent back to Gordon.

"What did you find, Gordon?" she asked softly.

"The Tabuga pisces darter. Everyone assumed the fish was extinct. But it isn't. I found one!"

"Yeah, and it almost cost you your life," Russ said, eyeing the gathering darkness with distrust. "Let's get back to camp before we all get whacked in the head."

THE RUMBLE of angry voices mingled with the sound of the river as Miranda and the rescue party neared the camp. Miranda heard Betty's clear voice raised, followed by a deep bass voice. The exchange was sharp and loud.

A tiny drum of pulse sounded in her inner ear. What now!

"Betty!" Kurt heard the argument, too, and he started forward, but Tom's hand restrained him. "Caution," Tom urged in a single breath. "I'll move in from the north side."

Tom disappeared in the darkness, and Miranda found that she was alone at the edge of the woods with a groggy Gordon and Russ. She felt the reporter move up to her side.

"More trouble?" he asked.

"Maybe not." Miranda was too worried to even attempt a subterfuge. "Sounds like Betty is holding her own."

"I don't believe it!" Betty's voice came to them, that phrase clear and distinct.

"She's only interested in herself. She isn't capable of saving this river." The man's voice was also clear.

"Miranda Conner is very capable—" Betty's voice became garbled in the sound of the river.

"Let's go," Miranda said, pushing forward. What on earth was going on now?

She broke into the clearing with Russ and Gordon at each side. Betty was sitting in front of the fire. Beside her was a short, stocky man with flowing white hair and a handlebar mustache, also white. The man's face was flushed red, and he was waving his hand in the air. A little to the side, Cynthia was making notes and Fred was hanging back, the perpetual observer, his face absolutely expressionless.

"This river is my home and I won't have it jeopardized by some woman who thinks she can save it by hosting parties for a bunch of city folk!" the man exploded.

Betty caught sight of Miranda just as Tom and Russ leaped into the clearing from the opposite side.

"Now that's a sorry excuse for an ambush," the white-haired man said as he got to his feet. "I heard you forty yards back. You sound like rutting deer." He looked at Tom and snorted. "I thought you was a better woodsman than that."

Miranda saw the two men exchange a look. "Who are you?" she demanded. "Betty, are you okay?"

"Hell, no. She's more ornery than a coon with fleas," the man said. "But at least she ain't no—"

"Miranda, this is Clark Presley," Tom interjected. "Clark owns several hundred acres on the Tabuga. He's vehemently opposed to the idea of a dam, right, Clark?"

"I can talk for myself."

"Then you'd better start, and fast," Miranda said in a level voice. "What do you know about an attack on one of my party?"

The anger left the man's face and was replaced by a look of confusion, and then fury. "You think I hurt one of you? Is that what you think?"

"Someone attacked Mr. Simms," Tom explained in a soothing voice. "Everyone in the area could be considered a suspect."

"That's right. So, I attacked him? Did I steal his billfold?" When no one answered, he went on. "No, I didn't take anything, I just whopped him on the head and left, right?"

"Not exactly." Miranda wasn't amused by the man's behavior. "What are you doing here, Mr. Presley?"

"Looking for that renegade." He nodded toward Tom. "He took off and left me last week. Promised to take me on a tracking trip and then left, but I tracked him." He gave Tom a smug look. "I been your shadow for the past week, son, and you didn't even know."

Tom rubbed his chin, the feel of his stubble rough against his palm. "Could we discuss this later, Clark? I promised to check things out, not to take you with me."

"Well, I'm here now, and I want some answers." Clark looked at Miranda. "Why'd the WDC send you down here? The Tabuga needs someone who'll fight for her."

"I intend to do that, Mr. Presley," Miranda said, her gaze shifting between the older man and Tom. "I'll do whatever I can, within the law, to save the river."

"Within the law." Presley echoed her words with a grim smile. "That's a new attitude for you, isn't it?"

Miranda felt her heartbeat quicken. She didn't want a showdown in front of Russ and Cynthia. Her past was the last thing she'd ever want to drag out in front of the press, but she wasn't going to let some stranger come into her camp and impugn her reputation. She'd paid for her mistakes—they all had.

"Clark, let's discuss this privately," Tom said. His voice was so cool that it made goose bumps on Miranda's arms. She watched with amazement as Presley lowered his defiant chin.

"If they dam that river, my entire place will be gone," he said slowly. "Tom, here, talked all of us landowners into agreeing to let this fancy environmental group have a shot at stopping this. Well, this ain't fair. That woman—" he pointed at Miranda "—is going to ruin me."

"How many acres will you lose?" Cynthia asked the question, but she and Russ both held pencils aloft.

"Six hundred, give or take a few."

"The dam will put all of your property underwater?" Russ followed up.

"Every foot."

"Do you object to Ms. Conner heading the WDC expedition?" Russ asked.

"Clark is a known sexist," Tom cut in. "He thinks having a woman on a camping expedition is bad luck. Right, Clark?"

"Worst luck I know of," Clark said with his forehead knotted in a black scowl. "Almost as bad as having members of your party attacked," he said sarcastically. "That kind of violent luck seems to follow that Conner woman."

"I'm not hurt," Gordon managed. "I have a pounding headache, but I think I'm going to be fine."

As soon as he spoke, he stumbled to his knees and dropped face-forward only inches from the campfire.

Chapter Three

"My truck isn't too far from here. I think that would be faster than trying to raft the river at night." Tom watched the controlled panic in Miranda Conner's eyes. She was worried about the biologist. Very worried.

"We should have carried him," she murmured. "He seemed fine." She placed a hand on Gordon's cool forehead and adjusted the sleeping bag they had thrown over his prone form. He moaned but did not open his eyes.

"My brother's a doctor in Tabuga Springs," Tom said as he knelt beside Miranda. "Kurt and Betty know where he lives." He gave her hand a reassuring squeeze. "Doc's a pretty good medicine man if I do say so myself. He'll take care of Gordon."

"I can't leave the rest of the expedition alone." Miranda looked across at Tom. "We can't all fit in your truck." She nodded to Russ and Cynthia huddled together at the front of a tent. Fred Elton was nervously pacing some thirty yards away. Every noise seemed to startle him. Clark Presley sat smoking a pipe, an occasional glance of disdain falling on Fred's nervous behavior.

"Let Kurt and Betty take Gordon. I'll stay with you and the others and tomorrow we'll raft out. Devil's Hole is the only rough part of the trip left. I know you can handle one raft, and I'll take the other." He had a second of hesitation. He'd never intended to get involved in the WDC's

business. It was almost a conflict of interest, but he was
concerned about the camping party. Miranda Conner had
done a remarkable job, but there was a limit to one person's control. She needed help, and he could give it. Besides, he was more than a little curious about Gordon
Simm's babblings about a fish species.

Miranda finally saw light at the end of a dark tunnel.
She checked her watch. It was nine o'clock. If she could
just prevent another tragedy for nine hours, they would be
on the river and headed toward Tabuga Springs. "Kurt!"
She called the guide over. "Are you and Betty okay with
taking Gordon to Tabuga Springs?"

"Take him to Doc Wilkes's house," Tom said.

"Sure, we know Doc," Kurt nodded. "You two related?"

"Brothers." Tom stood, helping Miranda to rise.

"Yeah, Betty and I could do that, and to be honest, I'd
like to keep my wife with me," Kurt said. He looked into
the shadows of the forest. Darkness seemed to have crept
closer to the small camp. "I'd be just as glad to leave
here," he said, almost to himself.

"Then let's get busy," Miranda said. She bent down and
spoke softly to Gordon. "We're sending you to the doctor. Just relax and try to rest." She felt his cool head again
and checked his eyes for shock. Except for his inert state,
he seemed okay. That was what worried her the most. His
color was good, breathing normal, pulse steady. *Please,
don't let him have a concussion,* she thought as she helped
Kurt and Tom put him on a litter. Soon the small party was
ready to leave.

"I'll help get Gordon to the truck," Tom said. "I'll be
back as soon as possible." He looked at Clark, who was
still impassively smoking his pipe. "Do you want a ride
back to town?"

The old man shook his head. "I'll go back the way I
came."

Tom nodded, casting a long, concerned glance at Miranda. Clark walked up to stand beside her, and Tom had
a twinge of unease. It was bad timing for Presley to show

up. Clark was an eccentric, opinionated old cuss, but he wasn't dangerous. It was just that Miranda had her hands full without Clark Presley's comments on her past. There was nothing he could do, though. He gave a last wave and hefted one end of the litter. Kurt took the other, and they left with Betty in the lead with the most powerful flashlight.

"I knew when I heard you were coming here that trouble would start." Clark pointed a slightly crooked finger at Miranda as soon as the darkness had swallowed Tom and the guides.

In the flickering light of the campfire, Miranda saw the anger in the older man's face. "How did you know that I was here?" she asked. The WDC had not advertised the expedition. In fact, they'd gone to great lengths to keep it as hush-hush as possible to prevent the possibility of trouble. It was odd that Tom Wilkes *and* Clark Presley should show up at her campsite.

"I remember you," Presley said. "I remember."

"How did you know about this expedition?" she asked for the second time. A quick look about the campfire let her know that she and Clark were alone. Fred had finally retired into one of the tents, his silhouette a dark shape against the nylon material. Cynthia and Russ were nowhere in sight, and she felt a moment of tightening panic.

"I knew you were on the river two weeks ago." Clark picked up a piece of wood and threw it onto the fire. "I know who you are, Miranda Conner."

Miranda momentarily forgot her concern for the two reporters. "How did you know?"

"Folks on the river know who comes and goes. We remember, too."

"Mr. Presley, I love this river. I'll do whatever I can to save her. If you want to keep the Tabuga wild and natural, I urge you to give me all the help you can." As she talked, she tried to read his eyes. Why did he hold her in such contempt?

"You can't save the river. Not you. There'll only be trouble if you're involved. After what you did, no one's ever going to have respect for you or what you say. I remember. Other people remember, too.''

The sound of the leg trap went off in Miranda's head. She was positive that Clark Presley knew something about that incident, but she didn't know how to drag the information out of him.

''Were you up at Three Rock Split two weeks ago?''

Presley shook his head as if he'd just heard bad news. ''I saw the signs. That trap could of took your leg off. That should tell you folks around here want you gone.''

''It tells me that someone wants to stop the WDC from saving this river. You people should work with me, not against me. We both want the same thing.''

His clear blue eyes held her in a long, steady gaze. ''I'm not so sure I believe that. A woman doesn't testify against her man. That kind of woman isn't to be trusted.''

Miranda drew in a sharp breath. ''I did what I thought was right and I'll be damned if I have to explain my reasons to you or anyone else.'' Her heart was pumping with anger. ''The Tabuga has nothing to do with my past!''

''Nobody believes that. Not even you.'' Clark tapped out the cold tobacco in his pipe and scattered it on the fire. ''If you care about this river, you'll leave. There are some others who think something stronger than words is needed.''

''What other people? Who wants to make trouble?''

''I grew up on this old river. My parents, my grandparents and my great-grandparents all before me lived on the Tabuga. It's my whole life, and I don't want to risk it. I want those wilderness people to send a man down here to take care of this.''

It wasn't the first time that Miranda had confronted that sentiment. ''Mr. Presley, I'm more qualified to defend the Tabuga than any male we have in our office, regardless of what has happened in my past. Even more importantly, I care more than anyone else. The river is special to me, too.'' She tried to reason with him, though she didn't think it would do much good.

"If you don't get off this river and go back to Washington or wherever you came from, you're going to get hurt." He stuck his hands in his pockets. "Now, that's a promise. Now that you've been warned, I'm going home. You'd better round up those other two and stay close to the campfire. Some things out in those woods ain't real friendly."

"I know," Miranda said calmly, "but thanks for the warning just the same."

She watched him retreat into the darkness. There was a sound of a few limbs rustling, then silence. She hadn't asked how he'd arrived. Floated over on a raft, maybe. Or walked. She knew the Tabuga wilderness fairly well, but there were hundreds of small trails, new and old, that led away from the river. Chances were good that he'd been following them the entire trip.

"Russ! Cynthia!" She called the two missing members of her party.

"Right here."

Russ's answer came a little west of the camp, and soon he stepped into the glow of the campfire with Cynthia in tow. "We were trying to find those fish Gordon was talking about," Russ said. "An endangered species should help your case, Miranda."

"Gordon could have been delirious." She didn't want the possible existence of an endangered species to become bantered about in the press. If Gordon had found something, she wanted solid, hard, indisputable evidence—not speculation and a rush of WDC foes on the Tabuga.

"Well, aren't we being negative?" Russ put his hand on her shoulder.

"Not negative, just realistic. Gordon has been seriously injured. There's a good probability he was dreaming out loud. My primary concern now is keeping you safe and then finding out who did this."

"Hey—" Russ's sharp eyes took in every nuance of her behavior "—the attack wasn't your fault."

Miranda knew he was watching for a reaction. The trouble was that she felt as if she were responsible. Maybe

Clark Presley was closer to the truth than he knew. The attack on Gordon might not involve the current WDC project. What if it was something from her past? The group of young people who camped on the Tabuga that summer many years ago had never been popular. They had always been viewed by the mountain people as outsiders, intruders, and ne'er-do-wells. She'd never dreamed, though, that people like Clark Presley would have remembered her personally. It was just another bitter lesson in the fact that there was no escaping the past.

"Miranda?" Russ grasped her shoulders lightly. "Are you okay?"

"Of course." She pushed her anxieties down. She could sort through the matter later. Now she had to feed Russ and Cynthia and prepare the camp for night. "I think we should make an effort at finishing that meal," she said. "Tomorrow we're going to need to be rested and strong."

"Kurt and Betty were talking about a place called the Devil's Hole," Cynthia said nervously.

"We'll be fine," Miranda said, forcing confidence into her voice. "Tom is an old hand at the river and so am I. You'll enjoy tomorrow, and then we'll be headed back to D.C."

"It's going to make one great story," Russ said as he handed Cynthia a plate of cold fish.

TOM APPROACHED the camp with a lot on his mind. He was torn about possible development of the Tabuga. On one hand, he could see so many benefits of the development. On the other, the thought of changing the wild and savage river with a series of dams was almost an obscenity. He loved the Tabuga, but he also had to consider the people of Laurel County. It was a situation where he honestly didn't know the right path to choose—that was why he'd been so determined to involve an environmental group. His partners in the newly formed Clearwater Development had selected the WDC, a choice he couldn't fault. But why would an environmental concern as reputable as the WDC send a representative with a questionable past? That question had bothered him, but not so severely, until Gordon Simms had been attacked.

He went over the scene of the attack again in his mind. Gordon had been found a short distance from the path. He'd claimed that he'd captured several fish that were reportedly extinct. By a strange twist of fate, whoever attacked him had also crushed his samples boxes and there was no sign of the fish. Was it possible the WDC had planned the entire incident so that they could claim the Tabuga pisces darter was still inhabiting the waters? Such a ruse would definitely delay the dam projects, at least for a while.

He had to admit that he'd never have concocted such a theory if it hadn't been for Clark Presley. When Clark had discovered that Miranda Conner was leading the WDC expedition, he'd had some pretty harsh words to say about her character.

Part of it was Clark's old-time beliefs about women, but there was another, valid, issue that he'd raised. What was Miranda's real character? Would she stoop to faking an attack and fabricating the discovery of an endangered species?

He spied the flicker of the campfire through the trees and took a deep sigh as he approached. The only thing he could do was spend a little time with the WDC staffer and try to decide for himself if she was on the up-and-up. Well, he'd spent long hours with people far less intriguing, and not nearly as beautiful.

He caught sight of her sitting on a tree trunk, shoulders slumped and expression worried. She looked in need of a good hug. That thought stopped him in his tracks. He couldn't afford that kind of thinking. Clearwater had donated the funds for the raft trip, and that was as far as he ought to go. Sure, he'd lent a hand with an injured man, but he had no business even thinking about offering solace and comfort to Miranda Conner. No business at all.

"Come on up to the fire," Miranda called softly. She'd caught sight of him standing uncertainly at the edge of the camp. If Clark Presley was a concern, Tom Wilkes was a godsend.

Tom entered the small circle of light and noticed the plate of untouched food on Miranda's lap.

"Better swallow some of that grub," he said in a cowboy twang.

"You're right," she agreed, but she made no effort to eat. "I put your plate in the ice chest."

Tom retrieved it and took a seat beside her. He bit into a cold fillet. "It's still pretty tasty," he said.

Miranda picked up a hush puppy and took a bite. She had no appetite, but she knew Tom was right. She had to eat.

"How many times have you been down the Tabuga?" Tom put the question in a casual tone.

"A number of times, but it's been a while," Miranda said.

"How long?" he asked, digging into the food.

"In the '70s," Miranda said, almost too softly to hear. "Another lifetime ago. But I've rafted a great deal in recent years out west."

"You were just a baby in the '70s," Tom said, reaching across to drop a piece of his fish on her plate. Russ and Cynthia came out of the darkness, said their good-nights and retreated to their respective tents.

"I certainly thought I was grown and knew all the answers." For some reason Miranda found it easier to talk with Tom than anyone in a long time. It was undoubtedly the fact that they both cared so much for the river. He was also a darn good listener.

"Is he okay?" Tom pointed to the morose figure of Fred Elton sitting hunched on a log. He was staring at the glowing embers with unfocused determination.

"The attack on Gordon has really undone him. I don't know Fred that well, but he's a very influential aide to Senator Fremont. I wish we could have made him enjoy the trip more."

"You did everything you could," he answered, responding to a strange need to reassure her before he'd even thought through his answer. "We were talking about the wisdom of youth, weren't we? And now? Still have all the answers?"

"Less with each passing hour." She wanted to change the subject away from the past. "But I still know enough about rafting to get us through Devil's Hole unscathed."

His hand reached out and unexpectedly removed her empty plate. "I'll clean these up," he said, "but you—" he easily pulled her up to her feet as he rose "—have to get some sleep."

The fears that had been bubbling in the back of her mind forced a question to her lips. "Do you think we'll be okay tonight?"

"If you're asking if I think the attackers will come back, I'd say no."

There was such assurance in his tone that Miranda felt immediate comfort, and also a pang of curiosity.

"How can you be so sure?" she asked.

"Well, from my experience, I'd say whoever attacked your party accomplished their goal. They could have easily killed Simms, but they didn't." He waited for her reaction.

"So you think it was just a scare tactic?"

"Sounds that way to me." Tom's deep voice, calm and logical, put a veneer of sanity on the cold horror of his words. "The attack came just as you reached the river, when you were on the most vulnerable point of your journey. Actually I'm surprised they didn't try something before now."

Well, they had. Tom just didn't know about the leg trap. "You think they were watching us the whole time?"

"More than likely." He'd seen signs of someone else along the trail, but he'd put it down to campers. "We need to be careful." In the flickering light from the campfire, he could see the strain his words had put on her face. Surely if the attack on Simms was a setup, she wouldn't look so afraid.

"Thanks for staying around tonight," she said. "I've never been afraid of the wilderness, and I'm not now."

Her smile was slightly self-deprecating, and the dimple marked her cheek. "I'm glad you're here, though. Really glad." There was something extraordinary about Tom Wilkes. Whenever he was around, she felt a little more . . . alive. It was exciting, and a little unnerving.

"We'll get back to town tomorrow." His voice was slightly rougher. Miranda's green-eyed appeal was so natural, and so irresistible. She acted as if she had no idea how she affected him. "Just remember, if someone intended to hurt you, they would have by now."

"You're right." Miranda sighed. "Whoever they are, they want to stop me from stopping that dam."

"Something tells me that won't be easy." He meant it, too. He didn't know her well, but he had the distinct impression that she would put her whole self into any cause she took on.

"No. They'll get a fight."

"And you need your rest," he said lightly. "I'm sending you to bed." Before she could protest, he put his arm around her and moved her toward the tent she shared with Cynthia, who was already sound asleep.

The touch of his arm was comforting, but it also stirred a stronger feeling in Miranda. She liked him. She hadn't allowed herself to like anyone in that way in a long, long time. Tom Wilkes was a handsome man with a lot of physical presence. The thing she had to remember was that she didn't know him, and his appearance coincided with a lot of trouble.

At the flap of the tent, Tom removed his hand from her back. He stepped back and said good-night.

Miranda had a clear view of him in the starlight that was so bright along the riverbanks. His face was strong, not classically handsome, and the beginning stubble of a beard peeked from his bronzed skin. In the moonlight she saw unreadable secrets in his amber eyes.

"Good night, Tom Wilkes," she said softly. "Thank you."

"Good night, Miranda," he replied with a wink, "and you're welcome."

Her last image of him as she quietly closed the tent flap was reassuring, and yet disturbing. He stood by the tent like a phantom guard.

Lying awake in her sleeping bag, she listened to a screech owl hunting prey. Smaller animals signaled warnings back and forth. Within a hundred yards of the camp there were squirrels, rabbits, a varied assortment of birds, maybe a few possums, raccoons and even a skunk or two. Wildcats were not as common, but even if one happened to be patrolling the area, she knew it posed little danger. Like the black bear, they preferred to avoid all contact with humans.

More dangerous than even the wildest animal were the person or people who'd attacked Gordon Simms. She went over the sequence of events again, hoping that a thorough examination would yield additional clues. On the surface it looked like the work of locals. They'd come up through the woods. She was certain that no one had passed them on the river, so whoever the attackers were, they'd either camped downriver and waited or trekked through the woods. That's why locals seemed the obvious choice. Somehow, though, that explanation was too pat.

She rolled to her side and made sure her restlessness wasn't affecting the sleeping Cynthia. The reporter was curled comfortably in a deep slumber. As quietly as possible Miranda eased out of her sleeping bag, found her shoes and slipped from the tent. The campfire was cold, and all of the summer heat had drained from the night. Wrapping her arms around herself, she stole to the edge of the camp and found a comfortable seat on the old fallen tree.

The night was beautiful, crystal stars crowding the velvety sky and the sound of the Tabuga gurgling only thirty yards away. She walked to the edge of the bank, watching the water pass into the deep pool beneath the waterfall where another small stream joined the larger current.

"It's too cold for a swim."

Tom's voice didn't startle her at all, and she realized that she'd hoped he, too, would be restless.

"And too dangerous. I wasn't planning on swimming," she said, turning to face him and brushing her hair out of her eyes. Feeling the tousled mass of curls, she thought how disheveled she must look and vainly tried to pull some order into the heavy tresses. "I usually wear it up at work," she said. He made her so aware of herself as a woman.

"That probably looks nice," he commented, "but I like it down." He couldn't resist picking up a strand and letting it sift through his fingers. "Mermaid's hair," he said, and laughed. "An ancient secret."

"That's twice you've mentioned mermaids," she said. "Were you a sailor?" There was a tremor in her voice. Even the slightest touch of his fingers in her hair triggered a reaction.

"In a manner of speaking," he said, turning to face the water so that she saw only his profile. The small scar on his cheek glistened in the starlight.

"Is that how you got this?" She traced it with her finger. She wanted to know about this man.

"Not hardly," he said. Her touch was delicate, almost tentative. He felt the sensitivity in her fingers. She was a remarkable blend of tough self-reliance and tenderness. "Sibling rivalry. My brother and I fought often, and hard, when we were growing up. There were times when we did our best to kill each other. Now he's a doctor. Time certainly changes everything."

She followed his gaze to watch the river sweeping before them. "Were you really born in Tabuga Springs?"

"No, I was born in California," he said. "My grandfather lived and died here, and the best summers of my life were spent on his farm. I came back about two years ago." He was telling the truth, as far as it went, but he had a pang of guilty conscience. He was withholding quite a few facts.

"And before that?"

"Now are you writing a book?" he teased.

"You never know," she replied tartly. "If the information is interesting enough, I just might decide to capitalize on it."

"Better find a different subject, 'cause you won't find much meat for public consumption in my life. I worked around the country in the building trade. Then I decided to come home. Now, enough twenty questions."

There were other things Miranda wanted to ask, but those were the same questions she didn't necessarily want to answer about herself.

They both heard the soft rustling of branches to the west of the camp. Tom's hand grasped her arm, signaling for her silence. Mingled with the breeze from the water, the sound came again, as if someone moved with deliberate stealth on the fringes of the camp.

Miranda froze. Tom's closeness was a stabilizing factor, and she concentrated on listening. They stood side by side, as if a magic spell had captured them in a single instant, his hand on her arm.

For a long moment there was nothing, and Miranda felt the tension begin to slacken. Then the noise came again, a little closer and more to the south. Tom moved so smoothly, she almost didn't see what he was doing until the starlight caught the barrel of a deadly-looking gun. Somehow she managed not to make a noise at the sight of the weapon, and his fingers closed more firmly around her arm as he slowly indicated for her to drop to the ground.

With her eyes on the weapon, Miranda eased to her knees, and then down to her side.

"Don't move," he whispered in her ear, his warm breath a contrast to the cold fear that seemed to run in her veins. "If you don't move, they can't see you."

Before she could respond, he was gone, moving across the empty campsite with a grace that belied his tall, powerful build. For one crazy moment Miranda thought of a moonlight dance, a dangerous duet choreographed to the music of the Tabuga.

When the noise came again, Miranda thought her lungs would burst with the air she held. Abruptly Tom lowered the gun. The noise came louder and she almost panicked, but there was no sign of fear in Tom's relaxed stance. Very slowly he eased back to her, lifting her to a sitting position as he bent to press his lips near her ear.

"Don't make a sound, but come with me," he said, drawing her up with him as he stood.

She looked up into his eyes, finding a sparkle of pure delight and the remnants of so many secrets, but no worry or fear.

"What—" But his finger at her lips gently stopped her question.

The noise came again, and Miranda couldn't stop her body from moving closer to him. His arm came around her, pulling her tight, and he pointed with his free hand into the woods. For a moment she saw nothing, and then the slightest movement gave away the location to which he pointed.

Miranda sucked in her breath in sharp surprise as she made out the shape of the deer, but it was unlike any deer she'd ever seen. He was completely white. The deer saw them, but made no effort to move away. Hugged against the warmth of Tom's body, Miranda reveled in the sight, watching the deer's nostrils quiver as he drank in their scent.

"Eight points, I'd say," Tom remarked softly. "He's a handsome rascal."

"He's magnificent," Miranda breathed. "Incredible."

"I've heard about him from some of the farmers," Tom whispered, "but I always thought he was more legend than fact. My grandfather believed that the albino buck was a symbol of very special magic."

"Should I wake up the others? They won't believe me in the morning," Miranda said. "They'll think I was hallucinating."

"Let them think what they will," Tom said, tightening his hold on her. "I'm afraid if you move, he'll be gone."

The deer suddenly froze, then tucked his haunches and bolted into the darkness.

Beside her, Tom tensed. His hand went for the gun again as he drew her protectively to his side. Eyes scanning the undergrowth, he turned toward the opposite bank of the river.

"What is it?" Miranda couldn't help the fact that her words were choppy. Tom's change of mood had terrified her. There was something in the darkness, waiting and watching. Something she couldn't see, but it could see her.

"They're still out there," Tom whispered.

"Maybe it was some hunters," Miranda said, her voice breaking several times in an effort to speak normally.

"Not hunters, or at least not animal hunters."

"But you said you didn't think they'd be back."

He looked down at her, anger and wariness reflected in his strong face. "I was wrong, Miranda. They're still here, and they're watching us right this minute.

Chapter Four

When the sun finally cleared the treetops and began to dispel the shadows of the night, Miranda allowed herself a deep breath. Not twenty yards away Tom Wilkes was also shaking off the stiffness of a night spent on watch. He flexed his shoulders, tightening the fabric of his flannel shirt. A smile of pleasure touched Miranda's face. Only the day before he'd been a stranger. Now he was becoming a friend. He'd put himself through a sleepless night, and the possibility of danger, to help her. His aid had come without thought of how it would benefit him. Maybe chivalry wasn't dead.

The rock she'd braced her back against was unbearably hard, and she rose slowly, giving her cramped muscles time to uncoil. Her eyes ached from constantly searching the darkness. There had not been another attack, but the sensation of being watched, even with Tom there, had taken a heavy toll. Across the distance of the camp their eyes met, and she gave a wry smile as he approached.

"Ready to break camp?" Tom's face bore the stamp of his tension-filled night, but he gave her a thumbs-up sign of encouragement. "It's been a long night, but it's over. No one seems in much of a mood for breakfast."

Miranda eyed her group, noting their drawn faces. Russ and Cynthia were struggling to make coffee. Fred was still in the tent, but she could imagine his face. Her expedition was in a shambles, and the attention she'd focused on the Tabuga wasn't exactly what she'd had in mind.

"Yeah, we look pretty pitiful," she said. "The best thing we can do is get back to Tabuga Springs. If you'll help load up, I'll see about getting Gordon's equipment. He said some of his traps were left in place in the river."

"Did you get a look at any of the fish he captured?" Tom reached out and caught a corner of the sleeping bag Miranda was rolling. He helped her stow her gear.

"No, I didn't see anything. He said he had five, but they were all killed by the attacker." She secured her backpack. "It makes you wonder who was the intended victim, poor Gordon or the fish?"

"Would a dead one serve as well? I mean, if there actually were darters."

Miranda shook her head, aware of the undercurrent of Tom's question. "I know what you're getting at. I don't have a prayer of making a case for the Tabuga without one of those fish. A living Tabuga pisces darter would be irrefutable, but a dead one would serve. Right now I've got the worst possible situation, a rumor that could make the WDC sound desperate." As she talked, she could feel her shoulders tightening.

"Miranda." Tom touched the side of her face where her dimple hid. "Remember that sometimes things take longer than you want. Whatever happens, I have a lot of confidence in the way you do your job."

The roughness of his fingers on her skin was pleasant, and completely unexpected. It had the desired effect, bringing a smile across her face. "Well, if Gordon actually had a Tabuga pisces darter, then there are more out there. If the traps are empty, I'll look for the ones Gordon caught. They're bound to be around the area where he was attacked. Dead is better than nothing."

"Miranda, don't get your hopes too high."

"I should have looked harder yesterday. I was so worried about Gordon, and dusk was falling. But I should have looked...."

"I did look, and I didn't see anything. Whoever attacked Gordon could have taken the fish, or simply thrown them into the woods." Tom saw the frown cross her face, and he could almost read her thoughts. Her forehead was lined with worry. "Don't look so glum. The WDC was working on a strong case before Gordon's discovery."

"Nothing we had came close to an endangered species, Tom. The darter would cinch our case."

He could see the importance in Miranda's green eyes. He'd spent a large part of the night thinking about Gordon and his find, and his attack. He wasn't certain what he believed, but one thing he had no doubt about was Miranda Conner's sincere desire to protect the river. "*If* the fish are in the river, we'll find more there."

"That's a mighty big 'if.'"

"But mermaids are lucky." He offered her a grin.

"I hope you're right." She answered his grin with one of her own. Tom's encouragement was infectious. "You always know the right thing to say, don't you?"

"I've never been accused of that before." His smile turned thoughtful. "Words aren't that much help in this situation." He'd given his position with the WDC some thought, too, and he wasn't comfortable with his involvement. The trouble was, he couldn't have walked off and left anyone in trouble. And Miranda in particular.

"You'd be surprised how a few words can improve a situation. You know, I get the impression that the Tabuga may be as important to you as it is to me." Miranda was watching the play of emotions across his strong features. He was a complex man, a man who had hooked her interest in more than a professional way.

Tom bent to lift their gear. His face hidden, he answered, "Maybe in different ways she is. That river is a lot of things to a lot of people." He straightened and nodded toward the rafts. "We'd better get busy or dusk will fall before we make Tabuga Springs. I'd like to get this party off the water with lots of daylight to spare."

"Good thinking." Miranda tied her bandanna around her forehead. "I'll be back in an hour or less."

"We'll be ready to go," Tom said, waving her into the woods. "Be careful."

Her mind was still on Tom Wilkes when she left the camp behind. The fresh scent of firs made the morning seem bright and hopeful, but Miranda was puzzling over Tom's comment about the river. She had felt a strong bond between man and river, a bond that she thought she knew and understood. But he had denied it in a backhanded sort of way. It was strange. He was strange, and she had to admit that was part of her fascination with him. He was strong and self-contained.

"Need some help?" Russ asked as he fell into step with Miranda. "I don't like the idea of you in the woods without some protection."

"Have you spotted any ravenous bears?" she teased.

"Hey, I was trying to be a gentleman," Russ replied. "I can see my sincere concerns are wasted on the WDC's legendary river woman."

"Okay," Miranda said, her laughter breaking some of the tension she'd felt since the night before. "I deserved that. I keep forgetting that you and Cynthia are much better at this game of verbal sparring than I am. I'll be very pleased to have your company, Russ. Help is always welcome." As she started down the trail, she signaled him to follow.

When they had left the camp behind, Russ tugged gently on her sleeve. "Hold up a minute."

Surprised, she turned to face him, her eyebrows arched in a silent question.

"Don't you find it a little strange that Tom Wilkes shows up at our camp, followed by that old mountain coot, just about the same time Gordon is attacked? Tell me if I'm stringing innocent coincidences together in some kind of paranoid conspiracy."

For a moment Miranda said nothing. "I've thought about the same things," she admitted. "I'm not certain how any of this fits together."

"Me either, but I'm beginning to develop some very serious theories."

"Like what?"

"Like Presley and Wilkes are sent to keep us busy."

"But why?" Miranda shrugged.

"Little fish, perhaps."

"Who could have known that Gordon would find anything? That's a wild leap of logic."

"Someone who knew all along that an endangered species lived in the Tabuga. Someone who knows the river well, and stands to benefit from the development. Someone who might pretend..."

Miranda held up a hand to stop Russ. "I know where you're going with this, but I sincerely believe Presley is opposed to development. It's just that he's also opposed to me personally."

"To you?" Russ rubbed his chin.

"Long story, very personal. It has nothing to do with the WDC or the antidam faction. When this is all over, I'll give you the gritty details." She smiled. "Word of honor."

"And what about Wilkes? Is that personal, too?"

The speculation in Russ's tone stunned Miranda. "What do you mean?"

"His eyes have been glued to you since he stepped into camp. He's been very handy, very helpful. He offers a ride for your wounded biologist because he's so conveniently parked downriver. It's just a bit more than my cynical reporter's mind can take in, I'm afraid. It looks to me like his interest is very personal and very well planned out."

Miranda did not try to deny it. The attraction between her and Tom Wilkes was unexpected, and definitely unprobed. She took a deep breath. "I'm not a cynic, Russ, but I'm not a fool, either. I'll have Tom's background checked as soon as we get home."

"Will there be a copy for your favorite reporter?" He grinned and winked.

"On one condition."

Russ groaned. "I hate conditions."

"Don't print anything about what Gordon thought he found. That is, unless we hit it lucky and have a thousand little darters trapped."

Russ looked over the wilderness, calculating the bargain he was about to make. He had plenty of material, and if the Tabuga fight went to the congressional subcommittee on the environment, it would be around for several months. He could afford to hold off, at least for a while.

"I'll hold it for a few days, but that's all I can promise."

"That's good enough," Miranda said. "If I don't find those darters in a few days, then it will be too late anyway. The hearing date should be set by the time we get back to Washington, so let's check those traps."

They found the place where Gordon had carefully set up the sample traps, but to Miranda's dismay the small fish collected in them were of such an ordinary variety that even she could identify them. She released them and reset the traps.

"Coming back?" Russ made sure the line holding the submerged traps was secure.

"I may have to," she said as she dried her hands on her shorts. "If there's a chance of finding an endangered species, I'll camp on this river till the winter freeze hits."

"I hate to be the one to remind you, but you don't have that much time."

"Let's check the place Gordon was attacked," Miranda said, uncomfortably aware of the limited time she had.

They located the spot where Kurt had found the biologist and began a careful search of the underbrush. There was no sign of any fish.

"This is getting stranger and stranger," Russ said after they'd covered the area for the third time. "There's not even a fishy scent. You'd think there would be some remains."

"We should have found something," Miranda agreed. She felt her hope sinking.

"Unless Gordon made the whole thing up."

She felt Russ's gaze as he waited for her reaction. "I'll be frank with you." Miranda picked up a handful of leaves and twigs and sifted through them. "I've thought of that possibility, but it doesn't make sense. Gordon has no personal stake in this, and he has a lot to lose by lying. I mean, his reputation would be shot to hell."

"What if…someone offered him money to say he found an endangered species?"

"Someone like the WDC?"

"That's one possibility."

"We don't do business that way, Russ." Miranda wasn't even upset by the accusation. "Our reputation is impeccable. We're by-the-book every step of the way, and we have the records to prove it."

"I'm not making any accusations, I'm just thinking out loud."

"And that's exactly why I don't want this fish story to break in the paper before we have a sample. Everyone will think the WDC is trying to pull a fast one."

Russ grinned. "I see your point. And if that were the case, I'd think you would be trying to get me to print a story about some fish that were hijacked by a mysterious assailant."

Miranda chuckled. "Well, I haven't thought it through that far, but yes, I guess that's what I would be trying to do. Right now, though, we've sifted every clump of dirt around." She checked her watch. "Tom will be waiting for us to break camp. We'd better head on back."

"What about the fish?"

"I can't manufacture something that isn't there." She forced a cheerful note. "If the fish are in this river, I'll get one some way or another."

Miranda set a fast pace back to camp. It was time to get her charges on the river and get them home. The work was stacked a mile high on her desk, but she was also concerned about Gordon's health, not to mention the new worries Russ had handed her.

"Any luck?"

Tom stood in the place where her tent had been. There was no sign of anyone else.

"Nothing," Russ answered. "Not even a sign that a hungry mountain cat came by and ate the evidence."

"Nothing in the traps?" Tom directed his question to Miranda, ignoring the reporter.

"Nothing," Miranda confirmed. "Where is everyone else?"

"Ready to go. Cynthia just took the last bundle down to the rafts." He turned to the reporter. "She was asking for you, by the way. She said something about your notebooks getting wet."

"She's a funny lady," Russ said, but he hurried down toward the river with only a backward glance at Miranda.

Left alone with Tom, Miranda felt a sudden awkwardness. She didn't like the implications that Russ had made, but she was also smart enough to realize she had some checking to do where Tom Wilkes was concerned. She'd taken people at face value before—and the price had been high and painful. The Tabuga was too important to risk.

"You left the traps, didn't you?"

Tom's question threw her into a dilemma. She wasn't certain she wanted him to know that she planned to return.

"Instead of making a special trip, why don't you let me check the traps tomorrow and get whatever is caught inside? I can have them flown to you," Tom said. "I promise."

"That's asking a little much of a stranger," she said slowly. Was Tom's offer aboveboard? He was almost too willing to help. She wanted to kick Russ for planting seeds of suspicion.

"It would be less trouble for me to check the traps than for you to fly back from Washington." He sensed her reluctance. If he had good sense, he'd withdraw his offer and let the WDC fend for itself. He'd never intended to get so deeply involved.

Miranda ran through the calendar of days. If Tom actually found the darters and flew them to her, he could save her a lot of time. If he checked the traps the next day and found nothing, she would still have a day or two to get back to Tabuga Springs and check the traps herself.

"I shouldn't impose on your good nature, Tom, but it would save me a trip. Time is at a premium in this case, as you know."

"Glad to help," he assured her. "I don't think anyone involved in the dam would want to do anything to damage the river or upset the ecology of the area."

Miranda chuckled, a sound with little mirth. "I wish I could believe that. Developers are notorious for putting profit before environment. That's why the WDC has such a hard fight, and why we lose sometimes. We don't lie, but the other side does."

"Let me add a word of caution, Miranda. Don't tar all developers with the same brush."

"When I find one that is truly honest, I'll..."

"What?" he asked, amused at her inability to finish the sentence.

"I'll ride down Pennsylvania Avenue on a white horse with a banner proclaiming the developer."

The mental picture of Miranda perched on a white horse, long hair flowing behind her, was both sensual and amusing. "I'll remind you of this one day," he warned her.

"Yeah, well, I won't be too worried about boning up on my riding skills," she said. Tom's direct gaze challenged her. "Is there something else?"

"I have a long memory," he said, then broke the tension with a laugh.

THE RIVER SWEPT them along at a pace that kept Miranda's mind involved in maneuvering the raft. Tom led, his familiarity with the river putting him in a better position to pick and choose among the rocks. The sound of the river increased as they neared Devil's Hole, and Miranda braced her body for the challenge of the swift water.

The Hole was a deep gully that filled with a treacherous current where the river narrowed and plunged down a series of small waterfalls. The drops were only a couple of feet, but a miscalculation could thrust the raft too far to either side, where swirling crosscurrents were waiting. At this point the riverbanks were high, and five rocks appeared to block the natural channel. Miranda knew the course was navigable, but to an inexperienced rafter the appearance of the rocks could create panic.

Following Tom's lead, she steered through the foaming rapids in a series of maneuvers that took her whole concentration and only a few minutes. When they came through and were safely on the other side, she smiled and gave Tom the thumbs-up sign that indicated her renewed spirits.

As the river widened and flattened out, she caught up with Tom and the two rafts drifted together. Passing clusters of cabins that began to populate the riverbanks, Miranda told the group about the people of the Tabuga wilderness, a varied assortment of families who could trace their roots back to Scotland and Ireland.

She knew many of the local legends, and she recounted them with increasing passion. Pausing a moment for a breath, she felt Tom's steady stare on her. His amber eyes held the power of touch, and she felt a warm flush climb into her cheeks.

"Tom probably knows much more about this area than I do," she said apologetically. "Perhaps he'll tell us something about Tabuga Springs. By my best calculations, we should be there at any moment."

"I agree with your time schedule, but I don't believe I can add anything to your talk" he said. "Few outsiders can express such appreciation for a place. I'm impressed."

"Since the first day I saw the Tabuga, I've loved her," Miranda said simply. "Over the years I've thought about her many times, especially when things around me were unpleasant." She gave an embarrassed chuckle. "But personal testimonials won't make much difference to the developers. Beauty isn't an element to them, only money."

No matter how she tried, she couldn't contain the note of bitterness that crept into her voice. Glancing at Tom, she saw that he was looking away from her. He maneuvered his raft and pointed up ahead with his paddle.

"Tabuga Springs," he called, and the rustic wooden bridge across the river had all of the impact Miranda had hoped for. The questions came fast and furious.

"Yes, the dams will destroy Tabuga Springs and all of the settlements downriver," Miranda said. She was skillfully leading the reporters to explore the issues involved in saving the Tabuga when she saw three stout men, all dressed in army fatigues. They stood, unmoving, on the old bridge. With the sun behind the men, Miranda couldn't make out their features, but their stance was threatening.

"Tom?" she called over the noise of the river. If he heard, he didn't respond. His full attention was on the men whose features were hidden by the blast of sun at their backs.

"Hey, who are those guys?" Russ demanded.

"Ignore them," Miranda warned. Something about them made her uneasy. It was only an assumption, but she felt as if they were somehow involved in the attack on Gordon Simms.

Slowly the rafts drifted under the bridge. Above her the three men held motionless. Time ticked by in slow motion. When the first bottle splashed down an inch from her raft, Miranda wasn't even startled. She'd expected trouble of some kind.

The second bottle struck her shoulder, glancing off into the river.

"Hey!" Russ started to stand in the raft.

"Ignore them," Miranda hissed. "I'm not hurt."

The men laughed, and the third missile was a large rock. It hit the center of the raft but did no damage to the tough material. The men laughed harder.

"Cowards!" Russ called out.

"For God's sake, shut up!" Fred Elton urged. "We're sitting ducks down here. If you provoke them, they can hurt any of us."

"Fred's right," Miranda said. She saw the fear in Cynthia's face. "Everyone sit down and let's get through this without injuries. We'll do something when we get on shore."

"I'd do something now if I had a gun," Russ fumed.

"The best thing you can do is to sit down and shut up," Tom said calmly. "We're at a severe disadvantage. Right now they're playing with us. We don't want them to get serious."

The two rafts had separated, but they were within easy distance of each other. Looking at Tom's granite jawline, Russ settled back into the raft. They were ten, then twenty and finally fifty yards beyond the bridge.

"Tom, do you know them?" Miranda spoke softly, but her voice carried on the water. If Tom heard, he didn't answer. His gaze was locked on the landing that marked Tabuga Springs.

"If that's the people you're trying to save, maybe the dams should go in," Fred Elton said.

"We don't know who they are, and you shouldn't judge the whole river by three men." Miranda tried to be diplomatic, but Fred's comment was the worst type of prejudice. "They might not even be local people. Remember, for as much money as the WDC collects, the prodam forces probably have triple. Those men could have been hired to do that."

They docked the rafts without further comment and climbed onto the bank in front of a small cluster of curious townspeople. Miranda made her way through to Tom. "Did you know those men? I'm going to have a talk with the sheriff, and if you know who they are, it might be a big help."

"I have to take care of some business," he said brusquely, "so give me your address and I'll express those fish samples to you like I promised." His gaze shifted down the street, and though Miranda followed it, she saw nothing of interest.

"I'd like to thank you properly for all of your help," Miranda said, puzzled by his sudden frostiness. He was distant, his entire attention focused at the end of the small town. "Could I buy you a cup of coffee, or a very late lunch?"

"No, thanks. I was glad to help." He stepped away from her, his expression determined. "Now, if you'll excuse me."

"Tom?" she questioned. "What is it?"

"I'll be in touch," he said, avoiding all eye contact. "Good luck with your project."

Stung by his unexpected behavior, Miranda nodded. "As you wish," she said stiffly, and then turned away to make sure the equipment was safely off-loaded. The trip had been only six days, but she felt as if she'd aged at least five years.

"HARD TO FIND clues in a wilderness," Sheriff Uley Carter said matter-of-factly. Miranda was so tired she couldn't tell if she was being overly sensitive or if the sheriff actually seemed uninterested in the attacks on her group.

"Sheriff Carter, a man was assaulted and my entire party was placed in danger. Aren't you even going to try and find who did it?" Exasperation made her voice loud.

"Nobody was hurt. What's all the sqaukin' about? The egghead had a bump. No real harm done. You city folks need to toughen up."

"What does it take to get you concerned, a murder?" Miranda lost her control and shouted. "You're supposed to protect innocent people."

"Now it's a fact that mountain folks don't like outsiders stickin' their noses into our business." All attempts at friendliness were gone from Carter's rotund face. His blue eyes were cold and watery. "You want to play safe, stay in Washington and stay off the Tabuga." He pushed his flat face up to hers. "Or next time somebody might get hurt. And it might be you."

"Thanks for your *help*." She stalked out of the sheriff's office and onto the street. Gordon had rejoined her party, a white bandage around his head and a clean bill of health in hand. They had just enough time to make it back to the airport for their flight home.

"Tom Wilkes left in a big hurry," Russ commented.

"He sure did," Miranda said. She looked down the street once and then herded the group into the waiting van.

From his position at the end of town, Tom watched Miranda leave the courthouse and gather her group for a return to the airport and the flight back to Washington. He waited until she ushered her charges into the large van and drove away before he started walking toward the old bridge that hung over the Tabuga.

His stride was long, forceful; a grim expression was etched in his face. When he arrived at the bridge, it was empty. The three men were gone. He turned abruptly on his heel and kept walking north. The road took him past several offices, a beauty shop and finally to a country-style restaurant. He pushed through the door and scanned the room.

Cheryl Summers was sitting at a small table with a dark-haired man.

"Cheryl, Doc, what are you doing here?" he asked, taking a chair uninvited at the table. "I'll have some coffee," he said to the waitress.

"We were supposed to meet some of the crew from Mountain Terrace subdivision, but they haven't shown up," Cheryl said, annoyance turning her lips down slightly. "These people still haven't learned how important punctuality is. They come for appointments when they feel like it, *if* they feel like it, and that's the same way they work." Exasperation colored her tone.

"I was trying to explain to Cheryl that many of the Tabuga Springs people find it difficult to work for someone else. They're independent, and they don't like taking orders." Doc gave Cheryl a warm smile. "Not even from a woman as pretty as you."

"You know how to take the sting out of chauvinism," she said, her hand reaching out to squeeze Doc's arm.

"So, you had a little trouble on the river?" Doc said, turning the conversation to Tom. "What happened? I didn't realize we'd agreed to sponsor a dangerous trip. I thought the WDC was renowned for its competent staff.''

Tom sipped the fresh coffee the waitress put before him and leaned back in his chair. "Ms. Conner is competent."

"How gallant a defense," Cheryl said, a smile touching her eyes. "Tell us what happened."

"Someone clipped the biologist while he was away from the rest of the party. Then, as we were rafting in, three men threw bottles and rocks at Miranda."

"Three locals?" Doc's voice showed his amazement.

"I had the unpleasant feeling that it might have been three of our employees. Maybe Clark Presley's son."

"Why in the world would Jason Presley be involved in such a thing?" Doc asked. "His entire family should support the WDC effort. Besides, Jason isn't stupid. That kind of trouble can be serious."

"Clark has some kind of grudge against the woman who led the group, and you know how easily Jason is influenced by his father. No harm was done, but the implications were very clear."

"There's more support around here for the dam than you think," Cheryl said. "Some of the locals believe everyone will get a new home, a steady job and the great American dream. They might view an environmental group as troublemakers."

"If only it were that simple," Doc said softly. "Hey, that scientist was babbling about some great find. Anything to it?"

Tom hesitated. "He found something, but when he was attacked the fish sample was destroyed. He seemed positive that he'd discovered some extinct species."

"Now that could throw a cog in development of the river system," Cheryl said. "No developer with a pinch of ethics would want to risk destroying a species. I guess Ms. Conner was ecstatic."

"Cautious," Tom said, a smile touching his face. "She's a very cautious lady."

"Sounds like you have more than a passing interest," Cheryl teased. "Hum! Is the invincible Tom Wilkes actually weakening to female temptation?"

"Not Tom!" Doc insisted, shaking his head at Cheryl. "Not the man of steel! Never!"

"Okay, you two, that's enough." Tom finished his coffee and stood. "I was going to have a word with those three men I saw on the bridge, but maybe it would be best if I let it go. No real damage was done."

"That sounds smart," Doc said. He rose, too. "Now I'm supposed to be twenty miles north of town checking on an expectant mother. I'd better get moving."

"Me, too." Cheryl picked up her purse and stood. "The new housing project is moving along on target. Tom, those designs are fabulous. We should have twenty units ready for occupancy in another month. It's going to make a big difference for some of the poor people around here. They may actually be warm this winter." She linked her arms between those of the two men. "So let's get cracking."

MIRANDA'S SMALL OFFICE seemed even more cramped after the week-long stay in the wilderness, but she ignored her surroundings and settled down to read the files Connie had stacked on her desk.

The top of the stack was a report on the Tabuga pisces darter. Miranda scanned the file, noting that the fish species required a cold, fast-flowing stream of pure water. The creature was thought to be extinct. Her fingers drummed on her desk as she read on. Gordon had said the fish he'd captured were silver with a distinctive yellow stripe. The species had a ganoid scale that was three times heavier than modern darters and was a crucial link in the study of the evolutionary process. It sounded like the Tabuga pisces darter, and she studied the photograph that went with the file. It was possible that Gordon had actually found a darter. Just possible. She put the file aside.

She buzzed the intercom on her desk. "Connie, any word on who made that donation?"

"None," Connie answered. "The postmark was from this city. The note was typed, as were the instructions. Cash was enclosed. All efforts to trace it have failed."

"Thanks." Miranda picked up the next file. Tom Wilkes was written on the flap. She flipped it open. Wilkes was listed as a resident of Tabuga Springs. His occupation was farming. He owned over two thousand acres, some of it bordering the river. There was a plat of his property included, and Miranda could easily see how he would both benefit and suffer from any changes in the river. If the dams went through and a resort community was developed, Tom would become very wealthy. But the downside was that he would lose the natural beauty of the river. She held the file and thought. How important was that to Tom? Remembering him on the water, she thought it might be very important.

Returning to the file, she found that he was listed as single, had lived and worked in California, was self-employed as an architect. She found that interesting. Tom had never mentioned his work. Strange. There were several clippings, all old, where he'd won design awards. One for a home. The picture showed a modern structure that hung off the face of a mountain. Very Californian. There was a shopping center design, a renovation of an old waterfront area in Boston. He was a very busy, and talented, man.

She closed the manila folder and picked up another. This one was very light. Inside she found a single page with Clark Presley's personal information. Widowed, he had one son and a hunk of land that touched Tom Wilkes's. The Tabuga made for strange neighbors, she thought. There was little of interest as far as Presley was concerned. The WDC computer had turned up nothing of importance.

Tossing the file into the return stack, she stood and straightened her dress. "I'm going out for a paper," she told Connie as she headed for the door. "I'll be back in a moment."

At the corner deli she found a *Washington Telegraph*. Russ Sherman's front-page story was everything she'd hoped for. Wilderness Endangered By High Profit Dam. The story was played on the top half of the front page and opened with an account of Gordon's attack. Russ had skillfully crafted a story sympathetic to the WDC's plight. It also made Miranda out to be something of a heroine in the process. Scanning the story quickly, she felt slightly embarrassed by Russ's effusive praise.

She rushed through the article, thankful to see that though Russ had hinted at a possible biological discovery, he did not mention the fish Gordon had found. There were several paragraphs concerning Tom that were also flattering. She tucked it under her arm. She'd send a clipping, maybe. She'd been hoping all morning that he would call with some news about the darters.

Before she could close the office door, Connie waved her over to the desk. "You had a delivery while you were gone." Her voice sparkled with excitement. "I put it in your office."

"Is it the fish?" Miranda couldn't believe it. "Tom sent them?"

"That was the return address, Tabuga Springs, but I didn't open the case. It looked pretty well protected."

"Let's open it!" Miranda hurried into her office with Connie close on her heels. She peeled the tape off the box and removed the specially constructed carton. "I can't believe he found them," she said, wedging her finger in the lid to gently pry it open.

"The Tabuga may be saved," Connie said. "I'm so happy for you, Miranda. I know how much this means to you."

Miranda's face turned from excitement to ash. She covered the small case immediately.

"What's wrong?" Connie touched Miranda's arm. "What is it?"

"I'm not certain. Fish guts, I think."

"What?" Connie took the container and lifted the lid. "What sick person would do such a thing?" she asked. "That's exactly what it is. But there's something else." She pulled out a slip of paper.

Unfolding it, she read the message out loud, her voice breaking. "Be warned. Mind your own business or pay the price. Stay away from the Tabuga."

Chapter Five

"Sure you know how to handle a four-wheel drive?" the man at the Ashville, North Carolina, car rental counter asked, eyeing her with skepticism.

"I'm sure," Miranda said. There wasn't time to waste berating some local macho man for provincial beliefs. "Here's the money in advance, now give me the key."

"Okay, sweetie. Just be careful. Some of these mountain roads are steep and curvy. Sort of like you."

Thinking of several countries where such rude behavior would call for a tongue extraction, Miranda glared. She'd had plenty of fools to suffer, and he was just another in a long list. What was important was that she had the keys clanking in her hand. She was still two hours from Tabuga Springs. She wanted to get to the river, check her traps, find the fish and get out without anyone ever knowing of her presence.

The disgusting "present" and the note had frightened her secretary. She could still hear Connie's pleas, begging her to stay in Washington. But the dismembered fish had been a clear challenge—and an undisguised attempt to intimidate her. Well, she'd been a fool, but she'd never been a coward. She was going to the river and no one was going to scare her away. There were plenty of questions she wanted answered, and at the top of her list was who had sent the fish entrails and the note.

Only Tom had known she was hoping to get a fish sample. And Gordon. She thought, mentally checking off names. And Russ Sherman. Maybe Cynthia, depending how much Russ shared with the blond broadcast journalist. There was a spark of romance between the two, and it was possible Russ had told her everything. Possible, but not probable. Russ loved a scoop more than any woman, and Cynthia was career competition.

Well, once she had the darters, she'd worry about the threat. She could spend the rest of her life speculating. She needed hard evidence, and she'd look for that after the Tabuga was safe.

Gordon had told her exactly how to trap the fish without injuring it. He'd also told her that the chances were good the darters would remain in one location for at least a week. They liked the quiet pools near rapid water.

Whether it was luck or skill involved, Gordon had stumbled on what he hoped was one of the last remaining breeding grounds for the Tabuga pisces darter. When she'd called to tell him about her plans to get another sample, he'd been very concerned. Not for her but for the fish. She smiled for the first time that day, amused and heartened by Gordon's enthusiastic support for the WDC. He'd even volunteered to testify against the dams for no fee. That was sure to impress the environmental panel, and the politicians.

As she drew closer to Tabuga Springs, Tom's presence was harder to ignore. He was irrevocably linked with the river. She had not heard from him about the fish. The only message from the Tabuga wilderness had been the carton of fish entrails and the threat. Had he attempted to find the darters for her? There was every possibility he'd gotten involved in his farming. There was also the darker chance that he was responsible for the "gift" she'd received. Even as she thought it, she did not fully believe it. Not Tom. What purpose would it serve?

As she steered the Jeep toward the blue-hazed mountains, she pictured him again on the river. His sun-bronzed face was strong, filled with determination and what she'd read as honesty and integrity. She wanted to see him; there was no need pretending to herself that she didn't. The need intensified in the clear mountain air. This time, though, she had to use her brain instead of her heart. Her relationship with Tom was better unexplored until the Tabuga was safe.

Skirting the small town completely, Miranda headed downriver and found the old wooden bridge marked on her map. Stomach lurching at the narrow wooden boards, she pointed the Jeep forward and gently touched the gas pedal. She was halfway across when she felt the bridge tremble and a rusted-out pickup truck roared up behind her.

Three young boys were jammed into the front seat. The driver pumped the horn and hugged the rear of her Jeep as they all laughed.

"Get going or get off of the bridge!" they yelled at her.

Miranda felt like parking the Jeep and getting out to give them a piece of her mind, but caution prevailed. Keeping a slow pace, she finally cleared the other side of the bridge.

The pickup zoomed past her with a spray of gravel and a honking horn. Then it was gone. She settled her nerves and put the incident out of her mind. Locals were familiar with the rickety bridge and had little patience for intimidated out-of-towners.

She scanned to the right as she drove along, looking for the woodland trail that Tom had said he'd used to drive to their campsite. She'd packed a sleeping bag, a little food, an extra trap, the sample cases, a knife, a compass and a few first-aid items. She hoped the fish would cooperate with her, but she was prepared to spend the night, if that was what it took. The biggest complication was the impending hearing in Washington. Just before she'd boarded the plane for Ashville, Fred Elton had called and said the Tabuga issue had been given a tentative place on the environmental subcommittee's calendar. A definite time wasn't slotted, but there was a possibility the matter would be called within the next twenty-four hours

A large knot of tension crawled up Miranda's neck, and she forced her mind to relax. One thing at a time, she had to remind herself. The most important thing she could do was to get the fish sample. *And see Tom,* her heart threw in. That wouldn't be half-bad, she had to agree.

The drive through the forest began to work its magic on her as her fingers unclenched on the wheel and her jaw lost its rigid, unyielding look. The sun was hot, but the breeze through the open-air Jeep made it all seem pleasant, like summer days out of school when there was all the time and freedom in the world. She unbraided her long hair and let the wind whip it behind her.

Winding in and out of the mountains, the road required close attention. Miranda took her time, intent on making no stupid mistakes because of haste. She'd get the fish and get them back to Gordon. He'd warned her that the small creatures might remain in one pool for several days or a few weeks. They might move on to a pool with similar qualities, leaving no trace of a forwarding address.

Taking a hairpin turn to the right, Miranda slammed on the brakes. The same rusty old truck from the bridge careened toward her, looking as if two wheels were hanging off the side of the mountain.

Jerking the wheel to the left, Miranda cut into the other lane to give the truck more room. One young boy hung out the passenger window, grabbing at her as they passed. He seemed oblivious to the fact that the truck was just barely hanging on to the road.

"Come back!" he called after her with a wild yell, thrusting his upper body out of the window.

They were gone as quickly as they'd come, but their wild antics had taken her breath away. Adjusting the Jeep back in the proper lane, she inhaled and pressed the pedal a little harder. The best thing to do was leave the truck and its wild occupants as far behind as possible.

The farther into the mountains she traveled, the more serene her surroundings became. The peacefulness seemed to seep into her, and when she thought about Tom Wilkes, her unprotected emotions suffered a pang. Remembering his quiet strength, the appreciation he'd shown for the white deer, Miranda felt her heart stir. Tom was a man of the river and the mountains, a landowner. He, too, would suffer if the Tabuga were dammed, wouldn't he? She had to be sure, dead sure, of his motives.

Pulling the map from the seat, she sought the unnamed paths that served as roads through the mountains. The forestry service had been kind enough to provide the WDC with extensive maps that showed every hiking trail and lane in the area. Tom had come in on one of the twisting dirt paths, but she wasn't certain exactly which one. Her task would have been easier if she'd contacted Kurt and Betty Murray, but such an action might have alerted the wrong people.

When the two-rut path turned left, Miranda pulled as far to the side of the road as she could and stopped the Jeep. She'd been driving for over two hours, and she sensed that she was getting closer and closer to the location she sought. The sun was past midday, and soon the chill would begin to invade the deep foliage of the woods. Her fingers rapidly traced the lines of the map. She wanted to check her traps and establish some type of camp with a clearly marked trail back to the Jeep before darkness settled around her.

"Need some help?"

The unexpected question made her gasp as she crumpled the map and looked up. A tall, curly-haired man stood next to the left front fender of her Jeep. He was dressed in camouflage fatigues and he carried a rifle.

"No, thanks," she said. There wasn't a sign of another car on the road.

"These woods can be mighty dangerous. You weren't thinking of driving back into them, were you?" His eyes never left her face as he talked.

"No, I was just stopping to check my map." She kept her gaze away from the trail that led to Devil's Hole. She would be damned before she gave herself away with some overt gesture.

"Not many tourists make it into these woods. Or could it be that you have some business around these parts?"

The stranger kept his tone friendly, but his eyes were calculating, as if he already knew the answers to his questions. It was as if he waited for her to lie.

"I've always loved the Tabuga wilderness," she said easily. "What about you? I thought most men would be at work." She waited to see if he'd rise to her gambit.

"Oh, I'm working." He took a half step closer. "My family owns some land on the river and we've been having trouble with trespassers and weirdos. We've been thinking we might be forced to take some drastic action, if you know what I mean."

"No, I don't. Maybe you should be more explicit. What do you mean?" Her heart was pumping madly, but she knew instinctively that she could never show fear to the young man who stood so tall before her.

"Well, the law don't look favorably on trespassers around these parts. A man has a right to protect his land."

"Does he have a right to attack innocent and unarmed people?"

"Now I suppose that depends on your definition of innocent, doesn't it?" He grinned. "Sometimes innocent people get hurt by mistake, you know."

"Oh, I know. Sometimes it's deliberate, too. Tell me, Mr...." She waited for him to supply a name, but he didn't. "I should think that you'd use some caution. There are environmentalists on the river these days trying to save the Tabuga from development. If you and your family really love this river, maybe you should cooperate instead of threaten."

"Oh, this is no threat, it's a promise."

The loud honking of a horn warned that a vehicle was flying around the curve of the road. Miranda heard the laughter of young men, and she felt another jolt of fear. The man before her was trouble enough. Her fingers slipped on the ignition key. If worse came to worst, she could try to outrun them. She had the better vehicle, but they had the familiarity with the roads. It would be a toss-up.

"Hey, baby!" The young men ground to a halt. The rusty truck burped a black cloud of exhaust. The man standing beside her vehicle threw an impatient glance at them.

"Hey, Jason, we didn't mean to cut in on your gig," the driver called out. He raced the motor several times. "Tell your old man we said hello." With a jerk of the passengers' heads, the truck sped forward thirty yards and then screeched to a halt.

"Hey, Jason, where's your truck?" the driver yelled. "Need a ride?"

Jason looked at Miranda for a full thirty seconds, then walked down the road and got in the back of the pickup. They roared around the curve and disappeared.

Miranda lost no time cranking her vehicle and pointing it down the narrow trail. When she was safely out of view, she stopped and uncrumpled the map. Tracing the road through the winding mountains, she found that it seemed to parallel the river at a location just above Devil's Hole. By her best estimation, it had to be the road Tom had driven.

The road plunged down a steep incline and reared up at a seventy-five-degree angle across the ravine. Synchronizing the gas and clutch, she moved downhill and then gunned the vehicle aggressively as she urged it to the top of the incline.

With loose rocks and dirt spewing from the wheels, she gained the top of the ravine and took a moment to rest. She'd never really driven in the mountains, and if this first hurdle was any indication of what it was like, she knew it was going to take all of her mental and physical reserves. There was no other option, though, so she put the Jeep in gear and slowly drove toward what she hoped would be the Tabuga.

Thirty minutes later she parked and withdrew her compass from her pack. Grabbing the traps, she headed due north down a barely distinguishable trail. She'd brought along the red marking flags so she could find her way back, and a hatchet was an extra precaution in case her flags weren't sufficient or she needed more firewood.

Walking as quietly as she could, she was delighted by the wildlife activity. Sassy from an abundance of food, squirrels ran from tree to tree, fussing angrily at her. She laughed at them, ignoring their bad tempers. Two does grazed quietly in a small meadow. Miranda watched them for several moments, thinking of the white buck she'd seen with Tom. That had been a magic sight. She could well understand why the Indians had imbued the albino deer with strange powers. The night itself had contained a little bit of magic. She was thinking of Tom when the does caught her scent. They sniffed the air and bounded away, white patches bobbing in the sunlight.

The trail was so overgrown it was barely visible, but she continued in a northerly direction until she heard the sounds of the river in the distance. Her skin tingled with excitement. If she'd calculated properly, she would hit the river about a half a mile up from Devil's Hole. There would be another short hike, and then she'd be near the location where Gordon had found the fish.

The Tabuga was as splendid as she remembered. The water roared past, determined to hurl itself as fast as possible down the mountain and into the ocean. She smiled as she thought how direct nature was. The water had a course to follow, and it did, with a singleness of purpose that could be deadly. There was neither malice nor benevolence in the water, only natural law.

The sun upon her back reminded her of her mission, and she hefted her pack again and headed west, following as close to the bank of the river as possible. At times the footing was precarious, but she made good time and arrived at the spot where Gordon had taken the first fish. The line that had once held the traps securely to the bank was floating freely in the water. She drew it out, noticing the clean cut at the end. A smile touched her face and her dimple peeked through as she dropped her pack and carefully opened it. She pulled out the makings of a new trap—

she'd anticipated trouble—and set about putting it together. It took only a moment to construct the replacement trap, and she set it just as she'd been instructed.

When all of the work was done, she started gathering wood and establishing a camp. As the afternoon drifted away, she repressed her constant urge to check the traps. Meddling in the water might drive the fish away and only complicate her mission. When she could stand the inactivity no longer, she picked up her towel and shampoo and hiked farther upstream to the pool where she'd bathed before.

The water was icy, but after ten minutes of determined stroking, Miranda was immune to the chill. Frolicking from one side of the pool to the other, she loosened the reins on her pleasure and enjoyed the last hour of good sun. Tom had found her bathing in the Tabuga. The memory made her smile. He'd been chivalrous, a man with rare sensitivity. But what about reliability? He'd promised to check the traps for her, but there'd been no word from him.

The possibility that he'd removed the trap crossed her mind. What if he was trying to locate her now, with some darters? She bit her lip and tried to think it through. She had to be back in Washington the next day, but it would have been wiser if she'd contacted Tom about her plans. The trouble was that she didn't completely trust him. She wanted to. She was definitely attracted to what she knew of him. But that wasn't enough. Not when the Tabuga was at stake. Still, the thought crossed her mind—what would it be like to camp with him? A pulse of excitement raced through her body, and she abandoned the water and her thoughts. Surely by now she'd learned the wisdom of caution. Surely, she chided herself.

Climbing to the bank, she shivered in the brisk air and hurriedly dried and dressed.

TOM SNAPPED OFF the desk light and pushed the pages he held into the bottom drawer. With a quick turn of the key, he locked the desk and stood up. So, old Clark Presley had not been completely off his bean with his accusations about Miranda Conner. Not completely.

He dialed the WDC number in Washington, wondering if Miranda would be able to detect anything in his voice. When the secretary answered the phone, he was told that Ms. Conner "wasn't available."

"I have some information she needs," Tom pressed. "It's about the Tabuga." He'd expected to find her waiting anxiously by the telephone. He knew how important the fish were to her.

"I'm sorry, Ms. Conner is out of the office. I'd be glad to take a message."

There was an undercurrent of suspicion in the secretary's voice, and Tom got the distinct feeling that something had happened.

"I was supposed to send Ms. Conner some fish," he said.

"And did you?"

"There was a problem with the traps. They were gone," Tom answered. "If there's some way to get in touch with Miranda, I'd like to speak with her. It's urgent. I'm trying to find some more traps for her, but there doesn't seem to be anything in Tabuga Springs to fit the bill."

"I'll be sure she gets your message as soon as she returns," Connie said.

Tom replaced the telephone with a sense of growing dissatisfaction. What was Miranda up to now? She should have been in her office waiting for his call.

Suddenly he knew she was on the river. She was just that kind of woman. She wouldn't rely on him, not when her river was at stake. He flipped the shades in his office and checked the sun. It was late afternoon. He'd make a stop by Ketchin's Cafe and let Doc know where he was headed. If he was lucky, he'd be able to find Miranda's camp before dark.

As he walked the board sidewalks of the little town, he went over again the information he'd gleaned from the report he'd ordered on Miranda Conner. Having money to hire investigators was a mixed blessing. A man could find out things he didn't necessarily want to know. Miranda had been in Washington for five years with the WDC. Her record was impressive. She'd fought, and won, three major environmental battles, two against oil companies and one against a fishing industry. She had a good education, an average family background—just the one little worm in the apple. Her ex-boyfriend, Gregory Henson, was doing time in a federal prison for blowing up an armory building in Georgia. Miranda had been the star witness in the prosecution against the man. She'd gone from girlfriend to snitch.

Tom had heard Clark Presley make the accusation, but he'd never believed him. Clark wasn't the most reliable source of information, but this time he'd had his facts straight.

"Tom!" Cheryl Summers called. The bright summer sun set her hair aflame. "Doc and I were looking for you. How about dinner tonight?"

"I've already made plans," he said with a rueful grin. Cheryl was a smart woman with a habit of making his brother happy. She was also a great cook.

"Your favorite, lasagna."

"Now that's cruel," he said, grinning. "I'll be eating beef jerky and cold beans."

"Camping again?"

"I thought I might."

"You've been spending a lot more time on that river. I'm beginning to think you don't want to start a development project." She turned down the corners of her mouth. "If this is so hard on you and Doc, maybe you should give up the entire idea of developing a resort."

"I've always been torn on this issue, just like Doc," Tom answered. "It's hard to change the place you've grown up."

"Even when you know how it will improve the life for so many people here?" She swept her hand, indicating the town. "I think we should take a poll and ask the people what they really want."

"That's not a bad idea," Tom said. "But as callous as it sounds, Doc and I have to make the decision. We own the majority of the land that will be affected, at least in the immediate sense."

"Well, camp on the river and let the wisdom of the wilderness influence you," Cheryl said. "As a second alternative, I'll save you some lasagna for when you get back."

"Thanks. Where's Doc?"

"Inside, chewing the fat with Clark and some of the other men. It was more masculine chatter than I could stand. I'm headed back to the office." She gave a cheery wave as she started walking in the direction Tom had left.

Tom pushed the wooden café door open and stepped into the comforting smell of baking apple pies. He saw his brother at a small table with Clark Presley, his son, Jason and several other men.

"Your environmentalist is back at the Tabuga," Clark said. "I wonder what she's botched up this time."

"Could be she's dumping toxic wastes in the Tabuga," Tom said easily, signaling the waitress for some coffee. "No telling about those independent women. They might do anything."

Doc chuckled and slapped his brother's arm, but no one else in the group laughed.

"She's trouble, and you can try to make a fool of me if you want," Clark said, his cheeks flushing bright red against his white mustache. "I hope I don't have the last laugh. Someone's going to get hurt bad because of that woman."

"I'm going to check the hardware store for those hinges." Jason Presley stood. "See y'all later."

Tom sipped his coffee and chatted until he could get Doc's attention. Together they paid their tabs and sauntered onto the street.

"I'm going up the Tabuga for the night."

"Looking for that river woman?" Doc teased, his brown eyes assessing his brother. "You be careful, Clark acts like she's Satan reincarnated."

"There are some things about her that trouble me," Tom said honestly. "We'll talk when I get back."

"It's not anything I need to worry about, is it?" Doc glanced quickly up and down the street.

"No, it's nothing at all. I'll see you tomorrow."

Tom checked at the hardware store, but the clerk hadn't been able to finish rigging a trap. It would be the next day. Disgruntled, Tom went to his truck. When the motor failed to turn over, he thought it was a loose cable. The truck was new, and it ran like a top. He opened the hood, and a vivid curse escaped his lips. The spark plug wires had been neatly severed.

THE FIRE WAS more for company than anything else since she'd brought sandwiches to eat. As soon as it was blazing, Miranda got up and checked her traps. The mesh grilles were dismally empty, and she dropped them back into the water knowing that she'd have to spend the night. It wasn't possible that the small fish had moved on permanently. She couldn't allow herself to think that thought! She just needed a little more time.

Darkness crept over the eastern horizon with the stealth of a hungry cat. Once the sun settled behind the western trees, the blackness was almost instant. With an ample supply of firewood, Miranda relaxed, enjoying the warmth of the fire, the thick blackness of an overcast sky and the sound of the Tabuga. Her sleeping bag was spread beside the fire. When drowsiness began to overtake her, she slipped into it and rolled over to watch the dying embers. Sleep came in easy, delicious degrees.

The crackling beside her was only the fire, a sharp snapping of a tree limb. She turned restlessly, sinking back into deep sleep that spoke of her grueling day. When the snap came again, she tossed onto her side, glad for the warmth of the fire on her face but disturbed by the noise. A frown lightly brushed across her lips, but her eyes didn't open.

Sleepily she reached from beneath the sleeping bag to push a stray curl of hair from her face. The snap came closer, louder, and her eyes reluctantly opened.

The three shapes that steadily moved in to surround her were indistinct shadows in the darkness, but Miranda reacted with complete intuition. Still zipped in her sleeping bag, she rolled away from the fire, catching one man in the shins and sending him toppling to the ground with a muffled curse.

"Grab her!" he ordered as he twisted to avoid falling into the fire.

Hampered by the bag, Miranda rolled as hard as she could toward the underbrush. Her fingers found the zipper and she pulled it down, freeing her legs. In the darkness she caught a glimpse of a large object hurtling toward her, and she threw herself sideways in time to avoid one of the men.

"Get her!" the same man ordered. "Don't let her get away."

Miranda gave herself to the instinct to survive. Freed of the sleeping bag, she dived toward her backpack and the hatchet. When the wooden handle was in her grasp she crouched, ready to spring.

"Stay away from me," she said, her voice low and determined. "I have a weapon, and I know how to use it."

The men were fanned out in a semicircle in front of her. They shifted from foot to foot, none willing to be the first to attack.

"We'll rush her together," the man in the center ordered, pulling out a gun. "Remember, take her alive. Now on a count of three."

Miranda tensed, knowing that she would be overpowered but ready to inflict as much damage as possible.

"One, two." The men crouched low, ready for the attack.

"Stay back," a cool, unruffled voice commanded from just outside the camp.

"Get her!" the center man ordered as he rushed forward. The words seemed to catch in his throat as a loud shot rang through the night. Slowly he sank to the ground with a moan.

"Any other takers?" The same unruffled voice came from the edge of the river. In the darkness Miranda could barely distinguish a tall, lean man walking toward her.

"Now, you gentlemen put your hands on your heads," Tom Wilkes said, almost as if he were talking to children. "That's right. Nice and easy." He came to her side, his arm circling her shoulders.

Before Miranda could move to thank Tom, she saw one of her assailants point a gun at her. Tom's warning came with a harsh push. She felt herself falling when the bullet tore into her left arm. The two uninjured men broke and ran into the woods.

Chapter Six

The pain was fiery and constant, but Miranda didn't flinch as Tom cut the sleeve from her shirt and examined the wound by the beam of his flashlight. She averted her eyes, focusing on the distant horizon. Her mind was still numb from the sudden, violent attack.

"It's a clean hole, right through the muscle," he said. "You didn't happen to bring any medical supplies?"

"In the pack." Her dull voice was barely audible.

Beside the pack a man that neither could identify was dead. Tom had carefully checked for signs of life and also for some identification. There were none. Nor was there anything distinctive or familiar in the dead man's features. He resembled a hundred other dark-haired Caucasian men.

As Tom stepped over the dead man, he stifled any regret with the thought of what might have happened to Miranda had he not arrived. Who wanted the Tabuga dammed badly enough to kill? Certainly not him or anyone else at Clearwater Development. Doc and Cheryl had the same mixed feelings that he had. Not Clark Presley. He hated the idea of any type of development. He also had pretty strong negative feelings about Miranda Conner. Were they strong enough to warrant an attack that would permanently remove her from the WDC? A mental picture of Jason Presley at the café came to his mind. Clark and Jason were rough-and-tumble, and they had a penchant for bad decisions.

As he rummaged through Miranda's pack, he eyed the wilderness around them. The other two men had escaped, but that was no guarantee they had fled the area. They could be waiting, watching to finish what they had only begun. He had to get Miranda to safety.

"Once again, Miranda, I'm impressed with your camping skills." Returning to her side, he held a bottle of antiseptic and cotton aloft. He did not want her to sense his thoughts, so he forced a light tone in his voice.

"You saved my life." Miranda's voice was flat, emotionless. "Those men intended to hurt me." She paused, as if considering what might have happened. "I should have been more careful. I guess I convinced myself that the leg trap was an isolated incident, that it wouldn't happen again. That I could do my job."

He could hear the edge of hysteria in her voice. "What leg trap?" He kept his tone casual, hiding his increasing concern.

"When I scouted the wilderness to prepare for the expedition, someone tricked me by calling me down to the river. I was in a hurry and I tripped. Lucky thing, too. Someone had planted one of the steel traps right in the path. It missed me by a few inches."

The idea of what a trap might have done to Miranda made Tom's hands clench into fists. His jaw tightened, but he forced a casual attitude. "Maybe it had been there for some time. Hunters can forget their traps." No one could honestly have set such a trap for Miranda. A person caught in a leg trap would die an excruciating death; a person traveling alone was almost certainly doomed.

"No, I'd been down the path once before in daylight. That trap wasn't there. Someone put it there, and it was meant for me." Her voice started to rise.

"It's okay," he said, his hands moving through her hair. His fingers touched her cheek, her jaw. "It's okay, Miranda. You're safe for the moment, but we have to take care of that wound and get back to town."

"If you hadn't come, Tom, those men would have..."
She didn't finish.

Tom knelt beside her. "We were lucky tonight, but then
I've told you before, mermaids have lots of luck." He had
to keep her mind off the shooting. Her glassy eyes had him
worried. "You're going to have to hold the flashlight, and
I know this is going to really hurt. As soon as we get back
to town, Doc will fix this right up. He may even have a little something for the pain. Until then, we'll have to make
do the best we can."

"Who's trying to kill me?" she asked slowly.

"You're going to have to help me dress this wound,
Miranda." He could hear the shock in her voice and he had
to keep her calm.

She automatically grasped the flashlight he placed in her
hand and directed the beam where he wanted. Glancing
down at her arm, she saw the wound wasn't as bad as she
expected. When Tom opened the bottle of antiseptic, she
turned away, gritting her teeth against the burst of pain
that followed.

A low gasp escaped her tightly shut lips, and Tom pulled
her into his arms. "Scream," he urged her softly. "There's
no one to hear."

Stubbornly she shook her head. "It's okay," she said
raggedly, though tears fell down her cheeks. "That damn
stuff burns."

"So I've been told," Tom said, hugging her to him. His
arms held her securely until she could not longer resist the
haven he offered and relaxed against him.

"That's it," he whispered. "Relax." The feel of her in
his arms created an unexpected sensation. He was attracted to her; that he'd known from the first moment.
They'd both recognized the physical chemistry—and so far
had chosen to ignore it. This feeling was something different, though. He admired her, valued her strength and
determination. And he also wanted to protect her from
harm. "You know, you don't make it very easy for a man,
do you?"

The smile that touched Miranda's lips was tentative, but healing. "Oh, I thought a night like this would be standard for a man from the Tabuga wilderness mountains."

"I was frightened nearly out of my mind that I wouldn't get here in time." A rough quality had crept into his voice, and his hold on her tightened momentarily. "Someone did a little rewiring in my engine. I knew then that you were in big trouble, so I borrowed a truck."

"I'm confused," she said, resting her head on his chest. "It would help a lot if you told me how you happened to get here in the nick of time. How did you know I was here? And in trouble?"

"You've been in trouble since the first day I met you," he answered. "And it wasn't hard to find you since you left clues from one end of the county to the other."

"I was very discreet," she said, lifting her head.

"You might as well have taken an ad in the *Tabuga Springs Times!*"

"What?"

"Miranda, everyone who saw you driving past with that blond hair blowing out behind you took note. While I was trying to fix my wires I heard three kids talking about some golden-haired princess flying around the mountainside in a red Jeep. Then, of course, I knew you'd come back for more fish. It didn't take a brain surgeon to put the two together."

"I guess not," she said tiredly. "And I thought I was being so efficient."

"We'd better get back to town." Tom shifted so that he was between Miranda and the dead man. "The sheriff will have to send someone for him." He tried to help her up, but she resisted. "Come on, we have to get moving."

"Forget that idea," she said, suddenly stiffening in his arms. Pulling herself away from him, she straightened her back. The pain and shock and confusion had almost made her forget why she'd come. "I'm not going anywhere without those fish! What happened to the trap Gordon left?"

"Miranda, you've been shot. It would be smart to go into town and see a doctor. Besides, someone destroyed the trap, that's why I didn't have anything for you."

"I can't leave," she said. Her arm was throbbing deep in the bone. All she wanted to do was lie down and sleep, but she couldn't give up. She was afraid of what might happen if she simply gave in and quit.

"I can come back for the fish." Tom glanced at the dead man. "We have to report this to the sheriff, Miranda. It was self-defense, but it's still going to require an investigation. We need to find out who that guy is, and we need medical attention for your arm."

"I'm not leaving this campsite until I have those fish. By tomorrow they could be gone. Gordon said so," she added with a quaver.

"Okay, okay," Tom soothed her. "I'll come back in the morning, when I have some traps."

"I brought another one. It's already in place."

"Tomorrow," Tom assured her. "First thing, but only if you come with me now, no more fighting." As he talked he gathered her belongings. One look at her told him that if she didn't give in voluntarily, in a matter of a few hours she'd be out cold and helpless.

Fighting nausea, Miranda rose. The slight motion sent a surge of pain through her arm. She bit back a curse and tried not to wince.

"Can you make it to the truck?" Tom asked.

"If I have to crawl," she replied.

"You aren't short on determination, are you?"

"No, Tom, just luck, despite what you say about mermaids," she said as she followed the direction of the flashlight he held in front of her. She couldn't stop herself from looking back at the dead man. "Should we just leave him?" The full impact of what had happened was beginning to register.

"We'll deal with that later. Right now I want you to see Doc."

The trip to Tom's borrowed truck took all of her energy. As she walked, the pain in her arm spread through her shoulder and on to the rest of her body. She had no extra strength to ask Tom the questions that slipped in and out of her mind, and she didn't resist when the path widened enough for him to walk beside her and offer a supporting arm.

Just when she thought she'd have to stop and rest, they found his vehicle. With a groan she lifted herself into the passenger seat, very glad that she didn't have to drive. The left side of her body was on fire with pain, and the soft bucket seat felt like paradise.

"Grab hold with your right hand," Tom directed, showing her the brace. "It's going to be rough."

"I remember all too well," she said, forcing herself to smile at him even though the night was still dark. She could tell by his tone that he was very worried. "I'm okay, Tom. My arm hurts, but I'm not going to faint."

"When I saw you holding off three burly men with a hatchet, I got the idea that you weren't the fainting type," he said. "Could you have struck them with the hatchet?" Maybe it wasn't a fair question, and it wasn't a fair time, but he had to ask. There was a lingering doubt in his mind about her involvement with the bombing of a federal building. He couldn't help it. It wasn't an easy thing to accept, especially about a woman he was beginning to care about.

Tired and hurting, Miranda's natural reserve was down. The question was an echo of the past, and she remembered the plans she'd actually made to commit another act of violence so long ago. The memory brought the familiar surge of sickness, and she was barely able to utter her reply. "I don't know." The pain was almost intolerable, and she was suddenly so very tired.

"Well, you had me convinced," Tom continued, talking soothingly as he drove through the dark wilderness. He felt a surge of relief. Whatever Miranda had done in the past, she wasn't a liar. No one could honestly say what they would do in order to survive. No one. He reached across the truck and squeezed her chilly hand. She was so beau-

tiful, even under the worst circumstances. Beautiful and...
He was startled when she spoke again.

"A long time ago I almost did something." Miranda
spoke as if she was unaware that she was talking out loud.
"But then I realized that violence wasn't an answer. We
were kids, and talk was too slow. But that was all a long
time ago." Her voice drifted away, and Tom slowed the
truck and then stopped.

He wanted to tell her that she didn't have to tell him the
story, but she wouldn't have heard. "You okay?" he
asked, gently touching her forehead. "Too cool," he
muttered. Shock was a dangerous possibility. Getting out,
he unrolled her sleeping bag and tucked it snugly around
her. She didn't seem aware of him, and he hurried back to
the driver's seat. He started forward again, this time going as fast as he could without wrecking.

The ride back to Tabuga Springs was something Miranda would never remember. Lost in a confusion of
thoughts, she didn't notice when they turned onto the
paved road. Though Tom cast frequent worried looks at
her, he didn't try to talk. His clenched jaw spoke of his
concern, but he put all of his energy into driving down the
twisting mountain road.

When at last they got to town where there were a few
street lamps, her pallor was clearly visible and more cause
for concern. He continued along the outskirts of the town
to a driveway marked by apple orchards on either side. At
the end was a large two-story house surrounded on three
sides by a porch.

Leaning on the horn, Tom split the peacefulness of the
night. Before the echo had died away, he was around the
truck and at Miranda's side, scooping her into his arms
and running up the steps. The porch light came on and a
tall, dark-haired man held open the door as he buttoned a
chambray shirt.

"Tom?" Doc Wilkes asked in disbelief.

"She's a friend of mine. She's been shot," Tom said
roughly. "It isn't a serious wound, but I'm afraid she's
gone into shock."

Doc didn't waste further words. He led the way to an examination room in the back of the house. Against the whiteness of the table, Miranda's pale face was even more disconcerting. Tom half supported her until Doc ordered him away.

"You wrapped it?" Doc asked, removing the bandage from her arm.

"I used the first-aid supplies she had. The bullet went cleanly through the muscle."

"The wound looks fine," Doc agreed. "Still haven't lost your touch." He removed the sleeping bag that still covered Miranda and replaced it with a clean sheet and several blankets. "She's going to be fine, Tom. She's healthy, strong, the shock will wear off and I'll give her something for pain." He filled a syringe with a clear liquid and quickly gave the shot in the uninjured arm. "Her arm will be impaired for a few days, but that's the worst of it. At least physically."

"She seems . . ."

"Whatever happened was just too much for her. She's retreated from it, but you know that's not uncommon. Often wounded people don't know they're hit until later. You've seen it before."

Doc pulled the stethoscope from around his neck and put it on the counter, catching the softening of his brother's face out of the corner of his eye. A speculative look entered his eyes and then faded.

Tom turned away and went to Miranda. He tucked the blankets around her and fluffed the pillow, his fingers brushing gently at her cheek. "Should we move her to a bed?"

"She's fine for the moment. Let me fix you a drink and we'll come back and watch her."

Doc pushed open the door and walked down a long hall. The big old house served as both office and home. In a few moments he had two drinks ready, handing one to Tom. "Now would you like to explain to me what happened?" His black eyes registered more than curiosity.

"I guess the first thing I should do is call the sheriff," Tom said, at last demonstrating the weariness he felt by straightening his powerful shoulders. "I left a dead man in the woods."

"A dead man?" Doc's face hardened. "What have you gotten involved in, Tom? Did you know the man?"

The urgency in Doc's voice caught Tom's attention and he paused. "No. Never saw him before. He was a burly guy. To be honest, I was more worried about Miranda than someone who tried to hurt her."

"Of course." The anger disappeared from Doc's voice. "I'm sorry. It's just that I've gotten to know most every family for a hundred miles around. This river business has torn the town and community apart. Maybe it wasn't such a good idea to bring that WDC woman here. There are some strange stories...."

"I know, but I'm not particularly interested in that kind of gossip," Tom said slowly. He looked at his older brother. Doc had gone through some interesting changes in the past few years. He'd taken his practice to heart, developing real concerns for the patients and families he took care of. Doc had pulled himself from the brink of personal disaster and become a crucial part of Tabuga Springs. "It's good to see a doctor take that kind of interest in his patients," Tom said. "The people here are lucky to have you. I'm lucky, too."

Doc sipped his drink before he met Tom's gaze. "No, I'm the lucky one. I found something I could care about, and I think maybe sometimes I care too much about this town."

"When you went to France for medical training, I never thought you'd come back to a hick town. I saw you practicing in some big city with modern facilities, research funds."

"My heritage was always more important, even if no one understood that." Doc turned back to the bar and mixed another drink. "And I never thought I had a lot of choice about coming back here." He met Tom's gaze. "You made me believe that."

"I understand, and I respect you for honoring Grandfather's wishes. I know what future you gave up by coming back here."

Doc swirled the ice in his glass and arched his eyebrows. "Yes, I gave up 'my French future.'" He chuckled, but the sound held no mirth. "I was a fool. My career, my wife—" He broke off.

"You haven't mentioned Glynda in a long time," Tom said.

"Talking about Glynda is a vice I've given up, especially with Cheryl in the picture." He finished his drink. "You'd better make that call to the sheriff," he added gruffly. "Ask Uley Carter to let me know who the man is. I might want to pay a call on the family. Even a criminal has family."

Tom took his drink to the phone. The conversation with Sheriff Carter was brief and bitter. He slammed down the phone.

"I have to go back up there with the sheriff." Tom didn't bother to hide his displeasure. "I'd rather stay here, but I guess I have to get those darters for Miranda anyway. That old fool Carter acted like I made up the entire story." He shook his head, as if to dislodge his anger. "I'm nearly dead for lack of sleep, and I'm leaving a wounded woman in your hands while I chase rumors of the Tabuga pisces darter."

"Rumors?" Doc asked with a crooked grin.

"So far, that's all we have. You'll take good care of Miranda, won't you?"

"Just like a loving brother." Doc gave Tom's shoulders a squeeze.

"I'd like to check on her before I go."

"Remember, she is sedated."

Tom nodded and then walked back down the hall to the examination room. Miranda's color was better, and she'd settled into a peaceful sleep, her blond hair cascading off the table almost to the floor. Quietly he walked to her side. Watching the slight movement of her eyes beneath the lids, he remembered the crystal green depths that reflected her passion for life. He lifted her hair, arranging it down her shoulder, then he bent to softly kiss her lips. She stirred beneath him, and her eyes opened slowly.

"Tom?" she asked, sounding as if she spoke from a long distance away.

"Everything's fine," he assured her, kissing her forehead.

"Where am I?" She reached for his hand and held it. "I was dreaming that we were camping together on the river. There was this white deer, a herd of them . . ."

"Miranda, you're at my brother's. He's a doctor, remember? You're fine."

"Will you stay with me?" She fought the drowsiness that seemed to hold her in a warm embrace. The dream had been so real. She wanted to slip back into the warmth of the sun and the sound of the river, to feel Tom beside her.

"I have to go somewhere for a little while, but don't worry. I'll be back before long, and Doc will take care of you."

"Okay," she agreed, smiling slightly. Then she drifted back into a deeper sleep.

"She's a lovely woman," Doc said from the doorway.

"Inside and out," Tom agreed, taking one last look.

MIRANDA AWOKE feeling as if a bulldozer had run her down. Every muscle in her body ached, and her left arm was throbbing with a mean, bone-jarring pain. When she tried to sit up, the fiery burst of torment from her arm almost made her yell. The events of the night before came back to her. There was no way to avoid the ugly truth. Someone was trying to hurt her, and there was one man dead to prove it. She forced herself to a sitting position so she could survey her surroundings.

She was in an old room that had been converted into a doctor's recovery room. Beside her were three other beds, all empty. A large window at the end of the room was wide open. Midday sun slipped through the sheer curtains with a gauzy, soft light. Gingerly feeling her shoulder, Miranda swung her feet out of bed. She'd been attacked, shot and, thanks to Tom Wilkes, saved. The memory of the dead man came back with frightening clarity. She could see his heavy face in the glare of the flashlight. A shudder rippled through her, and she forced her body to the edge of the bed.

Her shoulder was swathed in cotton bandages, and a bright orange stain ran down her arm and all over her shirt. The antiseptic Tom had so liberally used, she remembered. Where was he? And where was she?

"Welcome back."

The rough, masculine voice came from behind her, and Miranda swung around. The broad shoulders and black hair, partially silhouetted in the sunlit doorway, were very familiar.

"Tom!" she cried, struggling to her feet. Anticipation plain on her face, she started toward him.

"Sorry to disappoint you, dear." Doc stepped fully into the light. "I'm Tom's older brother, the town sawbones."

"Forgive me," she said, her welcoming smile dropping slowly from her face. "In the window light you looked so much like him."

"We do favor," Doc agreed as he walked closer to her, "but only in appearances. We both resemble our Cherokee grandfather, a dour, solemn old gentleman who had very strong ideas about everything in the world. Tom's like him, and I'm the relaxed member of the family."

"Where's Tom?" It was easy to figure that Tom had brought her to his brother for medical attention.

"Tom should be back soon. He had some business with the sheriff."

"To identify the body, I assume." Miranda felt no need to skirt the issue. "Tom saved my life. He had no choice in what he did. Those men intended to hurt me."

"So Tom told me." Doc checked the closing on her bandage. "Do you feel well enough to talk about what happened?"

"It might actually help me get it straight in my mind," Miranda agreed. "I was asleep, and I remembered hearing something. These three men came out of the darkness. I'm not really clear about everything, but it seemed like they wanted to capture me. I remember one saying to take me alive, if possible." As the images came to her, she shook her head. "They had me surrounded. I only had my small hatchet. Just before they all rushed me, Tom came out of nowhere and shot the one in the middle." Her pulse increased and her words began to rush together.

"Did you know any of the men?" Doc's black eyes watched her closely, taking in her physical reactions.

"I couldn't see anything." She shook her head. "Not even the color of their hair. I looked at the dead man, but I didn't know him."

"Such a shame." Doc gently led her back to bed. "But I must point out, it isn't safe for a lovely woman to camp alone. Not on the Tabuga or any other river." A chiding note crept into his tone. "Especially not such a controversial river. Especially not such a controversial woman."

Miranda's reaction was instant anger. "I'm sorry, but I won't accept responsibility for what happened. I have a job to do and I'm doing it the best way I know how. I'm not out trying to shoot and kill the people who want to dam the Tabuga because I don't like their plan. They have no right to send someone out to hurt me because of what I believe is right."

"How can you be certain that what you believe is right? Maybe it isn't right for the people who live here. Have you ever thought about the people instead of the river?" Mild curiosity registered on the face that so much resembled Tom's.

For a second Miranda weighed her words. Doc was Tom's brother, a Tabuga Springs resident and a member of the healing profession. He deserved the best answer she could give.

"I was on the river to obtain some important fish samples. Getting those fish to Washington is part of my job, and it could mean a lot to everyone around here. If there is a species in the Tabuga that matters to the environment, then the Tabuga is a lot more important than just a North Carolina river, or a personal crusade.''

"A few fish?" There was mild disbelief in the doctor's voice.

"Very important fish."

"Let's put this discussion aside for a moment so I can take a look at that arm. I don't think getting overexcited is going to benefit my patient."

Doc had his brother's charm and an air that inspired her confidence. She knew doctors were trained in developing a good bedside manner, and he had taken his lessons to heart. As he helped her back into bed, she automatically lay down and let him drape the sheet over her. When he pulled his stethoscope out of his pocket and bent to listen to her chest, she stopped talking and tried to relax.

"How about we take a look at that wound? The bullet went straight through, small caliber, Tom did a great job, but it never hurts to keep it extra clean."

"It hurts, but since I got up and moved around, I feel much better."

After unwrapping the wound, he examined it, applied more medicine and bandaged it again. "It's coming along fine. You're really very lucky." He helped her to sit up. "Is there anything I can get you?"

"What I'd really like is a bath and maybe the loan of a shirt." Tom had cut the entire arm out of hers, and she knew her appearance was bedraggled and pitiful.

"That can be easily arranged." Stepping back, Doc cast her a critical glance. "If you're sure you're feeling up to it."

"I'm positive. A hot bath would be the best medicine." She gave him a grin. "I like to prescribe for myself."

"Not a very healthy practice, but in this instance I agree. A hot bath would be excellent. Did you realize that Tabuga Springs was named because of a series of natural hot springs?"

"No. I've never heard that." Miranda tested the floor with her feet. With each step there was a tiny jolt of pain in her arm, but it was bearable.

"It's a well-guarded family secret. The springs are located about twenty miles from here, on the land that Tom inherited from Grandfather." Doc led the way down the hall to an enormous bathroom with an elegant old claw-foot tub. He opened the cabinet and showed her the towels.

"Are the springs large?" Her curiosity was piqued.

"Fairly. Grandfather discouraged tourists, said they'd disturb the spirits of the land, but of course when this development thing comes through, Tom has created a fabulous design for a resort. It's a totally new treatment of this type of idea." Handing her a clean chambray shirt from another closet, he smiled.

Miranda felt her hand tremble as she took the shirt. "Tom's going to develop his land?" Somehow she kept her voice steady.

"If he hasn't told you, please don't mention to him that I did," Doc said, his warm brown eyes showing his tolerance of his brother. "Tom is very secretive about his future resort plans. You'd think he was up to something illegal, and he's very sensitive about it all."

"I won't mention it." Her words were more vow than simple promise.

"Enjoy your bath. Tom should be back any minute."

Chapter Seven

"Need anything?"

Tom's voice, coming from behind the closed bathroom door, surprised Miranda. She rose from the hot water where she'd been soaking and grabbed a towel.

"No, thank you." Her words were cold.

"Sure?" Tom's relief at her recovery was so great he couldn't resist the urge to tease her. "I could scrub your back for you since your arm is hurt." He rattled the door threateningly.

"I'm warning you!" Her voice held danger.

"Got your hatchet handy?"

"I don't need a hatchet, Tom Wilkes. I'll—why I'll drown you in the bathtub with my bare hands."

Her only reward was a warm, completely amused chuckle from behind the closed door. "Without a trial first? I thought you didn't believe in capital punishment."

"Try me and see," she warned. Her heart was pounding irrationally. Tom's brother had dropped a load of information on her, and she still hadn't had a chance to sort it all out. She was too stunned by the fact that Tom owned a development company with plans for a resort on the very river she intended to save.

"You're certainly feeling better. A little on the nasty side of mood, but it sounds as if you're fit and ready."

"I'm perfectly fine." She dried herself as fast as her injured arm would allow and began throwing on her clothes.

There were several things that weren't clear yet, but as soon as she got back to Washington she intended to find out the name of the company. It was possibly a small concern, an adjunct to the main development plan. She didn't want to jump to any hasty conclusions—and she didn't want to risk her feelings for Tom any further. She was trying hard to be objective, but she couldn't help the distrust that came from the fact that Tom had deceived her.

"Hungry?" Tom asked.

She wanted to lash out at him, to tell him that she'd learned about his so-called farming life-style. She was mad at herself, too. She'd conveniently overlooked his architectural background. She'd thought perhaps he was modest. Why was it that she was always ready to believe the most honorable thing about perfect strangers? Hadn't she learned her lesson?

"Food is the last thing on my mind." She managed to speak without growling, but it was an effort.

"How about some coffee, eggs, bacon, biscuits? You haven't eaten in almost twenty-four hours, and Doc recommends a hearty meal."

Her mouth actually watered. "I said I wasn't hungry."

"That's too bad. I'm going down to the Ketchin's Café. Miss Velma puts down the best breakfast in the country. Red-eye gravy. Biscuits so light they float off the plate."

Sudden inspiration struck. "Wait a minute and I'll be there." If she was smart, which she was, she'd learn a lot more from Tom over breakfast than sulking in a bathroom. Besides, she had to discuss the fish samples with Tom.

Her wet hair was wrapped in a towel when she opened the door. To her surprise Tom was still standing there, leaning casually against the wall as he waited.

"I thought you might need a hand."

The offer sounded sincere, and the look of relief on his face seemed real. Miranda's chest constricted. She couldn't fall victim to that ploy. "I'm only wounded, not crippled," she said.

"Are you always this nasty tempered after being shot?"

Turning to confront him, she was ready to snap back with a short retort when she caught the look in his amber eyes. She turned away and stalked down the hallway. She could have sworn that he was concerned for her, deeply concerned. But it was something she didn't want to probe until she had all the facts about his past, present and potential future.

"I guess that means yes." His voice trailed lazily after her. "Maybe some food will put you in a better frame of mind."

"Don't count on it," she threw over her shoulder.

In the recovery room she shook her hair out and hunted through her backpack for a brush. Tangles had taken over her long tresses, and she plied the brush furiously, with a great deal of awkwardness.

She heard Tom's footsteps cross the hardwood floor, and though she didn't turn to face him, she spoke.

"Any luck with the samples?" She sat down on a small bench before an antique vanity. The old, blurry mirror gave back an impression of sparkling eyes and jaw tilted out in defiance.

"Miranda, the traps were empty."

"Were, or are?" She couldn't help the anger in her voice.

"What's wrong with you?" He walked behind her and firmly took the brush from her hand. "A few more tugs and you'll be bald." Starting with the ends, he skillfully began to work the knots from her hair. "I checked the traps and there wasn't a sign of the darter. I put them back down, and if there's time before you leave, I'll check again. If not, then I'll get something to you when we trap it."

The feel of his hands in her hair ignited a strange, confusing emotion. "I didn't realize styling hair was one of your many skills." She started to rise, but his hand pressed her good shoulder until she resumed her seat.

"Wait a minute here. I'm trying to get these tangles out."

He plied the brush again and the touch of his hand made her want to jump up and run away. He was a sensual man, and even though she didn't trust him, she couldn't deny that he affected her. With Tom she had to guard her heart, as well as her future with the WDC.

"Thanks, Tom, I'll finish later." She tried to rise again, but once more he held her steady.

"Styling isn't my forte. Brushing is. See, when I was younger my grandfather bought me a horse. I'd spend hours brushing Daniel, and his tail isn't much different from your hair."

Rounding on him, Miranda saw the humor hidden deep in his amber eyes, though he tried to present an innocent front. "So my hair reminds you of a horse?"

"A horse I loved," he clarified.

"Give me that brush!"

"When Daniel got nasty about being brushed, I'd sometimes have to tie him up. Hated to do it, but then it was necessary. For his own good."

Miranda held her back rigid as she felt him begin to work through the thick mass again. She closed her eyes, fighting the emotions that rose to the surface. The terrible truth was that she enjoyed the feel of the brush in her hair. The tenderness he showed her was almost irresistible, and somewhere in the back of her mind she'd even fantasized about Tom, about a moment when he would touch her... and she would respond.

Tom put the brush on the vanity. His hands gently picked up her hair and he held it lightly. "When my grandmother was alive, she'd sit in front of the fireplace and brush her hair for two hundred strokes." His voice was soft. "She said it put fire in her hair. Highlights, I suppose. She was right, too, because she had beautiful hair."

"Black, like yours?" She couldn't help the question.

"No, blond. Like yours."

"She wasn't Indian, then?"

"No. An Irish lass." The lilt was awkward but credible. "Shall I braid your hair for you? It's an old Indian tradition."

Before she could answer, she felt his hands divide her hair into three heavy strands. Then there was the comforting sensation of the weave as he worked in and out, gradually dropping lower.

"Now, want to tell me what's got you in such a painfully mean mood?" Tom spoke softly, beside her ear. He could see that she was in some terrible conflict, but he didn't understand. Perhaps she was exhausted and confused by the events of the night before. He certainly couldn't blame her. Now wasn't the time, but soon he wanted to tell her what he'd learned from the night's adventures. He could no longer pretend that he was helping her because of the WDC—it was strictly personal now. His motivation was purely his growing interest in Miranda.

"Why am I in such a mood?" she asked aloud. "Well, it could have something to do with a hole in my arm and the fact that some man is dead." She couldn't tell him the truth—that she was afraid she was falling in love with him. She couldn't tell him that his lies and half truths had cut her deeply. No, it was better to avoid all personal references.

"Who was the man you shot?" Her question was aggressive, and she saw the momentary shock reflected in Tom's eyes in the old mirror. She knew there had been no choice for him, but she had to put him on the defensive before he saw into her heart.

Instead of an angry retort, he sighed. He unbraided her hair and began to brush it out. He stroked her hair ten, fifteen, twenty times as the silence between them expanded. "I don't know," he finally said.

"He was a stranger to Sheriff Carter, too?"

"The body was gone. The sheriff and about twenty volunteers and I searched the woods thoroughly, but there wasn't any body to be found. Not even the first drop of blood."

She cast a look over her shoulder and caught the puzzled look on his face.

"So a dead man just got up and walked away?" Disbelief echoed in the room. Had Tom actually shot him, or could it possibly have been a put-up job? Something designed to scare her off the river.

"So it would appear." Tom watched her closely. Something was definitely different. There was an edge to her that wasn't there the day before.

"And the sheriff thought you made the whole thing up?" She remembered Sheriff Carter's reaction to her complaints. He'd treated her as if she were some hysterical tourist.

"As a matter of fact, he was reluctant to believe his woods were filled with potential murderers, or even potential bodies. Sheriff Carter doesn't want anything to happen that might mess up his plans for development of Tabuga Springs. A murder is bad publicity, you know. But I did find something that made him see my story in a more favorable light."

"What?"

"That Jeep you rented. Someone had stripped the distributor cap off."

"The Jeep!" Miranda touched her forehead. "I'd forgotten all about it. I just left it in the woods."

"You weren't in any condition to drive out," Tom reminded her. "Even if you'd gotten away from those guys, you'd have been stranded in the woods. Survival can be harsh in those mountains, if you're not equipped."

"And I wasn't," she admitted slowly. Not even after repeated attacks. Her heartbeat increased. Tom's brushing had become slow, deliberate strokes that began at her crown and traveled down her back. All of the tangles were gone, but he brushed anyway.

"Don't worry, we repaired the Jeep and one of the searchers drove it back into town. But I find it more than a little odd that I have wiring problems and then your Jeep is mangled."

"Someone wanted me in those woods, alone." She shivered and felt Tom's hands on her arms. The warmth was welcome, and for a moment she relaxed.

Tom pulled her back against him. He took care to cushion her injured shoulder. "Miranda, I want you to go home as soon as possible."

"I can't leave without those fish."

"Listen to me. You can't do any more than I'm already doing. What good will all of this come to if you're hurt? Please, you have to promise me that you'll go home."

Tom's concern, the feel of his strong body holding her, was tempting, but she could not give up on her mission. "Let's check the river once more."

"Then you'll go?"

"I'll think about it." She turned around to smile and found him looking at her. Before she could draw a breath, his lips were on hers. Her response was instant and powerful. She'd wanted his kiss. Right or wrong, wise or foolish, she was drawn to him. She felt his fingers on her throat, and she almost moaned. With a force of will she broke away. If she couldn't resist him, then she'd have to confront him. "Tom—" she took a deep breath "—why didn't you tell me you were thinking about developing a resort on the Tabuga?"

The clear green of her eyes was clouded with passion, and Tom resisted the urge to smother her question in another kiss. He owed her an explanation, and it was long overdue. The trouble was he didn't know how much to tell her without frightening her away. She'd been attacked twice, and he stood the most to gain by stopping the WDC. If she doubted him, she would refuse his help. God knew, she needed someone to look out for her. She was virtually a sitting duck.

"I didn't tell you because the development of the Tabuga is a mixed issue for me." He pushed a strand of her magnificent hair from her cheek. Her skin was so soft, so perfect. "I could make money if the dam is built. I do have a plan to build a resort. Or I can enjoy the river in its natural state. I stand to win both ways, so I'm not an advocate of either side."

"That's difficult to believe," she said, wanting to believe him. "Excuse my skepticism, but when profits are involved, most people have strong opinions."

"I don't really need money."

"Everyone needs money," she said. "If they have millions, they need more."

He felt the edge of her cynicism and he knew that she was speaking from hard experience. "Not everyone has my background," he said. "I was lucky enough to have an old Indian grandfather who loved this land more than anything else. He believed the wilderness was filled with a magic spirit that came from the river. To him the Tabuga wilderness was paradise." Tom paused. "I could use more money, you're right that everyone could. But not necessarily at the expense of something I love. Can you believe that?"

The light in his amber eyes was so honest, so real, that she wanted to believe. She forced herself to hold back. "I'm not certain," she said softly. "You lied to me."

"I didn't lie," he corrected her. "I withheld some information because I knew I'd get this reaction from you. I've meant to tell you, but I felt it was more important to help you. I was afraid if you knew about the development that you wouldn't let me help."

"So, there's a difference between withholding information and outright lying?" She had to know how far he'd go. Where did this man draw the line? Did the end always justify the means?

"Sometimes," he said, "I can't lie about that. To keep you safe, I'd hedge the truth. I'm sorry if that offends you." He couldn't resist touching her. His fingers traced the line of her jaw. "Miranda, I'll get those fish for you if I can. I promise you that. But you have to trust me enough to leave here. I won't help you unless you go somewhere that's safe."

"I see." She felt childish tears burning behind her eyes. "You withhold facts, and you're not above blackmail."

"No, I suppose when it comes to something I care about, I'll bend my principles enough to keep you safe." He brushed one tear from her cheek. "You're questioning my honesty, I know that. I also know how much you need to believe in my integrity. I may disappoint you, but keep in mind that when I care about someone, like you, I want to protect them." He lifted her chin so that their gazes met. "And I care about that river."

"Let me call my office and see how things stand." As much as she hated to leave the intimacy of the moment, she had to get busy. Tom Wilkes was a dangerous man. He spoke and her heart listened.

The sound of approaching footsteps echoed along the hardwood corridor. When Cheryl Summers opened the door with a tray of coffee, Tom and Miranda were several feet apart.

"Good news and bad," Cheryl said brightly. "The bad news is that Doc made the coffee, so be careful. The good news is that there's a phone call for Miranda. The man sounded very excited. Maybe it's some new development."

"You can take the call in Doc's office," Tom said. "Just down the hall to the left."

Miranda took a cup of black coffee, dark and strong, from the tray as she left the room. She found the telephone, expecting to hear the sound of her boss's voice. How had they tracked her down to Doc's private little hospital?

"Miranda Conner speaking."

"So, the gunshot didn't impair you too badly?"

"Russ!" Miranda couldn't believe it. "How did you find out about this? How did you find me?"

"I can't reveal my sources," Russ said disapprovingly. "Now, give me the facts. I've got to run with the story and I'd rather be accurate."

Miranda resisted the urge to beg him not to print the story of her shooting. Russ had a job to do, and she couldn't interfere. "Russ, I'm not hurt. It was an accident." She hesitated. Now she was caught on the horns of her own dilemma. Should she tell Russ about the man Tom had shot? The man who'd disappeared without a trace. Her answer was an emphatic no.

"Accident?"

"I was camping. Someone came up. There was some confusion and before I knew what had happened, I was shot."

"Any trace of those fishes?"

"No, and they aren't really part of this incident."

"You were just camping for the fun of it, exactly at the location where Gordon found those little evolutionary devils. Some coincidence," he added sarcastically.

"Russ, please. We haven't found the fish. A story like that could put every prodam proponent on the river, dynamiting like mad. If those fish are there, they won't stand a chance. And neither will the WDC."

"Guilt isn't very effective against reporters," Russ warned.

"You have a conscience, and you have one juicy story. Give me a little more time."

"Okay, and by the way, you'd better check in with your office. There was some type of break-in at the WDC. We have a reporter checking at the police station now. No injuries, but it seems the place might have been ransacked."

"My office?" She felt a dull stab of anxiety. "Connie wasn't hurt, was she?"

"No injuries was the word I got, but it's beginning to look like your job might be a little on the dangerous side. Take care, Miranda, and I'll be in touch."

"Russ, how *did* you find me?"

"We have our little secrets, Miranda, and believe me, it's better that way." He was laughing when he replaced the telephone.

Miranda stood for a moment, the dead receiver in her hand.

"Bad news?" Cheryl asked behind her. "Or has Doc's coffee put you into a terminal coma?"

"The coffee's a little strong," Miranda answered, trying to cover her distress. "Did Russ ask for me at this number?"

"Yes, is there a problem?" Cheryl took the coffee cup from Miranda's hand. "You look too pale. Maybe I should call Doc?"

"No, I'm fine."

"Should I have said you weren't here?"

"Not at all." Miranda forced a smile to relieve Cheryl's worried look. "It's nothing. Really. I was just curious how

Russ knew where to find me, but then reporters have their means, I suppose."

"I'll say."

"I'd like to make another call, if that would be okay?"

"I'll get some more coffee," Cheryl said, picking up the cup. "This time I'll make it myself."

As soon as Cheryl was gone, Miranda dialed her office. The sound of Connie's voice was a welcome relief, but the news was as bad as Russ had led her to expect.

During the night someone had broken into the WDC offices and wrecked Miranda's office. So far, there was no way to tell what, if anything, had been taken. The destruction was confined to Miranda's small cubicle, and it was almost total.

"It's a mess," Connie said, her weariness reflected in her voice. "The only good thing was that you were safe on the river."

Miranda hesitated, then recounted the story of her shooting. "I wasn't going to tell anyone, but you'll read about it in the paper," she said.

"Thank goodness you called and told me. I would have been worried sick."

"Connie, could you check to see if anyone on the WDC staff talked with Russ Sherman about my trip to the Tabuga?"

"I'm almost certain no one did. That reporter could have checked airline tickets."

"True, but he would have had to suspect that I would make the trip."

"He knew you'd go back after the darter. Anyone who knows you at all could have made that guess."

"Possibly, but I think someone's leaking to him. It could be innocent, or it might be trouble."

"I'll check on it. And what about you?"

Miranda knew the answer. "I'm staying until I get my hands on that fish."

KETCHIN'S CAFÉ was everything and more, that Miranda could have wanted. Tom's arm gave her an entrée she couldn't have obtained in fifty years of residency. It was without question the local dining area, and each of the booths and stools along the single counter was filled. Tables were jammed in the center of the restaurant, and Tom steered her to a large, empty one with several chairs.

"Why, Tom Wilkes, where you been hidin' this gorgeous creature?" A pretty woman in a spotless white uniform came from behind the counter.

Tom made the introductions with Velma Thompson.

"Pleased to meet you," Velma said as she took Miranda's hand. Velma's blue eyes sparkled with delight. She patted Miranda's arm with real affection. "She's a pretty thing!" She addressed the restaurant at large. About twenty-five people all stared at Miranda. "Would you look at that head of hair. It's gorgeous."

"I agree," Tom said easily.

Unable to say anything, Miranda pinched Tom's arm as hard as she could.

"Don't pick on her too much," Tom directed Velma as he seated Miranda at a bright yellow table. "She might not come back."

"It's your orneriness and stubborn ways that will drive her off," Velma snorted. "Listen, honey, this man gives you one whit of trouble and you come to Velma. Men in general are trouble, but Tom Wilkes has been alone so long he's probably meaner than a wildcat and more set in his ways than an Appalachian boulder. But—" she leaned forward "—there ain't no man in existence that a smart woman can't tame down to her needs!"

The restaurant roared with good-natured laughter, and Miranda was gratified to see the faintest tinge of color in Tom's cheeks. His eyes sparkled, though, and she had the strange sensation that he was proud to be introducing her to his friends. The thought was completely disturbing.

As Tom made the introductions around the restaurant, she knew she'd never get the names straight. It didn't matter, though. Whether it was Gibbins, Turk, Sam, Ida or Becka, the one thing they all had in common was deep affection for the man who sat beside her. If Tom was involved in capitalizing from a dam on the Tabuga, no person in the room seemed too concerned.

The only exception was a tall, husky man with a rugged face and light brown hair. As the others in the café laughed and joked, she felt the man's gaze on her. Whenever she looked in his direction, though, he turned back to his plate, slumping his shoulders against her gaze. He was dressed in army fatigues, but so was almost everyone else. Old army-issue clothes and jeans seemed to be the proper dress code for Tabuga Springs.

"Who is he?" Her discreet question warned Tom to look with subtlety.

After a moment he turned around. "Abe Tuttle."

"He doesn't like one of us very much," Miranda noted. "He's staring daggers at us."

"Abe and I had a minor disagreement about three years ago. When I went down to look at part of my land, I found his fence on it, along with a dozen starving cows and a wife so sick she couldn't lift herself out of bed."

The anger in his voice made her want to turn the conversation back to more pleasant planes, but she pressed on. "What happened?"

"His wife died after I took her to the hospital." Bitterness edged into his tone, and he gripped the table. "She had an infection. If he'd taken her to the doctor three weeks before, antibiotics would have cleared it right up. As it was, I got there too late. I forced him off my land, took his cows and put them in with my herd and the upshot is that he hates my guts."

Before she could ask another question, Velma arrived at their table, plates of steaming food on each arm. The food was another of Tom's understatements. Miranda ate until she thought she'd split, and then she ate another biscuit.

"Can I take some of these back to Washington with me?" she whispered to Tom.

"I don't know." He leaned back and gave her a critical look. "I think you could stand to eat a few biscuits. I'll ask Velma to put a couple dozen up for you."

The door of the restaurant swung open, and Doc entered with Cheryl on his arm, her red hair flaming in the morning sun.

"So my patient has regained her appetite," Doc observed as he brought the tall redhead to the table. "Cheryl has accused me of trying to poison my patient with bad coffee. I told her that after the night you'd survived, my coffee wasn't even a threat."

"You sound awfully brave," Cheryl said, taking Miranda's hand. "And you, too, Tom. You seem to have a curious knack for being on the scene when Miranda needs help."

"He certainly does," Miranda said. "Tom has designated himself my guardian angel, I think."

"You could do worse," Doc said, then laughed. "He's been the most eligible bachelor around these parts for too many years. We're delighted to see him with some female company." He settled down at the table after seating Cheryl.

"I didn't get a chance to ask you earlier, how is the WDC plan to block the dam coming?" Cheryl asked. "Everyone in these parts is interested."

Miranda looked at the redhead and Doc and understood that there were few secrets between the two. They seemed very much in love. "I'm sure you heard about the discovery Gordon Simms thinks he made with the Tabuga pisces darter. If that proves to be true, then we have a strong case for delaying the dam, if not stopping it. Even if we buy a little time, it could not seem so lucrative to develop this area in two or three years." Out of the corner of her eye, she watched for Tom's reaction.

"It's true, development goes in trends like every other business," Cheryl said. "Isn't that right, Tom?"

"Yes, it is," he addressed his answer exclusively to Cheryl. "But as we constantly debate, I believe good design exceeds trends."

"That's an interesting position—for a farmer," Miranda said, unable to hold back the remark or completely conceal her bitterness.

"Tom didn't tell you that he also designed?" Cheryl asked, amazement on her face. "He was one of the top in the residential field when he left California. In fact, he's—"

"I don't think Miranda wants to hear this," Tom said quickly.

In the bright light that filtered through the café curtains, Tom's face was completely exposed. Miranda couldn't help but notice the lines of weariness.

"I'm sorry," Cheryl said, looking from one brother to the other. Doc shrugged his shoulders. "I didn't mean to bring up a touchy subject."

"It isn't touchy," Miranda said, her gaze never leaving Tom's. "It's just something he never mentioned before."

"The truth is, Tom, I told her about your development company." Doc shifted uneasily in his chair. "We were simply talking, and I told her. I knew by the look on her face that she was unpleasantly surprised."

Cheryl leaned toward Miranda, touching her arm lightly. "Listen, Miranda, Tom would never do anything wrong. If you don't believe anything else, believe that."

"If you're finished, Miranda?" Tom stood, looking down at her. "There's something I want to show you."

Tom's eyes were compelling, and she rose and followed him to the front of the small restaurant. As she stood at the counter, she had a very uncomfortable feeling, as if pointed objects were sticking her back. Turning around, she found Abe Tuttle's eyes boring into her. His glare was so malevolent that she wanted to challenge him. His pale blue eyes shot a warning to her across the room. Then he lowered his head again and slumped his shoulders.

Unaware of Abe's threatening look, Tom signed the ticket for the meal. He was almost ready to leave when Velma leaned over the cash register and grabbed his wrist.

"Listen, Tom, there's been some strange talk around here lately." She shifted her gaze to Tuttle in the back of the room. "Don't turn your back on that one, and remember, those you think you can trust the most are often the ones who betray you."

"What are you getting at, Velma?"

She shook her head. "Just be careful. Check your truck before you use it. And watch out for your pretty lady. There're some mean folks about these parts."

"Thanks." He turned back to wave goodbye to Doc and Cheryl and then held the door open for Miranda. There was a troubled look on his face.

"There's something I want to show you. These hills are rocky and hard to plant. My grandfather eked out a living, but just barely." His voice softened as it always did when he spoke of the past.

"Your Indian grandfather?" She was remembering parts of Tom's family history she'd read so hurriedly. There was something about the land and the family.

"That's the one. He was a wise old man." Tom smiled as he opened the truck door for her. "Miranda, there are a lot of things about me you don't know. We'll talk when we get to my place."

"Did Abe Tuttle ever try to get even with you?" she asked when Tom was behind the wheel.

Pausing with his hand on the key, Tom looked at her. He seemed to weigh her question before he answered. "He tried to burn my house down around me. And for his trouble he did two years in the North Carolina State Prison."

"Is it over between you?" She could still hear Velma's words of warning.

"As far as I can tell. He's been home about eight weeks now. I pass him back and forth, but he's never tried anything. He knows I'll do what I have to when it comes to protection." Tightness crept into Tom's voice. "Let's not talk about this now. I feel like I've spent my entire life doing what was expected, or what I had to do. Right this minute I just want to drive with you beside me, so I can show you this country."

"With everything that's been happening, it's hard to ignore trouble," Miranda said. "Should we stop by Sheriff Carter's and see if anything new has developed? And I'd like to check for those fish again." She looked around at the picturesque town. "This place hasn't exactly been hospitable to their survival."

"We're headed toward my home. The sheriff has my number, and I made him promise he'd call. Just don't expect too much. He acts as if he thought I made up the story about the body." He gave her a tired smile.

"Okay," she agreed. When they were out of town and headed for the dark green range of mountains that rose in the east, she lightly touched his hand on the gear shift. "You're going to think I'm nuts to ask this, but is it possible the man you shot last night wasn't dead?" The question had nagged at her mind, a macabre idea, at best.

Tom pulled to the edge of the road. "I never would have left a wounded man, Miranda. When I went to get the antiseptic, I checked him thoroughly. He was dead."

"So where did he go?"

"I intend to find that out eventually. But right now the most dangerous thing we have to face is crossing that rickety old bridge over the Tabuga." He drove onto it slowly, stopping in the middle so they could watch the rapid current of the amber river beneath them.

"This bridge really isn't safe," she agreed. She looked across at him and remembered the touch of his hands as he'd dressed her wound, the way he'd brushed her hair. She had to keep a close grip on her emotions.

"If the dam comes through, this old bridge will be destroyed, along with a lot of other things."

"You sound almost nostalgic." She held her breath.

"I love this place. I love it the way it is, wild and rugged and untamed by bulldozers and power plants. But I'm not the only person who has to live here. There are others who are cold in the winter and who can't afford any better. A resort would open a lot of jobs. A power plant would make life a lot easier for some people."

"And it would also destroy the last remaining wild river in the entire system. Is it worth that sacrifice for convenient living?"

Tom stepped on the emergency brake and cut the engine. "Now, that's one I can't answer. That's why the WDC findings are so important. If we have objective facts about the dam project, then we can make sensible decisions. Right?"

"I hope that's the case," Miranda said, suddenly tired.

The sound of a motor coming up behind them made her glance in the side mirror. A battered old red truck was approaching the bridge. Instead of slowing, the vehicle picked up speed as it came toward their stopped truck.

"Hang on!" Tom ordered as he cranked the motor and jammed the gear shift into first. They lurched forward with a squeal.

Miranda swung around in her seat and caught a glimpse of a lone driver behind the wheel of the rapidly approaching red truck.

"He means to run us off the bridge," she said, her voice rising with each word.

"It's Tuttle," Tom acknowledged. "I would have thought he was smart enough not to do something like this." He pressed the gas for all he was worth, holding the truck on the road by sheer muscle.

They were speeding across the wooden planks while beneath them the river seemed to roar.

Miranda could see the end of the bridge, but it looked as if Tuttle would get to them before they cleared the old structure.

"Brace yourself!" Tom directed, jamming the truck into second gear. It bucked, then leapt forward. He stopped suddenly and threw open his door. Before Miranda could stop him, he was racing down the bridge toward Tuttle.

Miranda hurled herself out of the passenger side, but there was nothing she could do. Tom was headed for Tuttle with the obvious intention of jumping in his truck and driving it off the bridge.

"Tom" she called.

Tuttle stopped, threw his truck in reverse and started backing toward Tabuga Springs. Tom raced after him, but not fast enough to catch the truck.

"This ain't over yet!" Tuttle yelled as he made it to the side of the bank and spun gravel turning around. "I ain't through with you yet, Tom Wilkes!"

Chapter Eight

The mountains folded out before Tom and Miranda in a semicircle that shimmered golden green in the afternoon light. They had driven for a long time in silence, finally turning off onto a barely detectable path.

"Where are we?" Miranda asked when the vehicle stopped. She'd been waiting for Tom to talk, to say anything about the incident that could so easily have turned into disaster. Abe Tuttle was a dangerous man. Dangerous and erratic. With everything else happening in her life, it didn't help to think that some mountaineer with a grudge was trying to kill, or at least maim, Tom.

"This is part of my land," Tom answered.

They walked from the truck to the edge of the water. The Tabuga cascaded down a series of small falls and chutes at their feet. They were in a small valley with mountains on either side.

"This may be the prettiest part of the river." She leaned against a tall outcropping of rock where she could watch Tom's face. He was easy to look at, even with a hint of anger buried deep in his eyes.

"This was my grandfather's favorite place. The springs are about two miles from here. Sacred ground." He smiled, choosing to ignore the subject that was on both their minds.

"Sacred enough to protect you from more attempts on your life?" Miranda decided that Tom's silence had gone far enough. He'd certainly involved himself in her life. Well, now it was her turn. "What are you going to do about Abe Tuttle?"

Tom rested a hand beside her shoulder on the rock. "I'm not so certain I'm going to do anything."

"We should call Sheriff Carter." On the long, silent drive, she'd watched Tom. She'd seen the emotions flicker across his face. Anger. Concern. A moment of what appeared to be pity and sadness. Then there had come a cold resolve. She knew then that he wasn't going to involve the law. It was something personal between them.

"I'll keep an eye on him. Sheriff Carter wouldn't do much even if I called him. I think they're related in some distant way. Besides, Tuttle hasn't inflicted any physical damage. He's always been a bully, but bullying isn't a punishable crime."

"Tom! That's crazy! He could have caused us to run off the bridge!" She exerted a tremendous effort and got her voice under control. "We're safe because you didn't panic. I can't say I would have reacted so calmly."

"He didn't actually harm us, Miranda. Around here threats don't get too much attention."

"This is a strange and peculiar place where lawmen don't protect the innocent, dead bodies disappear and grudges from the past put people's lives in danger."

"My grandfather used to tell me that too much living in the past could rob a man's future." His smile was wry. "Then he proceeded to live his entire life in the past. He knew more stories, more folklore, more everything. But he didn't regret his past, and maybe that's the difference. The things he hung on to gave him pleasure."

"You loved him a lot, didn't you?" Miranda decided to let the issue of Abe Tuttle rest for a while. Tom Wilkes was a bullheaded man who wouldn't be pushed. She'd let the beauty of the place work on him, and if worse came to worst, she'd file a complaint against Tuttle. It might be personal, and Sheriff Carter might not want to do anything, but the law was the law.

"My grandfather was more like a father. He raised me and Doc."

"It's strange that two such well-educated men would choose to remain in a small, isolated mountain town. Didn't you ever think of leaving?" The sun had warmed the rock, and it felt good against her injured shoulder. Doc had been right. She wasn't badly hurt, but she was sore. She watched Tom's face soften as he talked. His eyes constantly gazed over the vista of white water and green mountains.

"Doc and I both left, and we both came back. It was a point of great conflict for Doc when he was younger. To be honest with you, I've sometimes wondered if he didn't make a mistake, coming back here to a small town with limited facilities. I was afraid it would destroy him, this place and the past. But since Cheryl has come here, I think he's really happy."

"So she isn't from this area. I didn't hear the native accent." Miranda smiled. "What does she find to do in a town like Tabuga Springs? I'd imagine Cheryl as some executive."

Tom started to speak, then paused. "Well, she works with Doc."

"As a nurse?" Miranda couldn't believe it. Cheryl didn't look at all like a nurse or receptionist.

"Heavens, no. Cheryl's no nurse." Tom chuckled. "I don't think she has the temperament for the healing arts— a little on the impatient side."

"What does she do?"

"Oh, she and Doc have a business. Doc practices medicine and Cheryl runs the business."

"Wedding bells?"

"I'm hoping so. Doc was..." He smiled. "A long time ago there was another woman. She hurt Doc, and I didn't think he'd ever get over her. But he did, and Cheryl came along, and I've got my fingers crossed that this will work for him. Grandfather would be happy at the thought of Doc marrying and starting a family. The idea of great-grandchildren would please him."

"And what about you, Tom? No offspring for you?" Miranda felt her heart accelerate. It was a bold question, and one that was suddenly terribly important to her.

He considered for a moment. "I've never given it much thought until now. Everything changes, one way or the other." He looked out over the water, and a frown crossed his face. "Even the mighty Tabuga." He took a deep breath. "Even me. Let's get going. There's some place I want to take you."

"Tom, is something else wrong?" For a split second a terrible sadness had touched his features. Miranda felt as if he'd been on the verge of some revelation.

Tom pointed to the sun sinking lower in the sky. "We're running out of time, and I have a promise to keep. Let's go."

"What about the springs? I thought we might see them."

"Another time." He took her arm and started back to the truck. "This is something we need to do."

Miranda knew she couldn't pry any more information from Tom, so she walked beside him back to the truck. In a moment they were roaring onto the main road, headed deeper into the heart of the mountains.

It was another twenty minutes before Tom pulled into a narrow lane that wound back into deeper and deeper wilderness. The first sign of civilization was a narrow wooden footbridge. It was built over a sandy-bottomed creek that paralleled the road.

"Burning Creek," Tom said. "Best trout fishing in the world."

"Where does it feed into the Tabuga?"

"About three miles from here. It winds a bit."

"And the bridge?"

"You'll meet the man who designed and built it."

The words were barely out of his mouth when Tom turned a corner and a small log cabin was revealed. A man with silvery white hair was sitting on the porch, rocking slowly back and forth in a cowhide rocker. He rose at the sight of the truck and stepped to the edge of the porch.

"Afternoon, Clark," Tom said as he got out of the truck and went to open Miranda's door.

"Almost the end of the day. I was beginning to give you up." Clark pulled his pipe out of his shirt pocket and lit it. "We'll have time for a walk, but we'd better make it quick."

Before Miranda could ask any questions, Tom hustled her to the west side of the house. A narrow, single track led back into the woods.

"I can't guarantee anything's there, but Jason said he thought you might find one of those fish you've been looking for," Clark said as he fell into step behind Miranda. "We set us a trap for it."

"A darter?" Miranda hardly dared say the word. "Did he see one? Was he certain?"

"Nope. Jason's a good boy, but he ain't no scientist. Neither am I, and besides, my eyes aren't what they used to be. Still, I saw something yesterday morning when I put my minnow trap down. I thought it was worth a shot, especially after Tom explained how important this critter could be to saving the river."

Miranda looked over her shoulder to find Clark's speculative gaze on her. "I'm surprised you called me," Miranda said bluntly. "I know you have nothing but contempt for me."

"No, contempt's too strong a word, Ms. Conner. I'm not certain I trust or respect what you are." There was no friendliness in his blue eyes. "You're here, though, and this river needs savin'. Now, if you can help us, fine, but we need to walk a little faster."

They followed Burning Creek until they could hear the Tabuga. At a point before the creek fed into the river, they came upon a large, quiet pool. In the shallows of the pool, Miranda could spot several different types of minnows and fish. Their movement was too rapid for identification, but she felt a thrill of excitement at the possibility. This was exactly the type of place that Gordon had described as the perfect habitat for the Tabuga pisces darter. If Gordon had found the species, then surely there would be others alive in the river. This might be the place.

"Jason and I put the trap in early this morning. Want to check?"

Miranda nodded. Tom grasped her hand and gave it a squeeze.

"Tom said you were shot." Clark's gaze searched her shoulders as he spoke. "Mighty nasty business. I can't hold with men attacking a woman in the woods. When we find out who did it, they'll pay a high price."

"One of them already did," Miranda answered. She gave half of her attention to Tom hauling in the trap and the other half to Clark.

"That's an interesting problem, isn't it? How does a dead man get up and walk out of the woods?" Clark lit his pipe. "Any ideas?"

"The most obvious is that his companions came back for him," she said as she watched Tom steadily pulling in the line.

"That's how I figured it. You didn't see any of them?"

"It was dark. They were average men."

"And you think they meant to kill you?"

Clark's question drew her full attention. "Now that you mention it, I couldn't say that they absolutely meant to kill me. They said something about trying to take me alive. Why do you ask that?"

"I told Tom. There's been talk from others than me who don't take too well to havin' you on the river. Maybe someone was trying to scare you off?"

"Scare me or kidnap me?"

Clark shrugged. "Could be the plan got away from them."

"Do you know something about this, Mr. Presley? A man was killed in those woods. This isn't some game."

"That's exactly my point, Ms. Conner. This isn't some game like the ones you played when you were younger. Folks got hurt then, too."

Miranda clamped her jaw shut. "That's true," she said. "And I was one of them. I was young and naive. I admit that. I've suffered because of those times, just as some others did. But no one was injured or killed. No one. And the past has nothing to do with my efforts as an employee of the WDC.''

"Bad judgment isn't something a man, or a woman, necessarily grows out of." Clark didn't flinch. He met her gaze fully.

"That remains to be seen."

"I'm watchin', Ms. Conner. Like an old hawk up in the sky, I'm watchin'."

"That's comforting." Miranda felt a chill move over her entire body. "How's it coming, Tom?"

He was standing in the shallows. "Come take a look. I didn't want to bring it all the way out in the shallows here."

"Good idea. It would take a long time for the bottom to settle." She went to his side. In the clear water she could see the trap. Through the mesh she saw several small fish dashing back and forth within the confines, but there was no fish with the distinctive yellow stripe of the darter.

She shook her head, and Tom set to work replacing the trap. She tried to hide her disappointment. "We'll have to keep checking."

"Not today," Clark said, nodding toward the western sky. The sun was low on the rolling horizon. "Down here in the valley the days are shorter, you know. When that sun sinks, it's night."

"Let's head back," Tom said. "I don't like the idea of three unarmed people on this river. We've got a bit more daylight, but I'd rather play it safe."

Clark patted his baggy pants pocket. "You might be unarmed, but I've lived hereabouts long enough to know the wisdom of carryin' something more than luck."

Trudging back through the woods, Miranda realized that she was utterly exhausted. In the late-afternoon light she could read fatigue on Tom's face and she realized he'd had almost no sleep. Maybe once she returned to Washington he could resume his normal life.

Tom helped Miranda into the passenger seat and closed the door before he turned to say his goodbyes.

Inside the truck Miranda could see them talking, but with the window rolled up she couldn't hear.

Clark made several motions toward the river, then he turned and walked toward his home.

"He'll keep an eye out, Miranda."

"He's a strange old man. I wish I trusted him more. There's something nagging in the back of my mind about him."

Tom gunned the engine and headed out. "Clark's a smart man. He's lived his entire life in these mountains, and he's plenty capable of thinking."

"The trap!" Miranda banged her hand on the truck dash.

"What about it?"

She turned so she could see him clearly. "It was my trap. Remember we left one down by Devil's Hole and it disappeared? Well, that was it."

"How could you be certain?" There was a shadow of doubt in Tom's voice. He knew Miranda didn't care for the old man. "Can you prove it?"

"Well, the trap isn't registered in my name, if that's what you mean," Miranda said angrily. "But it's Gordon's trap. I know because I helped haul that thing through the woods for a week. The mesh, the size. It was the same."

"Maybe that's a standard brand. Maybe Clark saw one and then built his own."

"How would he have known to make an exact duplicate?"

Tom drove for a moment before he spoke again. "Clark wouldn't take the trap."

"Can you be so certain? This river is important to him, and I think it's important enough that he might do something foolish." She shook her head and gave a brief bitter laugh. "If that's true, then he's guilty of doing exactly the same thing he condemns me for."

Tom reached across the seat and captured her hand in his own. "That's true, Miranda, and if it's true, then it's more than a little sad."

"It's a moot issue for now. But I'll check back into it. Where are we going?"

They'd turned back toward Tabuga Springs, Miranda thought, but she was almost lost in the wilderness. All of the roads were beginning to look the same.

"I thought we'd stop at my house, take a shower, change clothes and eat. I think we could both use some rest."

Miranda wanted to argue that she had to get back to Washington. Her office had been ransacked, and Connie would be desperate. She felt as if she'd completely lost touch with her old life in Washington. She couldn't deny that she was exhausted, though. She'd never be able to drive from Tabuga Springs to the airport. There was a dull pain in her shoulder, and she was fighting sleep. When Tom took a cutoff road that looked completely unfamiliar, she didn't say a word.

TOM'S HOUSE WAS perched, precariously in Miranda's opinion, on the side of the cliff.

"Are you sure a good wind won't blow this over?" She was awed by the boldness of the design, the way that the wall and roof blended and merged with the granite rocks of the mountain that barely seemed to support the building. It was not merely a building; it was a statement.

"Positive." He grasped her elbow and moved her down the natural stone walk to the front door. He worked the coded lock and swung the door wide for her to enter.

Miranda stepped into a small hallway that opened onto a wide den. In the foreground a grand piano caught her eye, but she was drawn past that to the series of glass doors that gave a perfect view of the sun setting behind a range of mountains.

"It's beautiful, Tom," she said.

"The house is small. I designed it for a single man, but it has everything I need."

"A modest understatement." She smiled at him. "Do you play?" She nodded to the piano.

"When I was in elementary school, I had great ambitions to become a jazz pianist." He shrugged his shoulders. "By my first year in college, I realized it wasn't going to happen. I didn't have the talent to make it to the level I wanted. Now I play only for my own enjoyment. How about a glass of wine?"

"A very small glass," she replied. "I may fall asleep drinking it. Your house reflects..."

"A lot of my work was on the West Coast, and abroad. The problem with that is I don't like to travel." The wineglass was elegantly tapered, and he filled it with light, golden wine.

"You and your brother are very different." She was thinking about Doc's old house, beautifully renovated into an office and living quarters. It was such a contrast to Tom's modern home, all glass and white walls.

"We are very different. Doc has always been more practical, more settled. He gave up a tremendous career as a researcher in France to come back to Tabuga Springs."

It was on the tip of her tongue to ask what he'd given up to return, but she decided to hold the question until they were rested.

Motioning her to follow him, he opened one of the doors, and she saw a porch that extended across the front of the house. It wasn't until she walked to the railing that she realized she was hanging over an eight-hundred-foot drop straight down into the Tabuga.

"This time of year the moon comes up right over there." He pointed southwest, where the ridge of mountains had a small broken chip in their outline. "Why don't you take a hot bath while I make us some dinner? By then the moon should be paying a visit."

"I should have called the office." She hesitated.

"Take a bath, then call your secretary at home. You can relieve both of your minds."

"You won't have to talk me into that," she said. Her body ached, and the thought of a hot bath was enticing.

Tom showed her the bath and left a comfortable sweat suit for her to wear while he washed her clothes. As soon as the tub was filled, she slipped into the warm water. It had been a long, grueling day. Abe Tuttle. Clark Presley.

The fish trap. Was there a link? She seemed caught up in different factions of a community that she didn't really know how to read.

She knew Tuttle was dangerous. He didn't bother to hide it. It was Presley who worried her. He was always johnny-on-the-spot when trouble came calling. Was it because he was the source?

"Hey, dinner's ready." Tom rattled the bathroom door. "I'd forgotten you were part mermaid. Better shake a leg and come and eat."

The bath had relaxed her, and she hurried into the sweats, rolling up the sleeves and pants. She was a sorry sight, but she felt much better.

"Your favorite, tuna sandwiches," Tom said sarcastically. "I didn't expect guests, and I'm afraid I don't keep the house well stocked."

"Sounds great to me." She took a seat at the wooden table in the center of the large, open room. She was ravenous. When they finished the sandwiches, Tom motioned to the telephone. "Help yourself while I get cleaned up. Your clothes are in the dryer. You look like you're going to disappear in those sweats."

"I'd better make some phone calls," she agreed. "Connie will be worried, and I'm going to have to book a flight home, fish or no fish."

"Telephone's in the kitchen, and there are others in the bedrooms."

When she replaced the telephone, she had a one-o'clock-flight reservation back to Washington, worried pleas from Connie to be safe and an urgent request from Gordon Simms to get fish samples to him. Tom had finished his bath and was sitting in a rattan chair on the porch, his feet propped on the porch railing.

He heard her and turned to smile a greeting. "In your absence the moon came for a visit." Above the mountains a three-quarter moon cast silvery light. "The mountains make for late mornings and early evenings, not so much in summer, but especially in the winter."

"I've never had much chance to spend winter months here. I..."

The jingle of the telephone split the night.

"Pick it up in the kitchen for me, would you? I don't think I could force my body out of this chair."

"Sure." She was only a few steps from the phone and she lifted the black receiver with a businesslike greeting.

"The Tabuga is dead, and so are you and your new boyfriend." The menacing voice paused. "Your past has caught up with you. Everything and everyone you touch gets hurt. Now a lot of innocent people will be blown away, and all because of you. If you aren't a coward, come to the river. You have ninety minutes to stop me." The connection dissolved.

She held the telephone helplessly in front of her, her hand frozen to the smooth black contours. "Blown away." The phrase rang a dangerous warning.

"Who was it?" Tom stood in the doorway anxiously watching her.

She opened her mouth to tell him and then firmly closed her lips. It was true. Everyone she touched got hurt. Only this time Tom wasn't going to. This was her fight, not his.

"Miranda, what's wrong?"

"Nothing," she managed. But something was terribly wrong. *Blown away.* Those words echoed from the past when she and her friends had sat on the banks of the Tabuga River and planned the bombing. *Blown away.* The exact words.

The caller had also warned that her past was catching up with her. The anonymous donation, the attacks on Gordon and herself. None of it made complete sense, but somehow she knew now that it was all tied up with her, with her past. The thought seemed to choke the breath from her.

"Who was on the phone?" Tom walked to her, brushing her hair from her cheek with a tender motion.

"It was Connie. She had to call me back. She'd forgotten to tell me about my office. They haven't been able to tell if anything was stolen, but it doesn't appear that theft was the motivation." She took a breath.

"Has anything else happened?" He saw the terror in her pale face and wide eyes.

"No. Just typical WDC folderol." She smiled. "How about another glass of wine?"

"Wonderful idea." He went to the kitchen for the bottle.

She could tell by his voice that he wasn't totally convinced by her answers. She eyed the clock nervously. The caller had said ninety minutes before a lot of innocent people were "blown away." She fought down the panic and tried to think. What had he meant?

"Miranda?" Tom lifted her chin with his forefinger. "I've asked you twice if you'd like something else to eat. Maybe some dessert?"

"It doesn't matter." She shifted away from him, guilty at her deception. "Something cold would be nice." The idea that came to her was sudden and terrible. The caller intended to blow up the bridge to Tabuga Springs—or possibly some part of the town. She had to get there before it happened.

Her breathing grew shallow. "Excuse me," she whispered, walking rapidly to the bathroom.

"Are you sure you're okay?"

"Fine. I want to wash my face." She kept walking, noticing the keys to the truck on the table near the front door. Her hand slipped out to grab them as she passed. A few seconds later she was sneaking down the hall to the front door, her nearly dry clothes clutched in her hands. Her heart thumped at the sight of the vehicle, parked on the very brink of the ledge. One slip of the clutch and she'd be over the mountain. But there wasn't time to hesitate. She shifted into reverse and pressed the gas. With a roar she was flying backward. She saw Tom rush out the front door but she didn't stop. She had to get to Tabuga Springs.

"Wait."

The confusion on Tom's face almost made her brake. "I'll explain later," she whispered, flying down the mountain toward town.

The drive was a nightmare. Her headlights cut the blackness like a candle in a storm-torn house. She drove so fast that at times the wheels hung on the lip of the road.

As she rounded a sharp curve the yellow beams picked up the eerie outline of the ancient bridge. Miranda's heart leapt with a gladness she never thought she'd feel for the decrepit structure. She was only a few minutes from town. Maybe she could make it in time. Maybe. And then what? Could she warn the people? Would Sheriff Carter believe her?

Leaning forward in anticipation, she caught a sudden movement beneath the edge of the wooden entry ramp. She swallowed the scream that rose in her throat. It was just some animal scurrying out of the headlights. A big animal, maybe a bear. There was something odd, though, a furtiveness in the way the creature moved. She tightened her hold on the wheel. Her imagination was in high gear. She had to get a grip on herself.

As she approached the bridge, the figure of a man jumped out from the side of the road. She swerved hard, somehow managing to avoid the man and keep the truck on the edge of the road. With an exclamation of pain from the wrenching in her shoulder, she slammed on the brakes and stopped the truck. Damn! Had she hit someone? She hadn't felt the truck strike anything. Surely she'd missed him, but where was he? Who was he?

"Hey! Anybody here?" she called into the darkness.

Feeling extremely vulnerable, she opened the truck door and got out to check the road. The twin lights of the truck cut through the darkness, revealing only the road and the surrounding trees. There was not a sign of a living creature. Teeth chattering, she climbed back into the truck. She had to get to Tabuga Springs and warn the sheriff. Something had to be done to stop all traffic on the bridge. If the call was a hoax, she'd rather look like a fool. If it wasn't, then a lot of people could die.

She roared onto the bridge as fast as she dared. The truck bounced from one wooden board to the next. The thought that she'd made it to the town in time came just at the same time as the first ugly rumble.

The explosion was slightly upriver, and the impact rocked the ancient timbers of the bridge. The truck lurched on the trembling frame, racing forward with a madness that made Miranda's heart and stomach collide.

She was barely able to stand on the brakes in time to keep from flying off into the black water below. The bridge shuddered in an effort to absorb the shock. A distant rumble farther upriver sounded, as if there had been at least two separate charges. There might have been more, all set up to explode in quick succession.

The form she'd seen at the bridge abutment was a man, someone waiting for her to drive onto the bridge. Whoever was behind the destruction had intended for the blast to send her hurtling over the unrailed side straight into the deadly currents of the Tabuga.

The bridge trembled as shock waves of water battered the wooden foundation. Somehow the ancient timbers held. With a final spurt of gas the truck lurched forward onto solid ground.

Thirty or so town residents had gathered at the banks of the river, drawn out of their homes by the tremendous explosion. She parked, allowing her rubbery legs a moment to recover. Before she could get out of the truck, she heard her name called.

"Ms. Conner?" Sheriff Carter's voice was tense.

"I need to talk to you." She had a lot to say to the lawman.

"What do you know about that explosion?" Accusation rippled in his voice.

"What is that supposed to mean?"

"It means we're aware of your past dealings with saboteurs." His angry mouth clamped shut with satisfaction. "You used to hang out on this river with those hippies, didn't you? The ones who made dynamite a specialty of their 'peace movement?' "

His charge almost sent her reeling. She'd expected help in finding the culprits, not a pointed finger. "I work with an organization designed to preserve the Tabuga, not destroy her." She spoke with cold formality. "If you have charges to make against me, you'd better do it officially, and you'd better be prepared to back them up with facts."

"That might not be as hard as you think. I warned you once about nosin' around here." His slow, insinuating tone made her skin crawl. "We got a call saying you were out on the river tonight. And lo and behold, here you are, right on time for the show." He walked to the back of the truck and shined a flashlight into the bed.

"What are you doing?" Miranda got out, anger giving her strength.

"Look at this." Carter reached into the truck and pulled out a black plastic bundle. In a moment he had out a pocket knife and sliced into the package.

"What is that?" Miranda demanded.

"Well, I can't be certain, but I'd say it looks like the makings for some type of explosive." Carter swung the light into her eyes. "Some old dogs can't give up their tricks, can they?"

"I don't know where that came from, but it isn't mine," Miranda said. Suddenly the meaning of the man at the bridge became very clear. He'd jumped out to stop her. He'd had just enough time to drop the bundle in the back and disappear.

"Whatever your plans were, Ms. Conner, don't be leaving town until I have the lab check this out. If that presents a problem, we can accommodate you in jail."

"That won't be a problem, Sheriff," Miranda said. "I wouldn't dream of leaving Tabuga Springs. Not now."

Chapter Nine

The lights of Doc's house beckoned like a haven when Miranda turned down the tree-lined drive. A sigh of weary relief escaped as she cut the engine and got out of the truck. As much as she hated to involve Doc, she had no place else to go. Sheriff Carter had warned her not to leave Tabuga Springs. In her mind she questioned his legal authority, but for the moment she was too tired to fight. She simply didn't have what it took to make the long drive to the airport, and there was no guarantee that she could get a flight at such an hour. The road to Tom's was not safe. Doc was her only option.

Carter had wanted to put her in jail, and only her position with the WDC in Washington had stayed his hand. He had told her he was going to take his time and gather evidence against her properly. He didn't want any mistakes in the bombing case against her. She could still hear the ugly edge to his voice as he'd pointed out that he thought she might have "grown out of blowing things up."

His words rang in her ears. Someone had used her past against her in a very successful way. She felt her anger climb another notch, but this time at herself. She'd been the perfect mark. She'd fallen for the bait like the biggest sucker in the world. The gunpowder in the back of Tom's truck was the ultimate setup, and she'd given them the golden opportunity to plant it.

"Doc!" She pounded the door. "Open up, it's me, Miranda Conner."

"Miranda?" Doc opened the door, a light robe around his pyjamas. He stood for a moment in confusion. "What's wrong? Where's Tom? What was that explosion?"

"Could I come in, please? I'll explain everything."

He hesitated a moment, then stepped aside. "Certainly."

As he ushered her into the back of the house, she told him what had happened. "I have to call Tom. He thinks I've stolen his truck, and I may have done worse. There's a chance Carter will suspect him, too, because I was driving his truck."

"I was just having a drink," Doc said, indicating a chair for her. "Let me get something for you."

In a moment he handed her a tall glass of bourbon and water. She politely took it, then stood. "Where's the phone?"

"You're pale as a ghost. You just sit down and I'll call Tom. It might be better if I explain."

"Thanks," she agreed, sinking back into the comfortable chair. Her body jangled all over, and fatigue had left her muscles feeling as if she'd been beaten. She closed her eyes a moment, trying to hold off the headache she felt building in each temple. Thank goodness for a friend like Doc. Not many people would get so involved. At last she heard his footsteps returning.

"Is Tom coming?"

"Not exactly." Doc gave her a sympathetic smile. "He wasn't thrilled by the fact that you took his truck and left him stranded. It's something of a long walk. I'll have to arrange to send a vehicle for him."

"But you explained to him, didn't you?" Things had gotten so crazy. She'd acted rashly by running off and leaving Tom, but it was for his protection. She had to make him understand.

"I tried to talk with him, but he isn't exactly in a listening mood. My advice is to give him a while to cool off."

Doc lifted his glass to her. "Tom has a hot temper, but he gets over it quick."

"I don't have time," she said grimly as she walked to the door. "I don't think you appreciate the jam that I'm in. Congressional hearings on the Tabuga will be scheduled any day now, and I don't have a sample of the darter. My reputation is on the line, as well as that of the WDC. I need to be in Washington, and I need to stay here and look for those fish. And now I've managed to involve Tom in something that could cause serious problems." She shook her head and allowed a soft, discouraged laugh. "I'd like to use the phone. I have to make Tom understand what I've done, and why."

"Don't push him, Miranda," Doc warned. "He isn't a man who takes that. Believe me, I know."

The urgency in Doc's voice stopped her. "If I don't explain to him, how will he ever understand?"

"Just give him some time. I told you he was the uptight member of the clan. Uptight and always right. That's Tom, and he can't help it. That's always been part of his appeal." His eyes flashed for an instant before he looked at the liquor bottle and poured another drink.

The bitterness in Doc's voice was so unexpected, Miranda was almost stunned. For the first time she noticed that the bottle of bourbon was half-gone. Doc's eyes were a little bloodshot, too. She didn't know him well, but it wasn't difficult to see that something was eating at him.

"Drink up," he said as if he read her mind.

"Mind if I have a Coke instead?" she asked, nodding at the counter where a supply of soft drinks could easily be seen.

"Not in the mood for alcohol?" Doc's smile was tight.

"I'm sorry to say that I am. It's been one hell of a day."

For a long moment there was only the sound of carbonation fizzing as Miranda poured her drink. She pulled the freezer door open and was drawn up sharp by Doc's startled question.

"Is there something you need?"

"Some ice. I can get it," she said, her hands already searching for ice trays. There were several small white boxes filled with medical supplies, and she pushed them aside. "Here we go." She found the tray, cracked it open and filled her glass.

She'd refilled the tray with water before she looked over at Doc. He was looking out the window, a pained expression on his face. "Doc, has something happened that I need to know about?" He looked so tormented that she felt a pang of sympathy for him. He was such a bright and giving man—what could have happened to put him so heavily on the bottle?

"I'm having a bad day." Doc smiled grimly. "And it's turned into a bad night."

"Is there something I can do?" Miranda could sense Doc's tenuous grip on his emotions.

"Not a thing, my dear." Doc smiled brightly and held up his glass. "I've found the cure for what ails me."

"Where's Cheryl?" Miranda looked around the room. There was no sign of any of Cheryl's possessions, but she'd somehow gotten the impression that Doc and Cheryl were a serious team.

"She had some business out of town. At least that's what she told me."

The pieces of the puzzle fell into place. Tom had told her that Doc had been through one bad relationship. Now he was suffering from Cheryl's absence and he'd done the worst possible thing, started drinking.

"She'll be back soon."

"And then Tom will send her away again."

Miranda laughed. "Doc, your brother can't send Cheryl away. Besides, even if he could, he wouldn't. He was telling me yesterday how glad he is for you that you've found someone to care for."

"Yes, Tom has always had my best interests at heart."

There was no missing the sarcasm, and Miranda decided not to answer. Doc was obviously on an alcohol-induced tear that had little to do with any reality.

Doc raised his glass. "To my brother, the man who lives by his own laws, and then makes people believe they're just." He finished the drink.

"What are you saying, Doc?"

"I like you, Miranda. You're a nice woman, dedicated. Watch out for Tom. He's single-minded. And in that single-mindedness, he can sometimes appear to be cruel. When he thinks he's right, there is no other way." He gave her a lopsided smile. "Just beware if your interests are at cross-purposes with his. That's all I have to say." He took a long drink, draining the amber liquid from the glass.

She could tell by Doc's posture that he was tired and drunk. Still, his words were unsettling. "If you don't mind, I'd like to lie down for a while. I'm not feeling great."

"There's a bedroom upstairs on the left. Help yourself to anything you need. I'm going to have another drink and then get some sleep myself. There's been too much activity going on in Tabuga Springs to suit me."

"I couldn't agree more," she said, walking up the stairs.

MID-MORNING LIGHT BROKE across Miranda's eyes, forcing her back to consciousness. Leaning on her elbow, she was amazed to find the sun halfway up in the morning sky. She'd had great difficulty going to sleep, but she'd slept soundly and much too long. As she slipped into her clothes, she heard the ringing of the telephone downstairs and felt a surge of hope that Tom was calling.

She ran a brush through her hair and bounded down the stairs. A chagrined and apologetic Doc was making breakfast in the kitchen.

"Was that Tom?"

He gave her a sheepish grin. "It seems I owe you two apologies now, instead of just one. Tom called earlier this morning. When I tried to explain about you staying over, and you'd wanted to call and I'd dissuaded you, he got even angrier. It's going to take him a couple of days to cool off now."

Miranda sank down onto a stool. "I should have called him last night."

"Now, now," he consoled her. "It's all my fault and I'll get it straight. I sent his truck back to him, and I had one of the local men who do mechanical work complete the necessary repairs on the rental Jeep."

"Thanks, Doc." Miranda meant it, but she couldn't help the disappointment she felt. She didn't want to leave Tabuga Springs without getting things straight with Tom. Now it looked as if she wouldn't have a chance to speak to him.

"And I owe you an apology for my maudlin self-pity last night. Tom and I had some earlier disagreements. He was Grandfather's favorite, and that was hard for an older brother. Some good has come of all of it, though. I've decided to give up drinking for a few months. I'm not very pleased with my big mouth once I have a few drinks."

Miranda found a smile for Doc. He was so ashamed, so much like a young boy. "You aren't the only person who drinks and talks," she said. "Forget it. Tom will cool off. Maybe I should drive up and try to see him before I leave for Washington."

"No, I wouldn't. He's mad right now. I'll go up later this afternoon after clinic hours. By then he'll be in a better mood."

Miranda started to protest, but the sharp ring of the phone interrupted. Doc handed her a heaping plate of eggs, bacon, grits and toast as he picked up the receiver. "My patients call relentlessly." He grinned as he put the phone to his mouth. "Doc Wilkes here."

The smile dissolved on his face. "I'm sorry Sheriff Carter, I have no idea where she could be. You say she dropped a couple of dynamite charges in the river last night? Uh-huh. Well, I find that hard to believe. She didn't strike me as the radical type." He gave her a long, worried look as he continued to listen. "Record of radical behavior? But that was years ago."

Miranda watched the expression shift over Doc's face. There was concern, doubt, worry and hesitation.

"You can't charge a person with such a serious crime unless you've got solid evidence, Carter. Now quit acting like a Wild West sheriff and talk sensibly. Anyone could have planted the gunpowder in Tom's truck. Anyone!"

He reached across the kitchen counter and took Miranda's hand, giving it a gentle squeeze. "Well, I can't help you, Uley. She didn't come here and I haven't seen her. Check up at Tom's. That's right." He put the phone down and came to her side.

"Miranda, Sheriff Carter is looking for you. He says you know something about that dynamite charge in the river last night. He actually thinks you were involved."

"Last night I was afraid this would happen," Miranda reminded him. "I know what he says, and I know what happened. Now I have to find out who framed me."

"Who'd want to do something like that?" Doc was startled.

"I don't know, but I'm going to find out," she answered. The hunger she'd felt a moment earlier was gone.

"Well, Carter's going to try to pick you up. He says he's got fingerprints and evidence. I told him you weren't here. I thought you might be able to use a little time before he gets you."

"Thanks, Doc, I've got to get home," she said, rising. "I'm nothing but trouble for you and Tom. I have to get back to the office and line up some legal representation. Carter's going to try and make this charge stick, I'm afraid."

"Carter said you weren't to leave town. Miranda, you could get in serious trouble."

"Maybe, but I'm innocent and I need some help. I must go home. He didn't serve me with any official papers. I'm not charged, at least not yet. Besides, I don't have those fish, and I'll be coming back for them. That's a promise." She forced a tentative smile. "Doc, if Carter calls again..."

"Don't worry," he interrupted, "I haven't seen hide nor hair of you, and I don't know anything about anything. It's the least I can do after messing you up with Tom. But

I'll get that straight, too. Now get on before Carter decides to come snooping around here.''

She gave the telephone a desperate look. "I'd really feel better if I made an effort to talk with Tom. Even if he hangs up on me, I should try."

"Carter may be heading this way. You don't have time." Doc grasped her elbow and started toward the door. "If you're going to get away, hon, you'd better move out."

There was no arguing. As she cranked the motor she appealed to Doc. "Please tell Tom I wanted to call."

"Don't worry, just get going. I'll take care of everything."

"Thanks, Doc." She smiled and pulled away.

"YOU LOOK PRETTY ROUGH." Connie's critical appraisal was softened with a hug as she grabbed Miranda at Dulles Airport's frantic baggage claim. "Let's hurry, I had to double-park to get in here at this hour."

"Thanks for meeting me," Miranda said. The past forty-eight hours were beginning to take a toll. "I didn't know who else to call."

"What's going on here?" Connie said as she led Miranda to the car. "I want to know everything."

On the way to her apartment, Miranda filled Connie in, trying her best to minimize her own gunshot wound and completely leaving out the part about the gunpowder in the truck she was driving.

After fifteen years with the WDC, Connie had heard plenty of stories of attacks on WDC members, but she couldn't hide the growing worry she felt for Miranda. She drove and listened attentively as the younger woman talked.

"I've got to find out who donated that money for our expedition," Miranda added. "Somehow all of this fits together. It all started with the donation and ever since that moment, someone has been playing me and the WDC like a fine fiddle. I've been in the WDC for five years, and no one has ever mentioned my past. This might even be coming from Capitol Hill," she finished grimly.

"It isn't inconceivable. Senator Fremont's record of protecting the environment is poor. I've heard several remarks he's made about environmental groups, and they weren't nice. If somehow the focus of the entire hearing could be pinned on you, and especially on some unsavory aspect of your character, then the Tabuga could be in serious jeopardy."

"It's a bitter irony that the thing I set out to save could be the thing I destroy." Miranda felt blacker than she ever had in her life.

"Finding out about that donor won't be so easy. I know the central office is a chaotic mess, and they don't even have a record of any donor. I've been checking. But if we set our minds to it, I'm sure we can turn something up." She reached across the car and patted Miranda's arm. "Don't give up. You're not a quitter."

Miranda nodded. "I can't stop now. Not even if I wanted to."

"You've had several calls from Mr. Simms."

"Gordon's going to be furious that I didn't get another sample," Miranda moaned.

"He was very agitated. Some of his preliminary findings should be in later today or tomorrow. And Mr. Cox—remember him? He's your boss—wants you to call." She gave Miranda a sympathetic look. "He's not happy with you. There's about a million other messages, and Tom Wilkes called twice. He was frantic with worry."

"Tom?" Miranda couldn't believe it. "He called the office?"

"He was so worried." Connie glanced at her and smiled. "He sounds like such a nice man. The last time he called was right after you called, so I told him you were heading home. That seemed to make him feel better, but he was still worried."

"Did he say anything else?"

"Well, something odd. He asked if you'd been at his brother's. Since I didn't know, I couldn't tell him that. Were you?"

"Relax, Connie. I did stay at Doc's, but only because I was too tired . . . to catch a flight home." She didn't mention Carter's order to stay in town. "It's sort of confusing. What about the hearing?"

"No definite date. Senator Fremont's aide did call the office today looking for you. I was very careful not to say much of anything." She pulled in at the curb in front of Miranda's building. "Want some supper with the family?"

"Not tonight, thanks. Maybe tomorrow." Miranda got out of the car and blew Connie a kiss. "I have a million things to do now." Number one was calling Tom. She ran up to her door and hurried inside.

She didn't waste any time but picked up the receiver and obtained his home number. Though she let the phone ring a long time, there was no answer.

She ran a hot bath and settled into the soothing water. Her arm was tender, but the wound was healing with amazing speed. The jar of the telephone made her heart lift with expectation. Maybe Tom was calling her!

She left a bubbly trail of footprints down the hall as she went to the phone.

"Miranda Conner?"

The brash, hurried voice jolted her. "Yes."

"Russ Sherman. I just got a hot tip and I wanted to check it out with you. That rafting trip, was it funded by someone we both know?"

"I told you the truth, Russ. I don't know who sent the money, but I'd sure like to."

"You don't have any idea?" Russ was elated to have a scoop, even if it only applied to her.

"No idea."

"I hear there's been some excitement up on the river in the last few days. I'd be willing to make a trade. Your version of the Tabuga incidents for the name of the man who donated the funds."

Miranda paused for a moment. What could it possibly hurt to tell Russ the truth? She'd tried to tell Carter, and no one believed her. It could be a real advantage to have a reporter on her side, especially if Carter got ridiculous and decided to try to file charges against her.

"Sure, Russ. Come on over."

She had sandwiches ready and two cold beers opened when he arrived. He gratefully sipped the beer as he settled on the sofa across from her.

"You go first," he said.

For the second time Miranda recounted the events. When she told of her attack and shooting, Russ scribbled furiously.

"You have a bullet wound for proof, but there was no body?" He scratched his head. "That's a tough one, Miranda. Did Carter ever see your wound?"

"No, but Tom told him." Miranda assured him. "And there was a body, but someone moved it. Either those two guys came back, or someone else took it."

"And now Carter wants to pin the river bombing on you?"

"That and whatever else he can."

"Why?" He gave her a questioning look. "What would it benefit Carter to hurt you in any way?"

"Maybe because I work for the WDC. If I'm nailed as some sort of criminal, then all of the years of work we've done will be reduced to nothing. We'll just be another 'radical' organization. No one will ever take us seriously again."

"You could have a point," Russ said, sipping his beer. "How many people knew about your past record? You were only charged with conspiracy and given a suspended sentence. I mean, you called the FBI and reported the bombing. You tried to stop it. How could that affect you now?"

"The man who called and warned me about bombing the river mentioned my past," she said, faltering, "as if I were responsible." She shook her head. "When I took the job with WDC, I knew that there was always the chance that someone would use the past against me to try to block a project. That's one reason I never told anyone at the WDC. The other reason was that I was ashamed."

"Carter didn't strike me as being sophisticated enough to put something like this together on his own. Did Tom Wilkes know anything about you before we met him on the river?"

Startled, Miranda stood up. "I have no idea. Why do you ask?"

"My sources indicate Tom Wilkes donated the money for your little raft adventure. He's the controlling member of the board of directors of the Clearwater Development Company, which is the company that stands to gain the most from development of the Tabuga. I find it very strange that when he conveniently shows up in the middle of our rafting party, all hell breaks loose. See what I'm getting at?"

"Oh, yes, I see." Miranda walked to the kitchen and got another beer for Russ. Her hands shook as she fought to unscrew the cap. By the time she returned to the living room, she'd calmed herself.

"Are you sure Tom made that donation? I asked him, and he denied it."

"So, you thought he might be involved?" Russ was pleased with his calculations. "He denied it, too." He scribbled a few more notes.

"Who told you Tom made that donation?" She was in control, but she couldn't stop the maddening hammer of her heart.

"I can't reveal my source, but I'll tell you it came off the Hill. Another reporter was talking about our big camping adventure. One of his sources knew about the trip and about Tom Wilkes. The exchange was sort of in passing, nothing serious, just gossip."

"So it isn't completely reliable? There's no record, no evidence?" She wanted to believe Tom hadn't lied to her.

"I doubt you're going to find an official document." Russ laughed. "Put it this way. I'm not going to print the information, because I can't prove it a hundred percent. But I believe it. My reporter friend covers Senator Fremont."

"I'm aware of Fremont, and his terrible record on environmental issues." She rose again and paced the room.

Russ gave her a curious look, started to comment and then gathered up his notes. "I'd better take off. My life is a deadline."

"Have you seen Fred Elton since the trip?" Miranda stopped pacing and returned to sit across from Russ. "The way this is shaping up, I might need a friend with some political clout. Fred seemed sympathetic to the WDC... and he's on Fremont's staff."

"I haven't heard a word from Elton," Russ said. "And I wouldn't put any trust in him. He's a political aide. They're supposed to appear sympathetic to whatever group they're with. I'd put more faith in a prayer." He stood up and patted her shoulder. "Look, sometimes I'm too cynical. Don't take it too seriously."

"Thanks for the warning," she said wryly. "And thanks for the information."

"You've given me one hell of a story." He paused for a moment, checking his notes. "What about those fish samples?"

"No luck yet. I'm afraid that blast in the river might have messed things up, but I plan to do everything I can to find a darter."

"Even going back to the Tabuga with Carter on your case?"

"Even that. But I'm asking once again, Russ, don't mention the darters until I have some proof."

"You're risking your neck," he said, bouncing his pen up and down on the pad. "What if I just broke the story? It might save you a lot of work and danger."

She shook her head. "It could ruin our case, especially if Fremont thought we were trying to pull a fast one on him."

"If you insist."

She saw him out the door and then locked and bolted it behind him. A sensation of emptiness crept over her as she went to the window and watched the traffic inch down the street. The beauty and peace of the Tabuga seemed like a lost illusion. The feelings that had begun to grow for Tom were now dangerous instead of magical. She stood for a long time watching the lights of the city push back the darkness.

Why had Tom lied? That was the crucial question. Why would the company that stood to gain the most from developing the river send money to fund an expedition that might foul the development plans? She turned the question from all directions. There wasn't an answer that made sense. Yet there had to be. She rubbed her forehead with her palm, trying to erase the weariness and depression. The image of Tom standing on the banks of the river refused to go away.

Across the street a tall man walked under the streetlight, and for a moment her heart beat rapidly. In the darkness the man resembled Tom, and for a few seconds she let her fancy rule her mind. Had Tom come to talk with her? Did he have an explanation for the hard facts she'd just received from Russ Sherman? She wanted to believe that he did. She started to lift the window, but stopped with her fingers on the wood frame. Tom had lied to her. Or would he prefer to say he'd withheld some information crucial to the truth?

She stared at the man again. He was walking slowly, without any purpose, into the night. Halfway down the street, he stopped and turned back to face her building. Miranda felt a pang of real fear grab at her stomach. It looked as if the man were staring straight at her. She flipped the light and moved quickly away from the window. Even if by some wild stretch of the imagination it was Tom, she didn't like the idea that he might have followed her back to Washington, that he was lurking around in the dark, spying on her. She started to lift the window, this time to challenge the stranger. Again she stopped. Unable to make up her mind, she watched as he walked out of her range of vision.

She pulled the drapes snug and went to her desk. She didn't have time to stare out windows, making up things to frighten herself. The answer to her questions had to be found, and soon. She picked up her personal file on the Tabuga project, which contained a copy of the instructions that had come with the donation. Russ and Cynthia. Herself. Fred Elton. A scientist. She tried to make the link.

She'd known the two reporters for better than a year. Both were highly regarded journalists. Gordon had done occasional field work for the WDC in the past. She tried again, lining up the people and their occupations, hunting for the common thread. It simply wasn't there.

Unless...unless! Her fingers clutched the desk. Russ certainly had a lot of inside information. It had happened before that a reporter had been used in a controversial story. The ugly possibility that Russ might have sold out was also there. He'd been named specifically in the note. He'd worked hard to gain her confidence. He'd even agreed to hold the story about the darter. What were his motives?

A rattling noise at her front door stopped her dead in her tracks. It sounded as if someone were working the doorknob very gently. She eased out of her chair and slipped silently from the desk toward the small foyer. Her feet moved noiselessly across the carpet as she inched closer and closer to the front door. She couldn't hear a thing. Maybe it had been her imagination?

As her feet touched the hardwood of the foyer, she saw the doorknob move ever so slightly. Someone was outside the door, turning it. Miranda froze, watching the knob twist.

There wasn't a weapon in the house, with the exception of a few kitchen knives. Miranda backed away from the door, her eyes never leaving the knob. Feeling behind her with one hand, she moved toward the telephone.

As her hand found the receiver, the motion of the knob stopped. There was the sound of rapid footsteps down the hall, then silence. After a second's hesitation she replaced the phone and walked back to the door. The brass knob was cold in her hand as she held it. The apartment building was quiet. As she pressed her ear to the wood, she thought she heard her neighbors coming in. There was the sound of laughter, then the closing of a door. Miranda slid the locks and pushed the door open.

A small white carton was beside her door. Her hand trembled as she reached for it. It was light, almost empty, but there was something inside.

With great care she opened it. A square of white paper rested on top. When she removed it, the small carcass of a Tabuga pisces darter was all that remained. She unfolded the paper. "They exist, Miranda. Pity you can't prove it. The Tabuga is lost."

The hallway was completely empty. Stepping back inside her door, she slid the bolts home again and reminded herself to breathe. On a hunch she hurried over to the window and eased back a corner of the drapes. The tall man was standing under a streetlight. He raised one hand in a gesture that could have been a warning or a threat. Then he turned and hurried off into the night.

Chapter Ten

Miranda's bag rested by the door. It had taken her less than five minutes to pack for her return to the Tabuga. Before she went, though, she had to speak with Fred Elton, who was obviously out making a late night of it somewhere.

She was on her third cup of coffee, and the combination of anxiety, waiting and caffeine had her nerves jumping. Not even the soothing motion of the old rocker that she'd bought years before from a craftsman in the Appalachians helped calm her. At her feet was the small white carton containing the dead fish.

She was almost positive it was a Tabuga pisces darter. It had the yellow stripe, now faded, and the scale structure was considerably thicker than most fishes. She was positive the fish had the ganoid scale that was so important for evolutionary study.

Too bad she had no proof that the fish had come from the Tabuga.

She picked up the telephone receiver, then replaced it after glancing at her watch. It was eleven thirty-two. She'd called Fred Elton's number only two minutes before. She *had* to talk with him before she left town.

The thought that she should have called the cops about her late-night visitor crossed her mind, and she brushed it away. It was unlikely that Sheriff Uley Carter of Tabuga Springs had put out a bulletin on her, but then anything was possible. She didn't have time for a visit to the station house and the arrangement of WDC bail. No, she'd avoid the law—and she wouldn't tell Connie, either. If her boss learned about all the things that had happened, there was a good possibility he'd pull her off the Tabuga case—for her own good.

She picked up the carton and examined the fish again. She was certain it was the Tabuga pisces darter! And she knew the fish had come from the Tabuga. Her stomach knotted at the next logical thought. She could lie about the fish. She could say she'd caught it in the Tabuga. Gordon would have his sample; the development of the Tabuga would be stopped for a long time. It wouldn't be a total lie. If she had more time, she knew she'd eventually find a darter in the river.

She put the carton back on the floor with a deep sigh. That would work, but she knew she couldn't do it. She'd never be able to get up on the witness stand at a hearing and say something she knew wasn't true. She could not back away from the truth and pretend. Not for the man she once loved. No, not for Gregory, and not even for the Tabuga. She lowered her head into her palm and closed her eyes for a moment.

Tom Wilkes might be able to hedge the truth, but she couldn't. That bitter thought got her out of the chair and rummaging in the refrigerator. She had a long night and a dawn departure ahead of her, and this time no one in Tabuga Springs would ever know she was there. She could no longer trust Tom or Clark Presley to check the fish traps.

When she'd finished her cookies and milk, it was after midnight. She dialed Fred Elton's home number and counted the rings. When he finally answered he sounded wide-awake and a little breathless.

"Sorry to interrupt your evening, Fred, but I had to know if there was any word on the hearing."

"Day after tomorrow. I understand the development companies are eager to push ahead on this, and someone has been applying the pressure. The date has been pushed up on the calendar."

"Great." It was the worst news she could have gotten. "Fred, can we delay at all?"

"Someone is eager to get this issue before the committee, Miranda. Someone with a lot more clout than the WDC. I'll do what I can, but I think you're asking for a miracle. I had hoped you might be ready." He cleared his throat.

"I'm still gathering evidence." She hesitated, then plunged on. "I have a specimen of an important endangered species, one of the darters."

"Get the reports over to me right away! This could change the entire proceedings. The opposition needs time to prepare their expert witnesses, that's true, but a specimen will knock them off their feet." Fred was thinking out loud. "When can I have the report?"

Miranda's fingers clutched white on the phone. It would be so easy to imply that the darter had come from the Tabuga. It wouldn't be a real lie, only a ... half truth.

"Fred, I have a problem. I can't guarantee that the specimen came from the Tabuga."

The silence was as bad as she knew it would be.

"Then you don't really have any evidence."

"I know. But I do have a lot of hope that I can collect my own sample. I'm going to take this fish over to Gordon Simms right now, so he can begin the preliminary tests to be sure it is what I know it is. Then when I get back with my collection, we'll be in serious business."

"The only problem is, you need more time."

She could hear the disbelief in Fred's voice. "This isn't a ploy to postpone because the WDC isn't prepared. I swear to you, Fred, those darters are in the Tabuga and I'm going to get one."

"You're not going back there, are you?"

"I can't trust this to anyone else. That's my problem now. I've let other people volunteer to do my job, and they haven't come through. This is too important. It's up to me."

"It's too dangerous!"

Fred didn't know the half of what had happened—and it was just as well that he didn't. "I'll be careful."

"Miranda, I'd feel better if you didn't go back there."

"I'll take care of the fish—you take care of the hearing."

"I'll do what I can, but I may not be able to do anything. Don't expect much."

"I appreciate all of your help and effort."

"Let me know the minute you have something."

"You're at the top of my list. Thanks."

Miranda checked her watch when she hung up. She had a six-o'clock flight out to Ashville. The only thing left to do was get the dead fish to Gordon. His lab was located in a bad section of town, and the idea of traveling there at the heart of midnight didn't hold a lot of appeal. She decided to try for a few hours' sleep and make the trip in the morning. She was packed and ready for the Tabuga, and this time she wasn't coming home empty-handed.

THE RINGING OF the phone was faraway but persistent. Miranda's first sleepy thought was that it might be Tom. Eyes still closed, she fumbled around the night table until her hand closed on the receiver.

"Hello."

"Gordon Simms is dead." The gravelly voice was unmistakably the same as the one who'd called her at Tom Wilkes's house.

"Who are you?"

"Keep up with your work on the Tabuga and you'll find out. Take a look at your biologist friend. He's dead because of you. And remember—this is the last warning. If you don't back off, you're next."

The phone hummed.

Rage blotted out her fear. Who was threatening her? Why did they think they could get away with such behavior? She dialed the emergency number for the Washington police. To hell with Uley Carter and his ridiculous charges. She'd had enough intimidation, and this time she wasn't going to be tricked.

"I received a threatening phone call," she began as calmly as possible to the police officer who answered the phone. She repeated every word the caller had said. The real possibility of what might have happened grew like a cancer. No one would actually hurt Gordon, a hired biologist. But then he'd volunteered. And she'd told several people! Tom and Russ among them.

"Ms. Conner, we'll check on Mr. Simms and get back with you. Will you be at this number?" The desk sergeant sounded tired and uninterested.

"Please hurry. I'll be here." She replaced the phone and dialed Gordon's lab. It was two o'clock in the morning. Not much chance he'd be working, but she tried. The phone rang twenty times without an answer. She pressed the switch hook and dialed again. Another twenty rings without answer.

"He's probably at home." She spoke aloud to allay her growing anxiety. With great care she looked through her files to find his home number. Another two dozen unanswered rings, and her heart was pounding unbearably against her ribs. Had she endangered Gordon by telling people the he'd volunteered to work for the WDC?

Calculating the time she'd called the police, she realized they hadn't even had time to arrive at the laboratory. Flinging her gown off, she dressed, rushed out and hailed a cab. She was a lot closer to Gordon's lab than the precinct station was!

There was no sign of the police when she arrived. She knocked loudly on the heavy metal door, but there was no answer. Gordon's lab was isolated, and the door opened onto a poorly kept back street. He'd taken the back of an old warehouse downtown. Completely dedicated to his field, he probably never even noticed the seedy nature of his surroundings.

A car turned down the road, creeping along toward the warehouse. Miranda searched for the red-and-blue lights atop the car, but the closer it got, she realized it was too big and too old to be a patrol car.

When she was caught in the beams of the headlights, the car slowed. For a moment she thought it was going to stop, and she felt trapped like a rabbit in the glare of the lights. But the car continued at a slow but steady pace. Miranda dropped her gaze to the ground to avoid the blinding lights. Something glittered in the dirt beside the warehouse door.

As she bent to examine the area, her fingers closed around a hard metal object slightly embedded in the ground. Carefully she pried it up. She held a ring, but the combination of dirt and poor light prevented her from getting a good look at it.

She fumbled in the pocket of the blue jeans until she found her house key. Poking and prodding, she loosened the dirt around the ring. There was something familiar about it.

Half a block down the street was a good light, and she hurried to it, feeling a thousand demons chasing on her heels. The ring was significant. She wasn't certain how, but she knew that it was.

In the good light she cleaned the rest of the dirt away and held it in the palm of her hand. It was a large yellow stone carved into a buck's head and set in gold. The ring was masculine, symbolic in heft and design.

She held it to the light and caught a flash of gold. A dim memory began to form. She was lying down, just waking up. There was a hand touching her chest. The face above hers was worried, drawn. Amber eyes were narrowed with tension.

Tom Wilkes!

Her fingers wrapped around the ring until the pain was too much to bear. She wanted to hurl it into the night, pretend that it didn't exist. Tom's ring was at Gordon's door. Had he stopped by for a little visit with the biologist, maybe to give him an "anonymous donation" for some project? The way the ring had been left, just barely in the dirt, it was almost as if he'd put it there to taunt her.

A black-and-white unit pulled up, and two uniformed policemen confronted her.

"I'm Miranda Conner, the person who reported the phone call. Mr. Simms is working on a case for the Wilderness Defense Center, my employer." She tried hard to present a professional appearance as she tucked the ring surreptitiously into her pocket.

Pointing to Gordon's door, she added. "That's Mr. Simms's lab and the door is locked, I've already tried."

When there was no answer to the loud knocks on the laboratory door, Miranda stepped back. "You'd better knock it down."

The men exchanged glances before kicking the door in with surprising ease.

"Damn!" The policemen paused in the doorway, surveying the total destruction in front of them.

"Gordon!" Miranda's worried voice called from behind the two men. "Hey, Gordon!"

His name seemed to hang in the air for a moment, and then disappear without an answer.

"Stay back," one policeman warned as they both drew their guns and entered the dimly lighted room.

Unable to obey, she stepped in behind them. The destruction was vicious, much worse than what had been done to her office. Beakers were bashed, tables splintered and wrecked. The lab was a total loss.

The room flooded with light as the cop found a switch against the wall.

"Oh, God." The sickened phrase came from the policeman to her left, and she turned quickly. A man's body hung half-out of a large fish tank. His cold dead eyes were turned directly at her.

"Oh, no!" Miranda's hoarse whisper cut across the room.

"I told you to stay back." One cop roughly grabbed her arm and pushed her toward the door, but she twisted away. There was something wrong. The face in the tank didn't belong to Gordon. Not the dark hair, the leaner face.

It was Fred Elton.

"Take her out!" the senior officer directed the other policeman. She was only too willing to go. The pain and terror on Fred's face were indelibly imprinted on her brain.

"I'll radio for an ambulance," the cop who held her arm yelled to his partner. "I'll get some backup, too."

"Don't let her get away, we'll need her down at the station for questioning. She knows more about this than she should."

The words were empty chatter crashing around her ears. She gave no resistance to the rough treatment the policeman gave. When he placed his hand on top of her head and shoved her into the back of the patrol car, she didn't even flinch.

Neither back door had handles, and the wire-mesh screen above the front seat prevented her from crawling over and getting out. She was locked in. She leaned back into the seat and waited. It wasn't her first experience in a patrol car. It didn't even matter. She was much too busy thinking about Fred Elton to worry about her own plight.

"YOU'RE FREE TO GO. For now, Ms. Conner." The chunky detective stacked his paper, rubbed his shoulder holster under his arm and stood.

"Thank you, Officer."

They'd questioned her for over three hours. Once they found her arrest sheet, she was fair game for whatever they wanted to throw at her. She was beyond them, though, far beyond in a personal agony that was never reflected in her calm, pale face.

Fred Elton was dead, a man who'd done nothing but happen into the wrong place at the wrong time. He was dead because of her. She picked up her purse and walked out of the precinct past the officers and a wild assortment of victims, muggers, prostitutes and God only knew what else.

She walked for a long time, not caring where she went or what time it was. When at last she stopped a cab and rode home, her feet were throbbing and her eyes burned dry and hot.

"Connie, I have to go back to Tabuga Springs. I'm leaving a fish sample in the refrigerator. Please get it to Gordon as soon as possible." She left the message on the office answering machine, took a hot bath and went out the door. The police had warned her not to leave town. She was sorry she couldn't comply, but she had some business to take care of. She clutched the ring in her pocket. Tom Wilkes had some answers, and she meant to get them.

WHEN DOC'S NURSE CALLED Miranda's name, she rose and walked back to the examining room she remembered so well. She had to force her legs to hold firm.

"We'll let Doc take a look at that wound," the nurse directed. "There wasn't a chart on you, but he said you'd been shot in some kind of accident."

"Miranda, dear." Doc entered the room, walking straight to her and giving her a warm hug. "I thought you'd let those Washington specialists take care of you once you got home. I didn't expect you to come all the way out here to see a simple country doctor."

"I had some other business here."

"Well, let's take a look." The examining-room light struck the unique ring on his left hand as he reached out to lift her arm. Her gasp was audible and he stopped.

"Did I hurt you?"

"No," she stammered. "I guess I'm a little gun-shy."

"In a manner of speaking," he said with a laugh that resembled Tom's so much that Miranda felt a physical pain in her heart.

"It looks fine, my dear. I presume you're here to give Tom a little surprise visit. He certainly needs it. He's been moping around like a lost moose. Is he back from his trip?"

"What trip?" Miranda tried to calm her heartbeat as Doc Wilkes listened to her chest. Her eyes kept glancing down to his hand. The ring was exactly like the one she had in her pocket!

"Oh, I'm not sure. He went out of town. Didn't say exactly when he'd be back, but he didn't act as if he'd be gone long. I thought maybe he was going to Washington to see you."

"No, not me." When Doc straightened up, she smiled at him. "Must be some other lady he's after."

"Don't believe that for a minute." He patted her back, his hand moving from her shoulder to her hand.

The ring was so conspicuous, how had she never noticed it before?

"Tom's smitten by you," Doc continued talking. "I've told you so."

"That's a lovely ring." She reached out and touched his hand, pulling it closer to her. A glow of perspiration began to break on her forehead. She had one ring in her pocket, and now Doc had another, identical one. What was going on?

"Very bold design. Grandfather had it made."

"I don't think I've ever seen another like it." She was fishing, but she had to try something.

"No? Tom has one. They're Wild Horse originals."

"Wild Horse?" The name threw her for a moment.

"My Indian grandfather, remember?"

"And your grandfather commissioned your ring?" She couldn't take her eyes off it. If she wasn't able to feel the lump of gold in her pocket, she would have sworn that Doc wore it on his hand.

"He did. One for me and one for Tom."

"How thoughtful."

"Grandfather was very involved in tradition, that's why he was so hurt when Tom—" Doc broke off, giving a chagrined smile. "I'm certainly talkative today, and not about my own business. Tom is a little sensitive about his affairs."

"It's nice to see two brothers so close." She would have given a year of her life to hear the conclusion of what he'd started to say. "I don't believe I've ever seen Tom wear his ring," she said.

"Tom's not a sentimentalist like me. He's also never been fond of jewelry. He says, and he's right, that rings are asking for trouble when he's on a construction site. Some of those jobs he does are rather dangerous.''

"He seems to have a minor addiction to danger." Her voice was warm and her lips curved slightly, but her green eyes were deadly serious.

"That's Tom. A little on the macho side, I suppose, but he can't help it. A lot of that is Grandfather's doing."

"How so?" She stretched her arms out behind her and propped back slightly on the table, striking a casual pose.

"I have to admit your interest in Tom delights me." Doc chuckled. "I suppose I am trampling in his garden, but since it's all for the sake of romance, I'll give you a little background."

"Closemouthed doesn't begin to describe Tom." Miranda smiled.

"He is tight-lipped," Doc agreed, "but you'll find that's an asset, as well as a liability. I'm much too inclined to spill my guts and tell the whole family history."

"Nonsense. You're being very helpful to me. If I knew a little more about Tom, then I'd understand him better."

"I guess I know him as well as anyone else, but after Vietnam he changed. As a young boy he was very open, very passionate about his beliefs. He and Grandfather would spend weeks camping, and he'd come back all excited about the things he'd learned, the history of the mountains and what he and Grandfather called the 'spirits.' Oooouuu!''

The eerie note was meant to be funny, but Miranda felt her skin crawl. "And what happened?"

"Tom went to Vietnam, strictly at Grandfather's insistence. You see, Tom was set to enter school. When the war issue came up, Grandfather encouraged him to go, and Tom obliged by joining the navy and training as a medic." Doc walked away from her and looked out the window. "I refused to go. I went to France instead."

Miranda remembered Tom's confidence as he tended her wound. His positive application of antiseptic, his professional demeanor. Now it made more sense.

"Tom saw some awful things overseas. In fact, his best friend, Howie Dalty, died in his arms. He was a changed man when he came back, and I don't believe he ever forgave Grandfather." He shook his head.

"I chose to continue my medical career in France." Doc looked down at the floor.

Miranda heard the regret in his voice, and she made no effort to interrupt.

"At the time, the medical team I was associated with thought we had a good lead on a cure for cancer. It didn't work out, but for several months we were so hopeful." Disappointment blended with regret.

"That must have been disappointing."

Doc shrugged. "It took Tom a long time to forgive me for disobeying Grandfather. When Tom came home from Vietnam, he changed the direction of his life. He started a whole new career for himself in architecture. All of our youthful plans to live in Tabuga Springs were gone, vanished."

"I'm sorry." Miranda was deeply moved by Doc. The suffering was in his eyes, the amber eyes so much like Tom's and yet so different.

"It's taken Tom a long time to recover. When he came back to Tabuga Springs, I knew it was a sign that he was on the mend. That's one reason I stayed in Tabuga Springs all these years."

"I had wondered," Miranda admitted.

"These people need medical help as much as anyone else. It gives me a lot of satisfaction to come here and bring technology and healing to the community that's forgotten by so many others. As it turns out, though, I may be just the beginning of advanced medicine."

"How is that?"

"With development comes many benefits. The people here will have a new hospital, the finest equipment, many services that aren't within their reach now. I know you're opposed to changing the Tabuga, but in many ways it will help the people here. If it comes about..."

"It will also change a unique part of America." Doc's words were true, but they still angered her. So much destruction was termed "progress" and hailed as an improvement. She wasn't opposed to improvements, but someone had to weigh the cost.

"Don't be too hard on Tom," Doc cautioned her, dropping a warm hand on her knee. "He isn't a profiteer. He wants to see this community thrive, grow and move into the twenty-first century with some of the benefits that other people, like yourself, take for granted. How long would you like to live without indoor plumbing, advanced medical care, proper law-enforcement protection, the little things?"

"Those things are important, but they have to be weighed against destroying an environment that can never be replaced." Her voice was soft and she didn't drop her gaze.

"Well, I can see this is an issue for you and Tom, not me. All I'm asking is that you remember he isn't a bad man for wanting certain things."

"I'm sure she will." Tom's flinty voice came from the open doorway, and both Doc and Miranda swiveled to confront him.

"A nice family chat about me?" He was furious, and badly in need of a shave.

"By way of pleasant conversation," Doc said lightly.

Tom's blazing gaze swung to Miranda. "What are you doing here, other than pumping my brother for something you should have asked me? The last time I saw you, you stole my truck and left me on top of a mountain."

"I came . . . I came to ask you something." She'd meant to ask him about the ring, but she refused to bring it up in front of Doc. There was enough dissension between the brothers. Their warm and loving relationship had grown over an old and ugly wound. For Doc's sake, she didn't want to open old scars.

"Since we're having such an intimate little family gathering, go on and tell me what you came all this way to say."

A muscle in his jaw worked, and his brown eyes were almost black with anger.

"Tom, really," Doc interjected. "It wasn't like that at all. I started talking, and Miranda was simply a very good listener. She didn't pry."

"So, my brother is now defending you?"

"Tom! Stop it." Miranda slipped from the table to face him. "We were talking, and very naturally the conversation turned to you."

"If you wanted to know something, why didn't you ask me?"

She riveted her eyes on him, driving down the impulse to look to Doc for assistance. Her hand instinctively dropped to her pocket and found the ring. Her anger and pain at Fred Elton's brutal death prompted her reply.

"Because I'm not certain you'd tell me the truth."

"What?" The harsh tone of his voice was exactly what she needed to push her into action.

"Fred Elton was murdered last night. What do you know about it?"

Chapter Eleven

The line of Tom's jaw was unforgiving, and the small scar burned white against his bronzed skin. "Is that a question or an accusation?"

"A little of both, maybe." Miranda refused to back down.

"We need to talk, uninterrupted."

"I have some things to talk to you about, too," she said angrily. "Like why were you in Washington? Why were you staking out my apartment? What do you know about how Fred Elton died?"

"Let's go," Tom said.

He walked out of the examining room, and Miranda followed. At the open door she turned back to Doc. "Thanks for trying to help." Then she walked through the lobby and out to Tom's truck.

They drove for fifteen minutes without speaking. Miranda used the time to study Tom's intense profile. She felt the ring in her pocket, but strangely enough she couldn't conjure up any feelings of fear.

"Aren't you afraid of me?" He gave her a dark look and kept driving.

"No."

He slowed the truck and pulled beneath the shade of a large hardwood. "You came here to accuse me of murder. Now you find yourself out in the woods with a man who you think killed Fred Elton, and you're not afraid? Why not?''

She couldn't honestly say. It was an emotion so strong, though, that she couldn't deny it. Looking at him, face to face, in the unforgiving glare of the mountain sun, she could not believe that Tom had hurt anyone. Her hand rested on the ring in her pocket. ''Were you in Washington last night?''

He rubbed his hand across his unshaven face. ''A blacktie affair,'' he said sarcastically. ''Miranda, I was on the Tabuga last night, looking for those damn fish and hunting down false leads.''

''False leads?'' She was thrown off balance.

''Is this your bandanna?'' He pulled the navy cloth from the glove compartment and dropped it onto the truck seat.

She nodded, picking it up. ''Those kerchiefs are inexpensive and easy to find.''

''Well, this one came with a rock and a note.'' He felt his anger seeping away. They'd both been played for suckers. He'd spent half the night worried to death about Miranda and the last half furious that she'd finagled him into a wild-goose chase. ''Late yesterday afternoon I found this. It had been thrown through the window of my office. There was a note that said you'd gone back to the river.''

''But Doc knew I went to the airport. Sheriff Carter...''

''Said that you'd left town against his explicit orders, and that you'd turned in the rental car at the agency. But he also said that when he notified Washington authorities to pick you up, you never got off the plane.''

''That's a lie!''

''That's obvious to me. Now. Anyway, the note said that you were in grave danger and that if I wanted you to live I had to get to the river and 'remove you.' ''

''So you went.''

''Yes, I went. And spent a futile night trying to track a nonexistent trail. Oh, there were a couple of clues, like the bandanna. They were all planted. I know that now.''

''And you have no alibi for your whereabouts last night. And your ring was planted at Gordon's lab, so you would be the first person I suspected when I went there." She leaned back against the seat, stunned at the intricacy of the setup. "Somebody wants us in a bad kind of way."

"My ring?"

She drew it from her pocket and gave it to him.

"The question is why?" He held the gold ring in his hand, turning it over as if he'd never really studied it before.

"The Tabuga. Someone wants that river dammed." Miranda looked at Tom and found skepticism in his eyes.

"I'm the developer, Miranda. I'm the main stockholder of Clearwater Development."

"I know. Russ Sherman told me yesterday."

Her softly spoken words were like a slap. "I should have told you before. I meant to, and I wanted to."

"You should have told me."

"I wanted an unbiased report from an environmental group. That's why I paid for the expedition. We researched the proenvironmental organizations and felt the WDC was the most qualified. We agreed to put up the money and then stand back until the results were in on how destructive the dam would be. We all agreed to abide by the WDC findings."

"Tom, you should have told me. Half truths aren't good enough." She took a deep breath and met his gaze. "Not when two people care about each other. Trust is the most important thing."

His fingers brushed her cheek softly. "I wanted to tell you, but so many bad things happened. I knew you'd feel betrayed and you'd send me away. I wanted to keep you safe, Miranda. I just made a mistake about the way I did it."

She touched his face, her fingers moving slowly across the stubble of his beard. A smile touched the corners of her mouth. "I've made a few of those myself. The truth is, I can forget other people's mistakes a lot easier than I can forget my own."

"Maybe we can work on that." Tom leaned over and kissed her cheek. "I'd like that a lot."

Miranda's heart hammered in her chest. For the first time in what seemed like centuries, she felt hope. With Tom by her side, they might save the Tabuga. At least she had a fighting chance now.

"I'd like that, too."

"So let's resolve this mess. I just want to tell you, Miranda. If the darter is in the river, Clearwater will back off all attempts to develop—without another question."

Miranda thought of the darter. Connie would deliver the specimen to the biologist, but it wasn't enough proof. Not nearly enough. Where had it come from, though? Who had made the strange delivery?

"Tom, what were you doing on the river that first day?"

"Clark Presley called me and said there might be trouble. He was upset when he found out you were leading the expedition. I was simply making sure that you were not in any danger."

"Clark Presley?" A link formed in her mind.

"Yes. He told me about your...background. He was concerned that you might lose the Tabuga because of it."

"But he didn't know you funded the WDC expedition?" Miranda was thinking fast.

"No, he didn't. We kept it a secret."

She thought hard for a moment. "It wasn't Clark who called me last night. It was the same voice as the man who called about bombing the river. It wasn't Clark, it was a younger voice." She slapped her leg. "Maybe his son, Jason!" In her mind she saw the man outside her apartment window. "Jason is a tall, strong man. It could have been him."

"Someone called you and told you about Fred?" Tom was following the rapid flow of her thoughts as fast as he could.

"No, this is the strange part. The caller said that Gordon Simms was dead and that it was my fault. And he said if I didn't stop my work to save the Tabuga, I'd be killed, too. That's exactly the same type of message I got when I ran out of your house. The man said something was going to be blown to bits and it was my fault."

"Did you recognize anything familiar about the caller's voice?" Tom watched her intently.

"It was rough, as if he had a sore throat." Her forehead furrowed as she tried to think. "No clear accents. He was very convincing."

"Could it have been someone you know?"

"The person was obviously disguising his voice, so it's hard to say. There was something familiar, but it could be that the threatening tone brought back some memories of television shows or whatever." She shrugged.

"I'm thinking that Fred was killed accidentally."

"I've thought that maybe it was supposed to be Gordon," Miranda said slowly. "Gordon had agreed to testify. If the WDC work is behind all of this, then Gordon is the most important person to our case. Not Fred."

"Have you talked with Simms?"

Miranda shook her head. "No, but I will as soon as I get back to town." She rubbed her forehead. "Before I got the telephone call, I had a strange visit. Someone left a dead fish at my door."

"A darter?" Tom asked.

"I think so. I saw a man outside my window. He looked like you, Tom." She touched his face again. "Then the fish was mysteriously delivered. I called Fred to try and postpone the hearing."

"Did you tell Fred about the darter?"

"Yes. I might have given him the impression that Gordon was working on the sample right at that moment."

"Haven't you wondered what Fred was doing at Gordon's lab after midnight?"

"I have wondered, with a certain degree of guilt. He might have gone there because he wanted those lab results."

"Or he wanted to destroy them."

"Why?" Miranda was shocked.

"Political pressure. Senator Fremont might have an ax to grind in this."

The idea was chilling. "We don't stand a chance if Fremont is involved. He's notorious for leading his committee members to rule against environmental factions."

Tom held up a palm. "This is all speculation, so hold on. There's another angle. I know the major shareholders of Clearwater Development. There are several minor stockholders who've come into the business. As soon as we get back to Tabuga Springs, I'm going to run a thorough check on all of them. It could be that they want development at any cost. They might not be real happy with the way I've run this show."

"Tom, there's another question. How did they get your ring?"

"It's been missing for several weeks. The last time I remember seeing it, I was at a construction site. I took it off and left it in the glove compartment of the truck. When I remembered to look for it several days later, it was gone."

"Doc said you weren't very sentimental."

"So Doc told you the story of the matching rings?"

"Some of it. I can't believe you left such a valuable ring in your glove compartment."

Tom laughed. "Now, that sounds like Doc talking. He was always better at taking care of valuable items than me. He used to hide my things to try and make me more responsible." The humor faded from Tom's eyes. "Grandfather loved us both, but I was his favorite. Doc was also so involved in his own studies, his research and his own thoughts. I enjoyed being outdoors with Grandfather. Doc and I have things settled now, but when Grandfather died, he left the bulk of his property to me. That was hard on Doc for a long time. That's one reason I started Clearwater."

"How so?"

"Doc and I are partners. Whatever happens to Grandfather's land, now we'll both share in it."

The quiet of the wilderness morning was interrupted by the sound of an approaching vehicle. Tom watched the rearview mirror. He cranked the truck, cut a sharp U-turn and pulled back into the road.

"What's wrong?" Miranda watched the battered old truck approach them.

"Remember Abe Tuttle? He isn't a stupid man, and talk is all over town about my interest in you. I don't mind tangling with Tuttle on a back road, but I don't want you involved. It would be old Tuttle's brand of justice to take my girlfriend, in retribution for his wife."

The possibility of cold-blooded revenge made Miranda shiver. "But you tried to save his wife."

"I butted into his business and his wife died. That's the way Tuttle sees it. Besides, he went to jail because of me."

The two vehicles passed, and Tuttle never looked in their direction.

"Because he tried to kill you!" she corrected him.

"Because of me is the way he reads it." He shifted into a higher gear and pressed the truck forward. They soon left Tuttle far behind. Tom's hand rested lightly on her shoulder, kneading the muscles.

"Dynamite is a handy tool in these mountains, and almost everyone who's lived here any length of time knows how to use it," he said. "Folks clear land or start a rock slide that's hanging dangerous before it comes down unexpectedly, little things. It's illegal, but everyone does it. It wouldn't be beyond Tuttle's capabilities. Stay clear of him."

"Don't worry, I will."

"I'm going to drop you at Doc's for a while. Stay there."

"I have to check those fish traps!"

Her protests were cut short. "I'm going to the office to get some files. I'll come back for you, and we'll check both trap sites together. I don't want you going alone." He pulled into Doc's yard and stopped. "Okay?"

"Thanks, Tom." She leaned over and kissed his cheek. Before she could withdraw, his strong arms came around her and held her tightly. His lips pressed against hers, and Miranda responded with a sudden hunger. The kiss seemed to seal a pact. They would work together to save the Tabuga. And to protect each other.

"I worry about you, Miranda," he said, giving them both time to catch their breath. "I'd like nothing more than to keep you here, right beside me. That way I know you'd be safe."

"I'll be as safe as I can," she promised. "And I'll be waiting here for you." She kissed him again and then waved him away. "Hurry back." Before she gave into the urge to kiss him once more, she got out of the truck and walked into Doc's house.

"Hello, Miranda."

Sheriff Carter's voice stopped her cold in the foyer. He was sitting in a rocking chair in the middle of the living room. He had a perfect view of the front yard and had obviously been a witness to her kisses with Tom.

"Have you come to tell me you have some clues to the men who attacked me?" Her tone was arrogant and angry. She was furious that he'd sat at the window spying on her. "If you'd listened to me when I told you someone was trying to hurt members of my group, maybe Fred Elton would be alive today."

"I haven't come to discuss theories, I'm afraid." He leaned forward, smiling slightly.

"Then why have you come?" For the first time she saw Doc standing in a corner. His expression gave away his distress at the scene he was witnessing.

"I've come to arrest you."

"For what?" she snapped.

"For the murder of Fred Elton and the willful destruction of the Tabuga River."

She took two small steps backward. She didn't believe what she was hearing. "For Fred's murder? That's preposterous!"

"Miranda, please stay calm. We'll get this all straightened out." Doc came to her side and put a protective arm around her. Outside she heard the roar of Tom's engine. She ran to the window and threw it open.

"Tom! Wait!"

She was too late. There was only a plume of dust thrown up by the rugged tires as he drove away.

Chapter Twelve

Tom gunned the truck through the small town and stopped at an old two-story building. He pushed open the etched-glass door that bore the legend Wild Horse Designs. He'd renovated the old boarding house for his private offices. Now it contained not only his architectural company, but also Cheryl and the newer Clearwater Development concerns.

"Well, the boss man returns," Cheryl Summers said. She handed a sheaf of papers to him. "We need signatures, and I'm due out on the construction site. I've already signed those, and so has Doc. We're only waiting on you."

"Grant applications?"

"Right on, and I think we should get the funding. Those designs you did are incredible, Tom. And I've reviewed all of those figures. We can bring them in at the price you quoted. It's almost a miracle. This may be the only reasonable single-family housing going up in the United States this decade."

He smiled tiredly. "At last some good news."

"This may be good or bad, depending on how you view it. Senator Fremont's office called early this morning. They wanted to alert us about Fred Elton's death, and I told them we knew. They've postponed the hearing for two days, but then they're going to proceed. They said they should have an answer for us within seven days."

Tom rubbed the stubble on his chin. "I thought they'd put it off at least a week. I had assumed that Elton was more crucial to the hearings, I suppose."

Cheryl got up and walked to Tom. She rested her hand lightly on his shoulder. "I know there's something developing between you and Miranda. I'm sorry that there's been so many terrible problems for both of you. I think, though—" she hesitated "—that Fremont's pushing for a hearing date because he wants to get this over before it gets worse."

"This has been a terrible ordeal, for Miranda and for everyone concerned."

"I'm afraid it's going to get worse." Cheryl squeezed his shoulder. "Fremont's staffer said that the Washington police were a bit upset with her for leaving town. They've issued a warrant for her arrest."

"Warrant? Is she a witness or a suspect?" Tom couldn't believe it. "Her job is in Washington. They have to know she's going back as soon as she can. Surely her office could explain how important it is for her to find those specimens. She's working! She isn't here hiding out."

Cheryl sighed. "*We* know that, because we know Miranda. They don't know her, and it would seem someone is very busy giving her a bad reputation. She needs to get home and clear all of this up before it gets out of hand."

"You're right. I'd better take her to the airport myself. She has a way of finding big trouble." He went to his desk and started to hunt for the file that contained all the names and addresses of the Clearwater Development limited partners.

"Can I help?" Cheryl asked.

"I want to take a look at our partners."

"Any particular reason? Have you come up with some clue?"

Tom shook his head. "I wish I had a solid lead." He gave Cheryl a weak smile. "I guess the most accurate description would be to say that I'm grasping at straws."

Cheryl went to the filing cabinet and in a moment she pulled out the file. "Here you go. Good luck, boss."

His fingers closed on the manila folder. "Thanks, Cheryl. I'll take it with me." His worries for Miranda were deepening every second. It seemed that everywhere she turned, something happened. She'd been attacked on the river, tricked into nearly getting killed by an explosion and hoodwinked into showing up at the scene of a brutal murder that appeared to involve the wrong victim. He felt as if a line of dominoes had been set up by some unseen hand. They were falling over one by one—each with a resounding crash—and Miranda was sitting squarely under the very last one. She'd be crushed.

"Hey! Not so fast, buddy." Cheryl grabbed his sleeve and held. "Sit down and sign these grant applications. The way it's been going, I might not see you again for several days."

"Right." He sat down on the corner of her desk and hurriedly wrote his name on several documents. "Doc was right when he suggested making you the third partner. I have no talent for paperwork, Doc has no sense of development and you are the best grant writer in the world."

"I'm glad you finally noticed." Cheryl stood up. "Of course, Doc is fond of some of my other attributes."

They walked to the door together, laughing. As they separated, walking toward their vehicles, Cheryl waved him to a halt. "Something just struck me, Tom. Sheriff Carter was in here earlier asking for you and Doc. He asked where Miranda spent last night."

"Did he say anything else?"

"Not really. You know Carter, slow and easy. Didn't seem to have much on his mind, but that's what made me suspicious."

"Thanks, Cheryl." Tom checked his watch. He had the files, but he wanted to talk with Clark Presley. The old man had been watching the darter traps. If someone had tampered with the fish traps, Presley would know. It might be a lead to the strange man who'd been casing Miranda's apartment the night before.

DISCOMFORT EXTENDED up the entire length of Miranda's back, impossible to ignore any longer. She rose from the narrow cot and stood for the first time in two hours.

Metal bars made three walls of the eight-by-eight cell. A leering deputy sat cocked back in a chair, watching her with what could only be taken as speculative amusement.

"Jails ain't your natural environment, are they?" he asked, laughing at his own little joke.

She was too tired and too worried to frame a scorching reply. "No. They aren't."

"It's a good place for someone who can't obey laws." He grinned wider. "Someone who may be a murderer."

"I didn't kill anyone."

"Yeah. That's what they all say." He stood up, deliberately jingling the keys he wore on the side of his pants. His actions were constructed to annoy, and Miranda turned away from him to confront the graffiti-covered fourth wall of her cell. The cement blocks had once been painted an institutional green, but a series of bored prisoners had added their own decorating touches.

The Washington police or possibly some branch of the federal authorities—she wasn't certain what crimes she'd been accused of—would soon be in Tabuga Springs with the necessary paperwork for extradition.

She was headed back to Washington as a suspect instead of a material witness. Carter had made it abundantly clear that the authorities felt she was more than a little involved in Fred Elton's murder. She was also formally charged with dynamiting the river.

Sheriff Carter had told her that a blood-soaked piece of her shirtsleeve was found in Fred's hand. There was no doubt that it was part of the sleeve Tom had torn away when she was wounded on the Tabuga. How it had gotten into Fred's hand was another story.

Tears of frustration stung her eyes. She couldn't stop them completely so she turned away, avoiding the deputy's gloating smile. She wouldn't give him the satisfaction of seeing her cry.

Now all she could do was wait. Carter had denied her a phone call, which didn't surprise her at all. He'd made some sarcastic remark about her *Miranda* rights. Her only consolation was that Doc had promised to find Tom and tell him about her incarceration.

With grim determination she fought back her useless tears, wondering if the fact that the main WDC project director was in prison for murder would be a justifiable cause for a postponement of the committee hearing. At least that would give other WDC staffers time to hunt for more evidence against development. So many loose ends dangled outside the prison bars, things that she needed to work on. A loud crash in the sheriff's office made her jump. It sounded as if a desk had been lifted and dropped.

"What's going on out there?" The deputy drew his gun and dropped to a crouch. "Sheriff? That you?"

There was only a rustling noise, then the sound of heavy, ominous footsteps.

"Who's there?" Panic gripped the deputy. His voice rose an octave and began to tremble.

Trapped in the cell, Miranda felt her skin crawl. Wouldn't it be convenient if she never lived to come to trial? If she were killed, they could always blame it on an attempted jail break. Her heartbeat accelerated with her imagination.

Another loud crash, metal hurling into a wall, spiked the atmosphere with tension.

"I'm comin' out there," the deputy warned, but he made no effort to move.

His answer was the sound of wood splintering.

Easing back to the bunk and as close to the wall as possible, Miranda never took her eyes off the door that led from the jail to the sheriff's office. Whoever was out there would come in. Sooner or later. And she knew he was coming for her. The deputy would never defend her. His hand was shaking so badly he could barely hold his gun.

A faint, acrid smell drifted lazily into the cell area. Another prisoner stirred farther down the jail.

"What's that?" the man called. "What's that smell?"

When there was no answer, his panic-filled voice came again. "It's fire. Someone's set the sheriff's office on fire!"

The deputy swung back at him, pointing the gun. "You shut up or you're dead."

"Let us out of here!" the man demanded. "Open these doors or we're going to burn to death, you coward. Let us out or get out there and do something!"

The smell of burning grew stronger, and the first wisps of smoke began to drift through the doorway from the main office.

Pressing against the wall, Miranda didn't move. The deputy would never open the cell doors. They were going to die. Her fingers gripped the harsh blanket that covered the bunk, lifting it to cover her mouth. She dropped to the floor, remembering that the smoke would rise. "Open the cells," she ordered the deputy. "You can't leave us here to burn to death."

With a grimace of desperation on his face, the deputy rushed through the doorway. The sound of a brief scuffle could be heard, then a body hit the floor, hard.

As Miranda watched, a big shadow fell through the opening, and the sound of a footstep seemed to echo for an eternity. Broad shoulders blocked the light, then a tall lean body walked lazily through the door.

"You do pick the strangest places to hang out." Tom Wilkes stood before her, grinning.

For once Miranda didn't know what to say.

"Close your mouth or you'll catch flies," he advised as he held the key ring in front of her bars and jingled it.

"What are you doing?" She stepped to the bars and wrapped her fingers around them, clenching to stop the trembling of her body. She was glad to see him, desperately glad.

"I came to save you." Inclining his head toward her, he continued. "Doc told me you'd been arrested."

"Let me out of here." She shook the bars. "The deputy might wake up."

Tom took in the whiteness of her face, the way her eyes were wide with fright. "Hey, take it easy," he said softly. "They didn't hurt you, did they?"

Miranda's throat closed. She shook her head rapidly. "No."

Tom threw the door open and pulled her into his arms. For hardly longer than a second he held her so close that she could feel the strong, steady beat of his heart. That sound gave her courage.

"The fire," she reminded him, but already the air was clearing.

"A small diversion in a trash can. All extinguished now." He clasped her hand. "The deputy is taking a little nap, but he'll be up soon."

She smiled, glad for his steadying grip. "Let's get out of here."

They slipped out a narrow back door. Tom had taken the precaution to park in a concealing cluster of bushes, and they made their way to the truck with caution.

"Now that I'm out, what are we going to do?" Miranda asked as he slipped into the driver's seat beside her and cranked the motor.

His arm came around her shoulders, and drew her against him as the truck moved through downtown Tabuga Springs. Tucked against him, she was conveniently hidden from sight.

The feel of his solid chest, his masculine warmth, helped her recover her composure. After a few heavy sighs she felt better.

They cleared the town, headed north, upriver. When she felt sure that her voice wouldn't betray her, she lifted her chin.

"Thanks, Tom. I realize how much you risked."

"I know you aren't guilty." He slowed, idling in the middle of the little-used road.

She looked at him a long moment before the beginnings of a tremulous smile touched her full lips. "That means a lot to me."

Flecks of gold shimmered in his amber eyes. "We don't have a lot of time to plan, but while you were busy getting arrested, I did some legwork. Guess who are limited partners in development of the river?" He put the truck in gear and drove on.

"Senator Fremont," she said, unable to think of anyone else who had enough power to make a difference.

"Close, but not quite accurate. Fred Elton. And Russ Sherman."

"That's a conflict of interest. Fred never made enough money to invest anything. He was an aide. They make about the same as a WDC staffer, and I know for a fact he didn't come from a wealthy family." Miranda felt a pang of warning. Something very wrong was happening. "And Russ never mentioned a word to me about his involvement. That's highly unethical."

"I thought the same thing."

"Did Doc tell you that the Washington police found part of my bloodstained shirt gripped in Fred's hand?"

"No, I guess Carter didn't tell him any details."

"It had to be the sleeve you cut out of my shirt when I was shot."

"And Carter could have found it. Carter or a dozen other men who were on the search party." He hit the steering wheel with his palm. "There are a dozen suspects every single time something happens."

"So we have to look for motive." Miranda felt some wonderful revelation hovering on the edge of her mind, but she couldn't call it into focus. She was tired, sore and on the verge of becoming frantic. "Let's keep moving."

Since they'd cleared the town, Tom pushed the accelerator to the floor, and the miles began to clip beneath their wheels.

"Tom, we can't go to your house. That's the first place they'll look."

"We aren't. We're going to a place Clark told me about."

Miranda hesitated, then spoke. "There's something not quite right about Mr. Presley. I know you've defended him before, but I don't trust him."

"He's old and ornery and a little eccentric, you mean?"

"He's all of that, but I think he knows more than he's telling."

"He told me where to find the Tabuga pisces darter."

Miranda took a deep breath. "Where?"

"Upriver from the place we checked his trap. He saw a school of them while he was fishing. He said he tried to catch one, but they were too elusive without the trap. He also said there were some footprints and tracks. It looked as if someone else had been hauling something out of the water." He gave her a quick glance to see how his disclosures were affecting her. "Maybe a fish trap. Maybe the one that was stolen from you from the Tabuga."

"Maybe." Miranda was noncommittal.

"I asked Clark where he got his trap, and he said he'd had it for a while. He said he bought it at a salvage store." He watched her face.

"I could be wrong about him," she finally conceded. "Someone else could have taken the trap."

"And they could be using it, too."

"Hence my little present," Miranda answered, remembering the dead fish that had been left at her door.

"That's exactly what I was thinking."

"We're going to that place on the river, aren't we?"

"I promised I'd help you get those fish. So far, that's only been empty words. We'll get some of those prehistoric little devils and then we'll go back to Washington and clear your name."

Miranda leaned across the seat and kissed his cheek. Words couldn't describe the swell of emotion she felt. She was certainly attracted to him, but this was so much more. She could believe in him, trust in his instincts and impulses. More importantly she was beginning to trust her own heart. She kissed him again, the stubble of his face tickling her lips.

His arm slipped around her and pulled her close. "Think the day will ever come when you can care more about a man than a river?"

"I think that day is here, Tom Wilkes, and you're the man."

He held her tighter. "You're a special woman."

"I'm a walking disaster. My mother should have named me Calamity Jane."

Tom laughed softly. "That has its good points. If you'd never been in any trouble, you'd never have given me a chance to help you. You'd have labeled me a wicked developer and never spoken to me again."

"I hope that isn't true, but it might be." She chuckled at the idea. "I do tend to get a little caught up in my beliefs."

"That's what I like about you. If you ever care for me that much, I'll be the luckiest man alive."

Miranda smiled and leaned her head against his chest. She already did, but she'd save that tidbit for a moment of her own choosing, not flying down the road in a truck after a jailbreak.

They'd driven for a long time, and Miranda was relieved when they finally turned off the paved road and onto dirt. Still, the journey stretched before them. They were headed farther upriver than she'd ever been. Bumping and bouncing, they inched their way deeper and deeper into the wilderness.

At last they stopped. The truck was wedged between a stand of young pines. It wasn't possible to go forward another inch. "I'm afraid the rest is on foot." Tom climbed out as he spoke. His movements were smooth and steady, and Miranda hurried to comply. Once again the passage of the sun was their most obvious enemy. They had to get to the river.

Gear, and the fish trap from Clark Presley's, was stowed in the back. Miranda took the pack Tom handed her. There was a tent, sleeping bags, provisions. She estimated they could stay in the wilderness at least a week. Did she have that long before the fate of the Tabuga was signed in

Washington? She couldn't think about that. She had to rivet her mind to one goal at a time—getting the fish.

Setting a brisk pace, Tom pushed deeper into the wild. She trained her eyes on the shifting muscles of his back and walked. Branches slapped at her face; mosquitoes feasted on her blood. She ignored them all, forcing herself never to let her eyes drop from the powerful man who slipped through the wild growth with the grace of a panther.

A lot of the upper reaches of the Tabuga were familiar to her, but now she was in an area she knew nothing about. She wanted to ask Tom about their surroundings, but the pace he set was so grueling she had no oxygen to spare for talking. Tom led like a man intent on saving his hide, and she followed.

Puffing with fatigue, she gladly stopped when he signaled to a flat rock. The roar of the Tabuga was only a short distance away, but Miranda couldn't see the water. The day was hot and sweat soaked her shirt. Her cotton jacket, once so white and clean, was in ruins. Several holes were torn in the yellow T-shirt, revealing scratches and bruises and the small bandage that covered her nearly healed wound. Deer flies hummed around her head.

Taking the canteen of water he offered, she dropped wearily onto the rock and gave a crooked smile. She pulled her yellow bandanna from her pocket and soaked it in water, then fashioned a headband.

"Clark said there was a homestead not too far downriver from here if we need a raft." Tom was consulting a roughly drawn map as he spoke.

"They'd give us a raft?" Hope lit her face, and she brushed an insect off her cheek. Rafting was far superior to trudging.

"Give isn't exactly the right verb." Tilting his head, he waited for her reaction. "We can't afford to stop and ask permission. Carter's looking for us by now, and if they catch us, we won't get another chance to escape. We may not need the raft, but if we do, we'll replace it as soon as we can."

"Let's get to the river," she said.

He smoothed a few loose tendrils of her hair away from her face. "I'm with you."

With Tom in the lead, they started toward the sound of the river. When they reached the water, they set the trap and established camp. They performed the ritual of setting up camp with few words. Both were tired and anxious, and they settled on the ground to eat a cold dinner.

"I'm so tired I could sleep sitting up," Miranda said. They'd agreed not to check the fish trap until the next morning. If necessary, they were prepared to camp several days beside the river.

Gently removing her plate, Tom stretched his long legs out, bringing his thigh in contact with hers. "Grandfather would have liked you," he said, putting her empty plate down beside his. "Grandmother would have kidnapped you for her own grandchild. She liked a child with mettle, or maybe she would have said pluck."

"Not many adults found me very amusing as a child," she warned him.

"It's the spirit, the belief in something bigger than your own needs, your own wants. I saw that in you from the first."

"And just look where it's gotten both of us."

His arm pulled her against him, and she leaned back into his shoulder. "I wish we could stay here forever, but under different circumstances," she said.

"Dark will be here soon, and very possibly rain." He leaned over her so that he could see her face. His left hand drifted from her shoulder down the length of her side. Holding her breath, Miranda couldn't believe the sensation stirred by his lightest touch.

His fingers reached to the top button of her jacket. "I threw some extra shirts in my pack for you. There wasn't anything I could do about pants." The third button came free, and his hand moved down to the last one.

The jacket fell open, revealing the soft yellow of her T-shirt. A tiny edge of lace drew his fingers. Ruffling it, he smiled at her. "Very nice."

"Even a girl who loves the outdoors can enjoy a little feminine touch every now and then." She took a small, shallow breath and felt a little dizzy.

"And some girls are very feminine, even without lace."

Before she could respond, his lips touched hers. His hands renewed their exploration. He pushed her jacket off her shoulders and freed her arms. Slowly the straps of the soft cotton shirt were pushed down her collar bones. His lips found the tender hollow at the base of her neck.

Her hands lifted to his chest, palms pressed against the muscles beneath his bronzed skin. Closing her eyes, she dropped her head back.

She felt him freeze, his lips still on her neck. At her first movement he pressed his hand against her ribs, a clear request to hold still. In the orchestra of the wilderness night, there was the sound of many small creatures. But there was also the sound of something else.

Miranda listened sharply. She wasn't afraid of the wild animals. At other times in her life she'd enjoyed the woodland sounds heard only at a campsite. But this sound was different.

"Wait here," Tom said, shifting to his knees so he could look in all directions. Slowly he rose, moving away from her.

"Tom," she whispered urgently.

"Don't worry, honey, Tom ain't goin' nowhere." The click of a gun cocking was followed by the appearance of a burly man. Abe Tuttle stepped into the glow of the fire, his gun trained squarely on Tom's heart.

"Hate to interrupt this sweet little scene, but Tom and I got some business to finish. Right, Tom?" His mountain drawl was soft and easy, but his words were flinty with hatred.

Eyes glittering with venom, he waited for an answer. "Nobody wants to talk to ole Abe. Well, folks, that's okay with me, 'cause what I got planned for you two don't call for much talkin'."

Out of the corner of her eye Miranda saw Tom edge toward his pack.

Don't try it, Tom. You're going to die, but I can make it clean or I can make it messy. Force my hand, and I promise you, it'll be messy." He grinned, his brown hair bobbing as he nodded.

"What do you want?" Miranda eased her arms back into her jacket and sat up straight.

"Well, pretty lady, I want a couple of things. One is revenge, and the other is a reward for you. See, the way I got things figured is I tracked the two of you down here to this camp." He grinned at his own brilliance. "I got here just in time to see you kill old Tom here when he tried to attack you. Wasn't nothing I could do to stop it. Then I do my civic duty and take you back to Tabuga Springs where some nice citizen has already offered a bodacious sum for your capture. Ain't that a grand plan?" He chuckled soft and easy, but his gleaming eyes never left Tom's face.

Chapter Thirteen

"Move over there." Abe swung the barrel of the gun toward Miranda. "Take it real slow, too, cause my finger might slip." He grinned as Tom eased to the rock and knelt down.

"You said someone has offered a reward for Miranda's capture. I don't imagine you would know who?" Tom's voice was cutting. Before Abe could answer, Tom leaned down to Miranda. "There probably isn't even a reward. That sounds like something Carter made up to get Tuttle to do his dirty work." His voice was just loud enough to carry to Tuttle's ears.

"There's a reward," Abe said, unruffled by Tom's assertions. "A big one."

"Nobody in Tabuga Springs has money for rewards," Tom scoffed.

"Didn't come from here. The money's comin' from Washington, D.C. A reward from some friend of that politician man she killed." He grinned at her. "He musta had some rich friends."

"There's no reward." She challenged Abe just as Tom had been doing. If they got him off balance, maybe they could get the gun away from him.

"The man who put up the reward is a big dog in Washington, some senator or something like that." Abe was completely at ease, enjoying his knowledge. "Maybe they'll even get around to makin' a reward for bringing in the folks who blasted Trimmer McCrory." He grinned.

"Who?" Miranda had never heard the name before.

"The man you and Tom killed on the river."

Miranda felt Tom's hand give support. She leaned against his shoulder.

Tuttle shook his head. "Poor Trimmer was a local, not worth much, I don't suppose. Anyway, I hear Carter told ole Trimmer's family that it was a poachin' accident. When he helped bring the body home he personally left a couple hundred bucks to ease their grief." Tuttle laughed. "That's a fine predicament, ain't it? The McCrorys don't want to go complainin' too much about Trimmer gettin' plugged because he was poachin' at the time of death. That Carter is a smart possum. He knows how to play the angles."

Tuttle crouched down, eyeing the remains of their supper. "What else you got to eat? I spent the whole day tracking you two."

When neither answered, he lifted the largest pack and began dumping food onto the ground. Every few seconds he looked up to be sure they hadn't moved. "Here." He tossed a can of beans at Miranda. "Put some wood on that fire and heat that up for me. And remember, try anything foolish and ole Tom here is going to hurt somethin' fierce."

Tom had already gathered a large stack of wood. From the pile Miranda selected a stout log as big as her arm and two feet long. Casually she turned to walk behind Abe.

"Hey!" He swung the gun at her, then back at Tom. "What are you doin'?"

"Getting the can opener." She swallowed her nervousness. If she could get behind him, maybe she could knock him over the head with the limb.

"C'mere." There was a new roughness to his voice.

Reluctantly Miranda edged closer to him, eyeing Tom with a warning not to interfere.

"Tom took my wife, did ya know that?" His eyes moved up the length of her body, then he smiled. "Seems it might be fittin' if I took his woman."

As he started to laugh, Tom sprang to his hands and knees. Dirt sprayed up in his face from the bullet that Tuttle put into the ground half an inch from Tom's hand.

"C'mon." Desire for a fight rippled in Abe's voice and face. "I waited a long time in jail, plannin' each day how this was gonna be. This is even better than I thought." He reached his free hand up and grabbed Miranda's wrist. "Even sweeter."

Tom's anger was hidden behind a cold mask of calculation. His amber eyes signaled to Miranda, and she read their meaning. Rising slowly to his toes so that he could rush with force, Tom balanced on his hands.

"Looks like you don't want to share this pretty lady, Mr. Wilkes. Maybe you need a shot in the arm for starters." Abe cocked the pistol again, his eyes focused madly on Tom, and his fingers dug into Miranda's wrist. "C'mon and get it, Mr. Wilkes."

As Tom shifted forward, Miranda lifted the limb. All of Abe's attention was on Tom, and she brought the wood down with such force that the resounding crack broke the limb in half. Abe Tuttle dropped to his knees and then fell face forward onto the hard ground.

"Did I kill him?" Instead of panic she felt numb.

Tom gave her a reassuring hug before he turned to the felled man. "He isn't dead, but he's going to have a headache. Get some rope from the pack."

Miranda tossed him the length of cotton rope and watched as he tightly bound Abe's hands and feet, neatly finishing by pulling his legs up behind his back in an effective hog-tie.

"Now give me your bandanna."

She obliged by pulling the yellow cloth from her head. Tom wasn't gentle when he stuffed it in Tuttle's mouth and stood up.

"Leave the tent, but get everything else together." He started packing as he talked. "Just take the essentials for survival."

"What are we going to do?" Looking around at the pitch-black forest, Miranda wondered how they would make it a hundred yards without getting lost. The smell of a big storm was in the air.

"We have to get away before Tuttle wakes up. It'll take him a while to get loose, but we want to be a long way from here by then."

"At night?" She couldn't hide the alarm she felt.

"There's no help for it." He stopped packing and came to her side. Pulling her against him, his strong hands caressed her back. "After what you just did, the Tabuga is a playpen. I've never met a woman like you, and when this is over..."

The hungry note in his voice gave her an added notch of energy. He was right; they had to survive. And they could, together.

"We'd better go," she said reluctantly after a warning rumble of thunder echoed ominously overhead. "What about the fish?"

"We'll check once more. If we don't have them, we can't wait."

In the darkness Miranda nodded.

"Clearwater Development can withdraw all plans to develop." He spoke softly.

"Tom, you and I both know that won't matter now. If it isn't your company, another will come along. It was only a matter of time."

Tom knew she was right. The fate of the river was beyond anything he could do now.

Pulling in the trap was awkward and dangerous in the dark, but he hauled it in with Miranda holding a light. "Careful," he called to her as she waded on the slippery rocks to get to the trap.

"Tom!"

He hurried to her side, spurred by the excitement in her voice. "Has our luck finally turned?"

With the flashlight in one hand, she threw her other arm around his neck. "There are five!" She returned to the trap, looking again to make sure.

"I'll get a carton," he said as he rifled through her pack. "Let's put those babies in something safe and get moving."

"Five!" Miranda was hardly able to believe it. "After all of those false attempts, I didn't hold out much hope."

"We still have to get them to Gordon, Miranda. It's not going to be an easy trip. We can't go back to the truck. We're going to have to go downriver."

Miranda scooped the fish into the container. "We'll make it, Tom. And maybe the Tabuga will, too."

"It's about three miles to the farm I mentioned." He adjusted her backpack straps as he talked. "We'll go and then I want you to wait while I steal the raft. Just keep your fingers crossed it's still there."

There were no moon or stars to help light the way, but Tom moved with a sixth sense. Following in his footsteps, Miranda concentrated on moving as rapidly as possible. If Abe Tuttle had found them, so could anyone else. A question she wanted to ask Tom when they stopped, was how Tuttle had found them so easily? She pondered the surprising issue of the reward offered for her capture. Who could possibly be behind the money? If only she could get to a telephone, Connie would almost certainly know.

The thought of Connie made her shudder inwardly. The WDC would be in complete chaos. She dodged a branch and trudged on. The wilderness was a lot friendlier than the scene in Washington that she imagined. There would be hell to pay when she got home and had to explain herself. But she had the fish! She had the key to save the Tabuga!

The downriver trek seemed much longer than three miles, but when Tom lifted a hand to silence her, she knew they'd finally made it to the small farm. Crouching in the thick underbrush, she watched his strong back disappear into the blackness. The sky was growing angrier by the moment. The sounds of the Tabuga a short distance away also sounded an ominous warning.

A few moments later a light bobbed for a second and then disappeared. She counted to twenty-five, as Tom had told her to do, and then moved slowly in the direction of the light.

Tom's hand grasped her wrist and helped her into the small two-man raft. Overhead a clap of thunder seemed an omen as he pushed them into the current of the Tabuga.

Miranda knew the water was swift, but in the darkness it was impossible to get an idea of speed because the banks were invisible.

Soon the river's current steadied and grew calm. Miranda relaxed against the raft, fighting the sensation of weariness that wanted to creep up her body and into her eyes. Lightning forked, illuminating the eerie banks speeding past the raft. The storm was coming closer and closer.

"Take a nap before the weather breaks." Tom's soft voice was almost a caress. "The river's slow through here. Before we hit the rougher places, I'll wake you."

"How do you know where we are?" Her question was lazy. With Tom at the helm, she felt safe. Drowsiness was settling over her like a warm blanket. The container of fish was clutched against her chest.

"I rafted this river for most of my life. I used to bet Doc that I could do it blindfolded. Now I can say that we did."

She smiled to herself, unable to stop the sleep that overtook her. She was too tired. They were fugitives from justice, their lives entrusted to the deadly currents of a river. Even so, the bond between them was growing.

"THERE'S WHITE WATER AHEAD."

Tom's voice urged her from sleep, and Miranda woke to the more urgent movement of the raft.

"When the current takes us, we need to stay to the right. Just paddle and pray. It's an easy run in the daylight. With caution we'll be fine." Tom handed her a paddle.

The confidence in his voice was for her benefit, she knew, and it helped. The river's song swelled to a crescendo. Miranda heard the crash of the water and felt her blood begin to churn with anticipation.

A furious roar of thunder marked their entrance into the swirling rapids and the opening salvo of the storm. Stinging rain began to pelt her face as she frantically paddled to keep the raft as far right as possible.

Plunging into the white water, the raft felt as if it were being torn to shreds. In the sudden deluge of rain, Miranda wasn't certain if they'd capsized or not. Somehow the raft managed to remain upright. She searched the bottom frantically with her fingers until she found the container of fish.

"Hang in there," she whispered to them. She took up her paddle again.

"That's it, nice and steady." The confidence in Tom's voice enabled her to throw more force into paddling.

Riding the black river in a tiny raft during a thunderstorm was insane, but she couldn't hold back the smile that turned up the corners of her mouth. The ride rocked her soul with excitement! Working so well with Tom was a heady experience, and for a few seconds she could forget the magnitude of her troubles. Whenever the lightning flashed she caught glimpses of his determined face. He was sometimes a difficult man, but she recognized their similarities. Tom Wilkes didn't give up when things got tough, and neither did she.

Her back and shoulders ached from using the paddle. They'd been at it for what seemed like an eternity—she couldn't judge time any longer. To ease the pain she retreated back into her own thoughts. The image of the man outside her apartment window came back to her. The man was so familiar, so much like Tom. Or Doc! Was it possible Doc was setting up his own brother?

"Rock ahead!" Tom called. "Go right."

There was no time to think as they fought the river. In a few minutes they'd returned to calmer water and Miranda rested her aching shoulders.

"Any idea where we are?" she asked.

"We'll be at Devil's Hole soon."

"Already?"

"You slept through some rough water," he answered. "I didn't need your help, so I let you sleep."

"After Devil's Hole, there's the Tabuga bridge," she reminded him.

"We're going under it, quiet as church mice."

Fear tingled her body. "They'll catch us, Tom."

"That's a chance we'll have to take. There's no other way out."

"And once we pass Tabuga Springs, then what?"

"Doc has a cabin in the woods. A retreat, really. I built it for him when he was having some problems with alcohol. No one knows about it but us."

Miranda's earlier thought about Doc came back to her, but she didn't speak. They had no other choice. "I've still got the fish," she said.

"I didn't doubt it for an instant. Now get ready for the rocks and thank our lucky stars that the storm let up. Remember the route?"

"I'm ready."

Once again they were swept into the white water. They worked as a team, riding the current with skill and precision. The landmarks along the bank blurred by them in the darkness, and Miranda settled down to watch for the lights of the small town.

"Tom, you rest for a while," she said. "I'll wake you when we get near the bridge."

He didn't offer a single argument, but slumped down in the bottom of the raft while Miranda took over the navigation. She had no idea how much time had passed when she finally saw the lights of Tabuga Springs on the right bank of the river. Tom was resting peacefully in the raft, and she decided not to disturb him. The river was wider and much calmer near the bridge, and Miranda let the current take them downstream. The bridge slipped by her and was left behind. Still the Tabuga carried them south.

She estimated the passage of another half hour when she finally woke Tom. She had no idea where the landing point for Doc's cabin might be, and she was afraid they would pass it. The sky was beginning to lighten, a sign that dawn was not far away.

"Take her to the left," Tom finally called.

With a shudder they hit the bank and disembarked. Miranda clutched the fish and her pack while Tom removed the other provisions. When she started to tie the raft up, Tom shook his head.

"Let her go." At Miranda's amazed stare, he continued. "We might give ourselves a little time. If they find the raft, they might think we drowned in the storm."

Together they managed to upend the raft, and Tom pushed it out into the current.

THE FAMILIAR OUTLINE of Tabuga Springs was on the horizon as the midday sun poured over the mountains. Tom stumbled into town, bone weary and exhausted. He'd caught two rides, but he'd also walked many miles. Somewhere in the journey he'd finally reduced his thought processes to two simple issues: Miranda had to be safe, and he had to make it to Doc's with the fish.

He skirted the main street, knowing that all of his friends and acquaintances would be headed toward Velma's for lunch. He wasn't paranoid, just careful. The twisted events that had disrupted Miranda's life had been choreographed by someone, and until he was certain who, he didn't intend to take any risks. Doc was the only person in Tabuga Springs he could trust implicitly. He sensed that Miranda had some unspoken reservations about Doc, but he knew his brother. Doc would never betray him.

He cut through a narrow alley, moving fast but with great stealth. He'd had to insist that Miranda remain at Doc's cabin, a fight he could never have won had she not been exhausted. He'd finally convinced her to stay hidden until he could get the fish samples to Gordon Simms. That would at least halt the Tabuga River hearings and give Miranda the opening evidence to defend the river. It would also help support her innocence—the very fact that the fish did exist would emphasize her credibility. Now the darters had become crucial to her survival, as well as to the river's.

He clung to the wall of a small dry-goods store and scanned the back street that led to Doc's. Two loggers were standing on the sidewalk chatting. They laughed, and Tom slipped by them, unnoticed.

He hurried through the town until at last he came to the apple-tree-shaded lane that wound to his brother's home. With a final burst of energy, he jogged up the steps and pounded on the door.

"What on earth?" Cheryl Summers, wrapped in one of Doc's comfortable old shirts and a pair of jeans, came to the door.

"How about some coffee?" Tom asked, smiling.

"How about a bullet to put you out of your misery? You look like warmed-over death, Tom Wilkes. Get in here and tell us what's been happening. Half the town is looking for you, and the other half, well . . ."

"Uley Carter's half is hoping I'm dead, right?" The smile disappeared off Tom's worn face. "Where's Doc?"

"He's getting dressed." She went to the refrigerator and began taking out food. "We took the morning off and decided to sleep in. We were up most of the night looking for you."

"Is Doc okay?" Tom took a seat at the table. "There wasn't any way I could get in touch with you or I would have. It's been a rough night for all of us."

"Doc'll be right down. Now, let's get some food into you, and then I think a little sleep."

"I'm starved," Tom admitted.

Cheryl threw together a late breakfast of eggs, bacon, toast and grits. She put a steaming plate in front of Tom before she spoke again.

"Where's Miranda?" Cheryl's eyes were drawn in concern. "Doc and I assumed you got her out of jail. Then we couldn't find you. We thought you might have hidden out at your house, but we checked it out and the house was empty."

"She's safe for the moment."

"But you're not, Tom. Carter knows it was you, even if he doesn't have any proof. That deputy of his is willing to positively identify you whether he actually saw you or not."

"That doesn't come as any real surprise." He'd never expected to pull off the jailbreak without getting caught. The important thing was that Miranda was safe.

"Why did you come back here?" Doc stood in the doorway, clothes hurriedly thrown on and his face unshaven. "You should never have come back. Everyone is looking for you!"

"I know," Tom said slowly, "but I need to finish something, and I knew the two of you were the only people I could trust. We found a Tabuga pisces darter. Several, in fact. I left the container on the front porch. They've had sort of a rough night, and I need to get them to Washington immediately. I need someone I trust to take them."

"It isn't a matter of trust," Doc said, taking a seat at the table. His hands clutched Tom's shoulder. "Carter has it in for you, and if he finds you. I don't know that he'll make an effort to take a prisoner. Tom, he's involved in something and when he came by here yesterday to tell me about the jailbreak, he as much as said he'd kill you."

"I know, but I don't intend to let him catch me." The food had restored Tom's confidence, and he gave them a grin. "Come on, Doc, you used to have a sense of adventure. If you get these specimens to Washington, then everything else will work out with time. I promise."

Cheryl's smile was skeptical. "I should know better than to get involved in a harebrained Tom Wilkes scheme, but I'll take them for you. Doc and I will take them together, won't we?" She looked up at Doc for approval.

After a second's hesitation he gave a rueful chuckle. "Okay, Cheryl and I will take them. But what will you do in the meantime?"

"Miranda needs to get back to Washington where she can get some legal advice and prepare herself against the charges that have been made. I know the airports are being watched, so I think we'll try slipping by on some of the back roads. But I'll need a four-wheel-drive vehicle.''

"Take my old truck. It has a big engine and lots of power. Some of those roads are going to be rough."

"Thanks, Doc." Tom rose and gave him a hug. "Thanks a whole lot."

"Don't thank me until you're safe.

MIRANDA RATTLED the switch hook on the telephone. A vague and fluttery dial tone hummed in her ear. The telephone worked for the moment. Tom had warned her that it sometimes went out for no reason—and stayed out for weeks. The telephone company didn't deem an old, seldom-used phone line as top priority in an area that begged for service.

"WDC." Connie's crisp voice answered on the second ring.

"I know you can't talk, but I wanted you to know I'm alive. I have the fish samples, and they're on their way!" Just hearing Connie's voice made Miranda feel better. "Is everything okay there?"

"Yes, the article by Russ Sherman did make some interesting points, but we at the WDC do not believe that Ms. Conner is involved in Fred Elton's death or Senator Fremont's death."

"Fremont?" Miranda was stunned.

"Regardless of the evidence, we do not believe Ms. Conner is guilty. The fact that her bandanna was found in Fremont's hand is circumstantial."

Miranda almost dropped the telephone. "Connie, that bandanna was planted, just like the sleeve of my shirt was planted on Fred Elton's body."

"I understand your position. No, as far as we know, the rumor that balance sheets showing payoffs from Tom Wilkes to Senator Fremont is not something that involves the WDC. We know nothing about Wilkes or his relationship to Fremont, and I'm not certain how you found out about the detail since it hasn't been reported in any news accounts. I'm certain Russ Sherman didn't tell you."

"Tom was giving Fremont payoffs?" Miranda couldn't believe it.

"That would appear to be the case, sir. Thank you for your interest in the WDC, but we can't tie up our phone lines any longer."

"Don't hang up!" Miranda had to find out more details. The click came before she could even draw a breath. Connie had done the best she could under the circumstances. It was obvious that someone was standing over her, listening to her every word. Lord, Senator Fremont was dead! That made three, counting the man Abe Tuttle had identified as Trimmer McCrory.

She checked her watch. Tom had been unable to estimate when he might get back to the cabin. It was a long way to town, and he was at the mercy of people who might or might not stop to give him a ride. She could feel her heart beating, racing against the frame of her ribs.

Fremont was dead, and there was some evidence that showed that Tom had been paying him! She was still trying to grasp the implications. It didn't make an ounce of sense. Why had Tom bothered to give funds to the WDC when he had Fremont in his pocket? Was it possible the WDC was being used as a cover for something else? But what? She slumped into a rocking chair.

She had to calm herself before she could make any headway. She rocked for several moments, clearing her brain. Tom had betrayed her. Every time she tried to make some sense of the new development, she came back to that thought. The result was an emotional wallop that fogged her ability to think. Tom had fought hard to earn her trust. He'd worked on her and worked on her until she'd finally begun to believe in him. And it had all been a ruse.

If he had already bought Fremont, why did he even involve the WDC? Did it possibly have something to do with the other landowners along the river? She had to put the facts together, and she had to do it in a hurry.

She forced her thoughts to Fred Elton and Senator Fremont. Both were politically involved. Both were brutally murdered. Their deaths had to have some significance.

The old rocker creaked back and forth, the pace of the chair a contrast to her thoughts. She picked through the facts at hand and tried to find similarities in the two deaths. The most obvious was that she'd been framed for both.

Connie had said that details of Fremont's death hadn't been reported by the press. Where had Connie gotten the information about Tom's payoffs? The most reasonable conclusion was that Russ had told her.

Miranda's first inclination was to call Russ Sherman, but she didn't move out of the chair. She couldn't trust Russ, either. Not since Tom had found him on the list of investors in Clearwater Development. Russ could be playing a double game. He'd always wanted to have time to write a novel. And he'd been so very willing not to report Gordon's finding of the darter.

The trouble was, she didn't trust anyone.

She stopped rocking.

What if Russ wasn't a shareholder? She never saw the list of names Tom said he'd found. It was only his word. Damn! She'd give anything for a television. Fremont's death would be on the national news, and she'd have a chance to glean crucial details. As it was, she was cut off from all news sources. She couldn't risk a call to any of the reporters she knew.

Nope. She was on her own. She had to think this thing through, and she had to do it before Tom got back. She only wished there was a way to figure it out that didn't have Tom smack in the middle of everything.

She checked her watch again. Doc! The image of Tom's brother formed behind her eyes. It was possible that everything that had happened had been orchestrated by Doc. He had the same access to everything that Tom did. He had a motive. Development would make him a multimillionaire. He'd be able to pursue his dreams of research. With megabucks he could build his own research facility and stay in Tabuga Springs if that was his choice. Yes, it could be Doc. Just because there was evidence with Tom's name on it didn't mean Tom had made the payoffs. Doc could have done it. There was certainly motive and means.

Her rocking slowed to a standstill. Tom was probably at Doc's house at that moment. So were the darters. And she was abandoned out in the wilderness with no means of transportation and a few days' supply of food.

She made a pot of coffee from the supplies they'd brought with them. She drank one cup, then another. When her nerves were twitching, she finally decided to explore the area around the cabin. If she had to make an escape, it would be in her best interest to have a route planned.

At the front door she got her bearings. Tom had said the path that led to the cabin was long and almost concealed. That would be a perfect place to start out. She needed to know how to get to the main road and how heavily that road was trafficked. Besides, a hike of several miles would help take the edge off her anxiety and maybe help her think.

When she returned two hours later, there was still no sign of Tom and she was no closer to discovering the truth. There were too many suspects. Too many motives.

She walked to the river and checked for signs of anyone rafting by. She was careful to hide in the underbrush in case a search party was looking for her. From her vantage in the brush, she could still see the tumbling river. For a moment it seemed as if everything that had happened was a nightmare. The Tabuga was there, wild and free. The blue sky was a direct contradiction of her emotions.

She was almost ready to leave when she heard a faint voice.

"Push it over!"

The words were not completely distinct. Aware that sound travels much farther over water, she pushed her body back into the brush to wait. If a search party was headed downriver, it would be helpful to see how many people were involved and to make sure they went downstream.

She felt the minutes drag as she waited. Had it been her overactive imagination? There was no sign of anyone on the water. An hour passed, and still nothing.

She shifted her position again and again. Her knees were screaming, but she couldn't leave the river until she was certain. There was always the possibility that whoever it was had docked upriver and was walking through the woods even now.

How much evidence had she left at the cabin? The backpacks and provisions were in plain sight, but none of the contents could be traced to her. The searchers would suspect, of course, but they wouldn't know for certain unless Tom had told someone where she was. She pressed back deeper into the underbrush. Her best bet for the time being was to try to wait them out.

Another hour passed slowly. In the west the sky brightened with the reds and pinks of sunset. When she thought she could sit still no longer, she made a decision. It was time for action. Dusk was falling, and she'd have a better chance of sneaking around undetected. If she was going to check out the woods upriver, she had to do it now. She rose on protesting legs and began to thread her way as soundlessly as possible through the thick wilderness.

She searched the bank of the river upstream for what she estimated to be a mile. There was no sign of a camp or even a landing. But she was certain she'd heard someone on the water. She was positive.

And she was just as positive that they'd never passed her on the river. They were still out there, waiting.

She returned to the cabin under the heavy blanket of night. Clouds scudded across the moon, warning of the possibility of another storm. At first she thought she'd lost her bearings. In the darkness she almost missed the unlighted hulk of the cabin. All around there was perfect silence.

There was no sign of Tom inside or out. The squeeze of conflicting emotions tore at her. She was glad he wasn't there, glad he couldn't look into her eyes and lie to her again. Yet she'd thought he would be there. She'd never really believed he would abandon her in the wilderness until Carter or some of the others found her.

The cabin loomed before her, empty and uninviting. Disappointment and a trickle of fear circled her heart. Tom! She almost spoke his name aloud as she eased up on the porch.

He'd broken her out of jail—risking his own life. He'd helped her find the darters and arranged for her safe hiding. No matter what evidence had been found, her heart refused to accept his guilt. Too bad that her brain would not accept his innocence.

Where the hell was he anyway? Had Carter found him on the road and made him pay for breaking her out of jail? She grasped the porch railing and steadied herself. No matter how much danger she put herself in, she had to call Doc and see if Tom had even made it as far as Tabuga Springs.

She pushed open the cabin door, hardly daring to breathe. It took a few seconds for her eyes to register the interior of the little house. Her gaze shifted over the open space of the kitchen and the bedroom area. All seemed quiet and undisturbed. She entered, making sure to lock the door behind her but taking care not to make any noise.

The cabin had electricity, and she felt in the darkness for the string that was connected to the overhead light. She found it and pulled. There was a muffled click but no light. Tom had warned her of the probability of sporadic utility service. She could only pray the telephone was still working. She had to find out about Tom.

In the darkness she found the phone. As she dialed the operator, she paused. Something was different. It took her a moment to recognize the change.

The window by the bed was open.

Someone had entered the cabin while she'd been gone. A gentle gust of wind blew the curtains lightly. They drifted like a lost soul, then settled back against the window. Someone had been in the cabin. And that someone might still be there, watching her. She replaced the telephone very slowly.

The hair on her neck prickled, and she fought down her first impulse to run as fast as she could. The nightmare vision of Abe Tuttle's mean, vicious face came to her, and she felt her knees quiver. The idea that he was hiding beneath the bed, one hand ready to snake around her ankle, made her step back.

Hardly daring to breathe, she dropped to the floor and lifted the edge of the quilt. Bare oak boards gleamed at her.

The low moan of a creaking hinge signaled a warning behind her. Drawing herself up, she turned to confront the noise.

The solid surface of the bathroom door opened a crack.

Edging quietly across the room, she picked up the backpack. There was nothing useful in it. The rough material slipped from her fingers as she searched the rest of the room with her eyes.

A bedside lamp offered the best possibility. Walking as softly as possible, she went toward it. She hit a board that gave with a loud creak, triggering a pulse of fear that felt like an explosion in her heart.

As her hand closed around the lamp, the crack in the bathroom door widened. A dark glittering eye peered out at her.

"Miranda!"

Grasping the lamp with all of her strength, she hurled it at the door. The sound of glass breaking drove her forward, and she ran for the front door.

Fingers fumbling at the lock, she twisted the knob. Her frantic efforts only froze the lock mechanism. Tearing at it, her fingernails broke, but she didn't stop. With a cry of success she felt the lock give.

A board creaked behind her, and she knew whoever was hiding in the bathroom had come out to get her. He was easing up behind her. Fighting the impulse to turn around, she yanked at the door. It swung open a few inches and then stopped, blocked by a large, powerful hand.

Chapter Fourteen

Before she could scream, she was spun around to face her attacker.

"Tom!" She was so frightened the word came out in a whisper. "What are you doing hiding in the bathroom?"

His hand covered her mouth with a gentle but insistent pressure. "Did you see anyone on the river?"

She shook her head. She wanted to struggle, to free herself from his grip, but she could not move. Her gaze locked into his, trying to read his intentions, but his amber eyes were secret, almost hidden in the dark cabin.

"No one around the cabin?"

She shook her head again. Her heartbeat accelerated. They were alone.

"Positive?"

She nodded, and he removed his hand.

"The roads out of Tabuga Springs were blocked when I tried to come back. Carter has pulled in help from all the surrounding counties, I'm afraid. They've decided to launch a real manhunt for us. I had to detour on a mountain trail. I drove in as far as I could, and then I left Doc's truck. The woods are crawling with search parties." His hands were on her arms, and he could feel the tension in her body. "Are you okay?"

He sounded so normal, so sincere. She nodded her head. She had to think clearly. She had to steel herself against her need to believe in him.

"Has anyone been around the cabin?" Tom asked.

"I heard someone on the river, but I could never track them down." She was amazed that her voice sounded so calm. She stepped back from him and felt his hands drop away. "I went upriver for a long way but there wasn't a sign of them."

"Chances are they're camped on the opposite bank. Probably pulled back in the woods so no one can detect them. Maybe someone will find that raft and assume we drowned. That's our best hope right now." He reached out for her. "While I was trying to get back here, I was worried to death about you. I had all of these visions of Carter finding you."

His fingers were in her hair, a gesture of affection that tore at Miranda's heart. Only the night before, his touch had been something special, extraordinary, and the passion he'd aroused had been the natural product of their growing feelings for each other.

She pushed his hands away and stepped back. "Did Doc tell you about Fremont?" She was no good at cat and mouse.

"What about him?" Tom stood with his hands still in the air. Slowly he lowered them to his side. "What about Fremont?" There was an edge to his voice.

"He's dead and my yellow bandanna was found in his hand."

"Dead! How? What was he doing with your bandanna?"

"Exactly my questions, Tom. If I'm not mistaken, that bandanna was left with Abe Tuttle." Her anger was rising to top form. "Maybe you didn't really tie him tightly. That thought crossed my mind."

"What are you talking about? You were standing right there. You saw the knots. And why would I pretend such a thing?" Confusion registered on Tom's face. He'd noticed the extreme tension in Miranda when he touched her. Now he understood that she was furious, but he had no idea why.

"I don't know the answer to that question, just like I can't imagine why you've been giving Senator Fremont money over the years." The words were out and there was no taking them back now. She saw awareness dawn on Tom's face, and she knew then that it was true. Deep inside she'd harbored the hope that Connie had been wrong, that Russ had been up to some manipulation. "So it's true," she said. In her voice was defeat.

"How did you find out?"

No denial, no attempt to even fabricate a half truth. "I spoke with Connie. Fremont's private books were found open on his desk where he was killed. Apparently he kept a written record of 'anonymous donors' to his career." She braved a look at him. "You know, Tom, those anonymous donations seem to be a bad habit with you."

Her voice was cold, beaten, and it hurt him. He'd much rather face her hot anger. "I'm tried and convicted, am I? No wonder you've had such a remarkably hard time forgiving yourself for certain past sins."

"I don't think I have to listen to any more of your partial truths."

"Wrong, Miranda. Dead wrong." He let his words sink in. Let her feel the scare for just a second; it might do her some good. She was too hard on herself and anyone she came in contact with.

"I'm not afraid," she lied, her green eyes holding his gaze.

"Good. Because you have no need to be." He saw the instant effect of his soft words. A crooked smile touched his face. "You aren't the only person in the world who's made a mistake in judgment. You aren't the only one who took a course of action that ended up badly. The trouble is, you *think* you are."

"I'm not the issue here. You are." She couldn't help but wonder where he was going with this conversation. She'd seen his smile. That certainly wasn't the reaction she'd anticipated.

"It's a shame about Fremont. Personally I never cared for the man and I certainly never trusted him. But in a way he was my ace in the hole."

His verbal acrobatics were confusing her. "What are you talking about?"

"How nice of you to finally ask an intelligent question." He knew he was baiting her, but he had to make her listen. "Years ago Doc was selected for the draft. He refused to go. He threatened to dishonor the family by going to Canada. It tore the family apart, and it nearly killed my grandfather, who had a great pride in this country. To resolve the matter I made a deal with Fremont to get Doc passed over, and Doc went to France."

"A deal?" Miranda interrupted.

"In essence I guess you could say that I bribed him, but it was carefully couched in the terms of a campaign contribution."

Miranda couldn't help it; she was shocked. She'd expected the payoffs to revolve around the Tabuga dam, not some distant draft issue.

When she didn't speak, Tom continued. "I was trying to protect my grandfather and my brother. I was young then. It was the only thing I could think of doing at the time." He reached out and let his fingers trace through a strand of her hair. "The war ended only a few months after that, but I'd already made the first payment. We all do rash things when we're young, especially when we're trying to protect those we love."

"Does Doc know this?" It was the only question she could think to ask.

"I don't know. I hope not. Doc is a bit like you, Miranda. He judges harshly, and most often that harsh judgment is directed at himself. He might hate me if he knew, but it's more likely that he'd hate himself."

"And you've given Fremont money all these years?"

"If your source of information was correct, and if Fremont kept accurate books, you'd know that the last contribution was made ten years ago. I went to him and told him that the past had been a mistake, that the actions I'd taken were wrong. There was no undoing them, but I told him I wasn't going to continue."

"And he said?"

"He didn't care. He had seniority at the Hill. He didn't need my paltry support any longer. We parted amiably enough."

"And that's why you think he would have helped you?"

"I said helped us." He paused. "No, Fremont never had a long memory. But I'll tell you, Miranda, I would have gone to him again. I would have given him any amount of money, right or wrong, to save you."

His final words seemed to hang on the still night air.

"That would have been wrong," she finally said, her emotions almost choking her. She knew the guilt of a bad decision, one that couldn't be undone.

"Miranda, sometimes the heart has more honor than the brain." He lifted her chin with one gentle finger. He could see the tears in her eyes. "What I did for Doc might be wrong. I've judged it both ways. But look at all the good Doc has done in Tabuga Springs. He's helped hundreds of families, given children who were sick or injured a chance at life. Is that such a bad result? Yes, my reasons for acting were selfish, but that doesn't mitigate the goodness of what Doc has accomplished."

"You can't go through life twisting it to your own end. Gregory thought he could do that. He believed he was right. He believed it enough to destroy a federal building, and in doing so he forced me to take an action that sent him to prison."

Tom could no longer resist touching her. His hands framed her face with the softest pressure. His gaze held hers a moment, reading the confusion and pain in her eyes. "You're forgetting one tiny thing, Miranda. You aren't Gregory. You're innocent of everything you've been accused of doing. I'm not trying to protect a guilty person from punishment. I'm trying to save the woman I love from a frame."

She felt his arms encircle her and she yielded, allowing his strength to mold her to him. Her arms reached around his chest, and she held on to him. He was solid, a man of flesh and heart. A man who loved her enough to risk everything he possessed to save her.

She lifted her lips to him, and he took them. Her doubts were gone, smashed to dust against the solid wall of his love. Her arms moved up to circle his neck, the fingers of her right hand catching his thick hair. He'd overcome her fears and routed out her guilt. He'd battered down her self-protective barriers and forced her to love him. And he did, with a fierceness and power that left her weak-kneed and frightened at her own vulnerability.

He felt her trembling against him, and he lifted her. The bed was only a few steps away.

The multicolored quilt was cool against her back. Miranda's fingers worked the buttons of his shirt as he undid hers. In a moment they were undressed, their fevered skin pressed close.

"I love you, Tom." Miranda spoke her confession into his ear. "I've fought hard against it."

"I know," he whispered. He kissed her cheek, her forehead and her lips. "We both fought against this, and I'm glad we lost." His lips claimed hers in a deep and possessive kiss, and then he began to slowly drop his kisses down her body.

CRICKETS AND CICADAS serenaded the darkened cabin. Tucked beneath the quilt, Tom pillowed Miranda's head on his arm. His free hand stroked her stomach, the curve of her waist, still marveling in the contours of her body. When dawn came, they would have to make a decision about their future. Their position was tenuous. Danger confronted them on all sides. For the next few hours, though, he wanted to devote his attention to the woman who rested beside him. She'd given herself to him with an abandon that excited every fiber of his being. When Miranda Conner loved a man, she held nothing back.

"Tom?" Her voice was a whisper in the darkness.

His answer was a kiss.

Her knuckles grazed the stubble of his beard. She'd been lying in bed, Tom close beside her, thinking. She had no future that she could see, but the past few hours she'd spent in Tom's arms had given her new hope and confidence.

"Who do you think killed Fremont?" she asked. If they could just unravel the first loop, then maybe they could get to the core of the puzzle.

"Someone who knew about my past contributions."

"I've been thinking about that. It looks to me like Fremont's death ties you firmly into this mess. I've been so busy trying to figure out the frames set up for me, I didn't see that you've been framed just as successfully. First your ring is left at the scene of Fred Elton's death. Lucky for you I found it instead of the police. You break me out of jail, then a U.S. senator is killed. I leave my bandanna and it is revealed that you've been paying kickbacks to Fremont. You're as much a fugitive as I am."

"Exactly."

"But who knew about those contributions?"

Tom leaned on his elbow. He traced her eyebrow with one finger. "I never told a single person. I never even told my grandfather. I was ashamed."

"Who do you suppose Fremont told? I don't believe he was sitting at his desk going over old accounts when he was killed. I think whoever went in there to kill him knew the account books existed and deliberately left them there."

"I could only guess at who Fremont might have told. I dropped all contact with him."

"You didn't know he'd been heading the committee on the Tabuga?"

"Of course I did, but that's why I wanted the WDC to investigate the development of the river. I couldn't trust Fremont to make an honorable decision. He was a pork-barrel politician, and he'd have sold out the Tabuga to the highest contributor. Clearwater is first in line to begin development, but if the door is ever opened, there will be plenty of other companies wanting to get in."

Miranda sat up in bed, struck by another thought. "Tom, did you send a list of instructions with your donation?"

"No. The money was delivered in a plain envelope. It was all cash. We did everything possible to make sure it wasn't traceable."

"Then you didn't know there was a list of instructions. Russ and Cynthia were specifically named as the news reporters to include. So was Fred Elton. And you don't know anything about this?"

"Not a thing." Tom pulled the quilt over her shoulders. The mountain night was chilly, and he wanted the warmth of her against him. Just for a little longer.

"Who actually mailed the package?" Miranda asked.

"I wrapped it up myself. Then it was left in the office for the postman."

"So anyone could have tampered with it."

"A number of people, yes."

Miranda didn't mention Doc's name, but he was the first person who came to her mind. Doc, the man with a motive and opportunity. The man with a drinking problem and a troubled past. Her fists clenched. Doc had sample boxes in his refrigerator! She'd seen them herself!

She slipped back down in the bed, shifting her body as close beside Tom as possible. She didn't want to talk anymore. Not tonight. The finger of guilt pointed directly at Tom's brother, and she was afraid she'd give her suspicions away if she continued the conversation. When it was light, when she could see Tom's face, then she'd tell him what she feared. For the moment, though, she wanted the comfort of his arms, and she wanted to let him know how much she loved him—before she had to hurt him.

MIRANDA AWOKE with a single thought. She had to speak with Gordon Simms and make sure the fish specimens had arrived safely. Tom had trusted them to Doc, and she had an overwhelming worry that they had not been delivered.

Tom slept, his arms and legs sprawled over the bed in a state of total surrender. She brushed the hair back from his forehead and resisted the temptation to awaken him with a kiss. He needed his sleep more than anything else.

The power blackout from the night before had been remedied when Tom replaced the fuse he'd taken, but Miranda was still uneasy about the cabin's appliances. The electricity had come back on with a sputter like an angry cat. She approached the telephone with some trepidation. Relief made her sigh when she lifted the receiver and heard the dial tone. So far, so good. She dialed Gordon's home phone.

"Simms here."

"Gordon, did you get the fish?"

"Miranda, where the hell are you? Your picture is smeared over every paper in the city. I don't think there's a crime on the books you aren't accused of committing."

"I know."

"Where are you?"

"I'm safe, Gordon, or as safe as I can be. I don't want to tell you because I don't want you to have to lie about it if the police ask."

"That's not a problem for me, but the police have already been here. This morning at 4:00 a.m., in fact."

Miranda sighed. "I'm sorry. You got a little more than you bargained for when you decided to raft the Tabuga with me."

"Stay off that river, Miranda."

"What?" She was startled by his remark.

"Since they found that Tuttle man's body, they're calling you a series killer. You've got about as much chance as a rabid dog, and the focus of the manhunt seems to be the Tabuga River."

Only Tom's firm hand kept her from dropping the telephone to the floor. Tom captured her and held her until she recovered enough to speak.

"Miranda? Are you there?" Gordon was almost yelling.

"I'm here," she said into the telephone, but she looked at Tom. "Abe Tuttle's dead," she said.

"I don't believe it," Tom answered sharply. "He was fine when we left him."

"How, uh, how did he die?" Miranda asked Gordon.

"A blow to the head. Miranda, I didn't believe it for an instant. Not for an instant. The officers who were here said it was all very hush-hush. It hasn't hit the newspapers yet, but be careful. I'm surprised they don't have bounty hunters after you. Oh, yeah, I got the fish. That doctor from Tabuga Springs delivered them."

"Doc Wilkes?"

"Yeah, Tom's brother. I thought that was very strange. Is Wilkes with you?"

"When can you have the report on the fish ready, Gordon? You are still going to testify, aren't you?"

"Nothing would give me greater pleasure. I was up all night and was able to do a lot of the preliminary tests. I should be ready to go with it by, say, three tomorrow."

"Gordon, do you think you can get the members of the Tabuga committee to meet tomorrow?"

"I don't know. Sen. Wayne Jaffe has been named to replace Fremont."

"Promise them that a surprise witness will be there."

"You!" Gordon was incredulous. "If you come near the Hill, the cops will swarm you."

"It's a chance I might have to take. Can you get Senator Jaffe there? We don't need the rest of the committee. In fact, it would be better if it was only him."

"I'll try. No, I'll do better than that. I'll make sure that he's there."

"Bring your findings, Gordon."

"Oh, I will."

"See you then." Miranda replaced the receiver. Her face was haggard as she turned to Tom. "Can we make it by three tomorrow?"

"Yes." He knew exactly what she had in mind, a sneak preview of the fish study. It was a daring move. She'd decided to plead her case in the public eye, armed with evidence that would surely bring the scientific community to her defense. She was not only smart but courageous.

"Get your things together. The truck isn't too far from here."

She nodded mutely and began to gather the backpacks.

Tom couldn't stand the slump of her shoulders, the blank misery in her eyes. He went to her and pulled her close against him. "You didn't kill Tuttle," he said.

"I hit him with that limb. When he fell down, I was afraid he was hurt, but he was breathing." She trembled against him.

"You didn't kill him, Miranda. I've seen a lot of injuries, and Tuttle wasn't hurt that bad."

"Maybe his brain was hemorrhaging." She pushed back from him.

Tom could see the fear in her eyes. "Miranda!" he spoke sharply to get her attention. "I swear to you Tuttle wasn't seriously injured."

"Then how did he die?" she asked.

"That, my dear, is the second-best question you've asked in twenty-four hours. I don't have the answer, but before all of this is over, I will. That's a promise." He kissed her forehead. "It's a long trip, let's get going."

MIRANDA'S PALMS WERE damp as she waited in the back corner of the small room that had once been Sen. Harry Fremont's private conference area. Outside the door she thought she heard Russ Sherman's voice, but she couldn't be certain. Gordon Simms was there. Tom had told her so. She took a deep breath. If Gordon's report was as dramatic as she hoped, today would mark a big step toward saving the Tabuga, and maybe even clearing her name.

She sipped the strong black coffee Tom had given her. Once they'd gotten to the truck, they'd spelled each other driving. The trip had taken much longer than normal because they'd skirted places where Tom thought roadblocks might have been established. Lucky for them no one had anticipated that they'd go straight to the heart of Washington—the Capitol. Now all she had to do was wait for Senator Jaffe to arrive. Once he heard her evidence, then he would be forced to take some action to save the

Tabuga and she could turn herself in to the Washington authorities until her innocence could be proven.

The doors of the conference room opened, and a small crowd of people entered. Tom walked beside a portly man Miranda took to be Fremont's replacement for the Tabuga dam hearing. Filing in behind Tom and the senator were Gordon, Cynthia Wickham, with her camper crew, and Russ Sherman. The latter looked about the room until he found Miranda seated in a far corner. He shook his head and pointed to his notebook, indicating he wanted an interview.

She nodded. She was more than ready to tell her side of the story.

The portly man took his seat at the head of the table. "I'm Senator Jaffe, and I'm replacing Senator Fremont for this hearing. This is slightly irregular, but I've been led to believe that the cause of justice will be served by this emergency meeting."

There was a rustle of papers and the sounds of switches snapping as Cynthia motioned her camera crew into action.

Jaffe looked around the room, stopping on Miranda. "Ms. Conner, I hope you know that I cannot allow you to leave this room. I have been convinced that I need to hear Mr. Simms's testimony before the police are called, but under no circumstances will I be party to protecting a wanted criminal."

"I understand," she said as she rose. "I appreciate the opportunity." She cleared her throat, surprised at her own nervousness. She'd given testimony at hundreds of hearings, but none had ever meant so much to her. "After careful analysis Mr. Simms has some testimony to give regarding a species of fish thought to be extinct in the Tabuga River. The Tabuga pisces darter is a species that still retains the ganoid scale. It is the belief of the WDC that all attempts to develop the wild and free Tabuga River must be stopped immediately. I would also like to mention that Mr. Simms is giving his testimony free of charge." She sat down.

"Mr. Simms." Senator Jaffe looked toward the biologist.

"My findings are irrefutable, Your Honor. I've run and rerun the tests in the hopes of coming to some other conclusion." He looked at Miranda with a strange cold stare. "But I cannot twist the evidence. The samples of fish brought to me by Miranda Conner of the Wilderness Defense Center are very close to the species of fish once thought to thrive in the Tabuga River system. But these samples are fraudulent. The fish are actually common to free-flowing streams and rivers in the North Carolina area."

"Gordon!" Miranda rose from her chair, her face pale and disbelieving. "What are you saying?"

"And furthermore, Ms. Conner has attempted to bribe me on numerous occasions to give false testimony in this case. I have repeatedly resisted her attempts at bribery, intimidation and coercion . . ."

Before anyone could say anything else, Tom grabbed Miranda's hand and pulled her out of the room. Together they fled down the long hall of the Senate building and out into the summer heat. Behind them there was the sound of whistles, running feet and shouted orders for them to stop.

"Tom," Miranda gasped. "What happened?"

"We got suckered, my dear," he said as he took her arm and forced her to run faster. "And if we don't hurry, we're going to be caught."

They ducked through the heavy traffic and ran. "Can we make it back to Tabuga Springs?" Miranda asked raggedly. She was out of breath from the mad dash.

"We can give it one hell of a try."

Chapter Fifteen

Miranda gave up the idea of sleeping as Tom drove to Tabuga Springs. The truck pitched and jerked on some of the rutted paths. Only his steadying hand kept her from spilling onto the floor on more than one occasion. When the roads were good, she drove. About midway through the long drive, they put together a plan. It was risky and bold, but it was the only option they could figure out.

As they drew near Tabuga Springs, Tom touched her hand. "I'm going to leave you at Doc's for a few hours, and then we'll put everything into action."

"No!" Of all the places she didn't want to go, Doc's was at the top of her list.

"It's the safest place, Miranda. Doc and Cheryl will take good care of you."

"And where are you going?"

"I have to see Clark Presley."

Miranda frowned. "I don't really trust him, and at this point I'm not so sure I trust your brother."

"I understand that, but you do trust me, and I trust them." He gave her a crooked grin. "I wouldn't risk your future on someone I had any doubts about, Miranda. Now don't argue, let's make a dash for Doc's house. No one will ever think you'd be brazen enough to go there."

Tom stopped the truck, and they left it hidden on the outskirts of town. Tom knew more dirt tracks and barely passable paths than she'd ever seen before. If there wasn't a path, then he made one.

Before she could protest again, Tom took her hand and pulled her after him as he struck out through the woods. Miranda was surprised when they stopped at the back of an old shed. They were already in Doc's yard.

"Tell Doc I want you at the cabin by two o'clock," Tom said. He lifted her hand to his lips. "Call Carter, like we planned. By the time the sheriff arrives, I'll be there to help you."

"Do you really think we can smoke them out?" Miranda had been instrumental in developing the plan, but in the light of day she wasn't so certain it would work.

"It has to, Miranda. We aren't going to be able to evade capture much longer."

"I know." There had been three roadblocks that they'd narrowly avoided. Tom was correct. The dragnet was closing in on them, and once they were caught they wouldn't have much of a chance to explain.

"Be there by two," Tom cautioned her. He kissed her goodbye, his fingers pressing deeply into her back as if he could imprint the feel of her into his hands.

He disappeared into the woods, and Miranda was left to dash across the open area of lawn and into Doc's neatly organized kitchen.

"Miranda!" Cheryl dropped the glass she held. Glass shattered and an amber cold drink spread along the tile. Cheryl bent immediately to clean it up. "You scared the life out of me. I had no idea you were in town."

"We just got here. I've been listening to the radio reports. I guess everyone knows about the Tabuga pisces darter."

"Yes, I'm sorry." Cheryl glanced nervously about the kitchen. "Would you mind stepping into the library? This is rather...open."

The two women stepped into the dark-paneled library, and Cheryl closed the doors. "What are you going to do?" she asked Miranda.

"I have to be at Doc's cabin at two o'clock. Can you take me?" She was much more comfortable asking the friendly redhead.

"Sure." Cheryl's gaze dropped to the desk in the library, and her eyes opened wider. She stepped across the room and closed the open books. Opening a drawer, she cleared the desktop. "I was just putting Doc's house in order," she said.

Miranda couldn't help but notice that her laugh was forced. "Anything wrong?"

"Nothing at all. It's just that I'm not the best book-keeper in the world. In case Tom hasn't told you, neither of the Wilkes brothers can balance a checkbook. It's a real problem, or it was until I took over the accounts, personal and business."

"Cheryl!" Doc's voice came through the closed library door.

"Coming, Doc," Cheryl called, then turned back to Miranda. "Wait here and let me tell him. One of us will make sure you get to the cabin." She smiled, but her lips were thin.

Before Miranda could respond, Cheryl left the room. The door closed firmly behind her.

Miranda hesitated for only a second. She went to the desk and pulled at the drawer. To her surprise it was locked. She didn't remember Cheryl having a key. A slender letter opener was the best tool available, and Miranda went to work on the flimsy lock. Within two minutes she had the drawer open and the account book sprawled before her.

"Good grief," she whispered as her finger traced column after column of debts.

She didn't hear the door open or Cheryl's soft tread on the carpet.

"I'm glad you know," Cheryl said at last. Two tears moved down her cheeks. "I've been so scared."

Miranda rose from behind the desk, her hand still on the ledger book. "How did this happen?" she asked. "Why?"

"Doc's drinking has gotten worse and worse." Cheryl angrily brushed the tears away.

"Tom doesn't have a clue," Miranda said, astounded. "This is going to kill him."

"It's partially my fault," Cheryl said as she approached the desk. "At first I helped Doc cover up the problem because I thought he could make it up. Instead of getting better, he just drank more and more and the gambling debts kept piling up. Whenever I mentioned telling Tom, he'd rail at me and threaten me. He never got over the fact that Tom was his grandfather's favorite." She stifled a sob with her fist. "My love was never enough. Never."

Moving around the desk, Miranda went to Cheryl and put her arms around the crying woman. "You have to get a grip," Miranda warned her. A sense of danger had penetrated under Miranda's skin. "Cheryl, have you told Doc I'm here?"

The redhead shook her head no. "I was afraid of what he might do." Her voice caught on a sob. "He went to see Senator Fremont when we were in Washington to take the fish. He went to see Fremont, and only a few hours later Fremont was found dead." She looked at Miranda with eyes that were drawn with pain and worry.

"Take me to the cabin, Cheryl. Right now. And you can't let anyone see me."

Cheryl nodded slowly. "I'll pull up to the rear and you can slip into the back seat while I load the laundry. I take Doc's office stuff to the cleaners for him and it's always a big pile. No one will see you or suspect anything."

"Thanks!" Miranda squeezed Cheryl's arm. "And whatever happens, I don't think Tom would ever abandon Doc. Tom will see that he gets the help he needs."

"I hope so," Cheryl sniffed.

THE SHRILL RING of the phone made Miranda spill a cup of hot coffee on her leg. Ignoring the pain, she was across the cabin in two rings.

"Tom!"

"I'm close by and on the way," he said. "I can't talk here, but begin the plan."

"Okay." She replaced the receiver and waited for her heart to settle down. She'd been on pins and needles waiting for Tom's call. Now it was time. With any luck they'd soon be forcing the entire chain of events to a dramatic close. Her fingers curled around the telephone receiver, and she took several deep breaths. She'd decided against telling Tom about Doc on the telephone. Such news deserved a face-to-face situation, one where she could offer comfort.

Before she picked up the telephone, she checked to make sure the brown manila envelope was sealed and in plain sight on the counter. Her hand shook slightly as she dialed the number for the Laurel County Sheriff's office.

"Carter here," a gruff voice snapped.

She took a deep, steadying breath. "Sheriff Carter, this is Miranda Conner. I need to talk with you, but you have to come alone."

The dead silence on the other end was more frightening than anything he could have said. "Where are you?" He was cautious, not giving any of his feelings away.

"I'm tucked safely away, with some very incriminating evidence. So if you would consider making a deal, then I might want to do business with you." She felt a jolt of self-confidence. She sounded tough and self-reliant, exactly as they'd planned it.

"What kinda deal you thinkin' about?" Carter played his hand with continued caution.

"You know I'm innocent of murder. I want my name cleared."

"Every cop in Washington, D.C., is looking for you," Carter countered. "If that's where you are, you'd better keep low." He spoke as if she were a disobedient child.

"When my name is cleared, they won't be interested in me," she parried. She had to keep talking until she convinced him to come.

"Best thing for you to do is come on into the jail here and surrender. That way we can work together to solve this mess you've gotten into. When I first saw you, I didn't think you were the kinda girl who would commit murder. Now talkin' with you, I see that you're innocent. But you got to come on in and settle this.''

She could hear the trap in his voice. He thought he was being so sly. Well, it was time to give him a taste of the stick instead of the carrot. ''I don't have to do anything! I'm the one with the evidence which shows your complicity in a series of crimes.'' Her voice cracked with anger. ''You're the one who has to do something, and I'm telling you right now, you'd better be quick. I'm at Doc Wilkes's cabin, but I'm gone in an hour. Be here if you want what I've got.''

''You have evidence?'' His voice prickled her skin. He was brash, but he couldn't hide his worry. ''What kind of evidence?''

''Come and get it if you want it. If not, I'll see that it gets to the proper Washington authorities.''

''Are you threatening me?''

''You bet I am. Now you have exactly fifty-eight minutes. Move it!'' She dropped the receiver back in the cradle, hoping the sound would hurt his eardrum.

Miranda returned to the old rocking chair on the front porch. Her spine was rigidly straight, but she moved the chair back and forth, back and forth, in an easy, singsong rhythm. The motion soothed her agitation.

When forty-five minutes had passed, she stood and walked to the edge of the porch. There was no sign of Tom, but then he always moved with the stealth of an Indian. He was out there, waiting for Carter to take the bait.

In exactly fourteen minutes the patrol car roared into the dirt yard, sending a plume of hot dust out behind it. Carter jumped out of the seat, a handgun pointed straight at her chest. He moved cautiously up the steps and onto the porch until he was only two feet away. Miranda had resumed her seat in the rocker, and she didn't budge at his approach. She scouted the woods with her eyes, but there was no sign of Tom. A spike of panic hammered down her spine, but she fought it back.

"How'd you get here?" Carter swung around, looking for a vehicle.

"I drove." She drawled the words, smiling at him. "I hid my Jeep for a quick getaway. Care for a cup of coffee?"

"I didn't come up here to drink coffee. Why don't you just get on up and get in the patrol car? A lot of people are looking for you." He kept the gun pointed at her while the other hand pulled her to her feet and quickly felt for a weapon. With a sneer he pushed her toward the car. "Get in."

"Aren't you forgetting something?"

Her arrogant tone stopped him in his tracks. "You don't have no evidence!" he sputtered.

"Would I have called you up here to capture me, unless I had some protection?" She smiled condescendingly. "I'm not stupid, Sheriff. I have something. If you don't believe me, look in the kitchen on the counter."

Where the hell was Tom? He'd told her to activate the plan, that he was on his way. What could have happened to him? She glanced toward the surrounding woods. There was only sunlight and shadows of a summer morning.

Carter edged to the door, keeping his gun carefully trained on her. She watched, willing him to go inside. That was the plan. Once he was in the door, then she was to run for the woods. Tom would take care of the rest.

The sheriff's florid face showed doubt as he hesitated. "You go in and get it," he ordered, thrusting the gun closer to her body.

"I'm content here." She leaned back in the rocker, smiling up at him. "There's a little envelope on the counter. Help yourself to a cup of coffee while you're there."

"Now listen, you!" He pushed the cold barrel into her shoulder. "Get up and don't make me hurt you." He emphasized his words by jabbing the barrel into her arm.

Cold fear swept through her. Tom was nowhere in sight. The envelope on the kitchen counter contained a blank cassette cartridge that had been in Tom's truck. When

Carter found out that the entire thing was a ruse, there was no telling what he would do. The fact that he'd come proved he was guilty, but of what?

She rose slowly, casting one final glance over her shoulder for Tom. The woods were beautiful but barren of his agile form. The gun prodded her back, and she had no choice but to enter the cool interior.

Reluctantly she walked to the counter and picked up the envelope. "This is your death warrant." She tossed it at him, playing for each additional moment she could.

"Where's a tape player?" His eyes scanned the small room.

For a second Miranda felt weak with relief. There wasn't a cassette player in the cabin. The place was bare of all luxuries. No music, no television. No tape player! She smiled.

"I'm afraid there isn't one, Sheriff. That's too bad. I think you'd be very interested in Senator Fremont's conversation." She stabbed blindly, based on her suspicions. Her strike was effective. Carter's face twisted into a red rage.

"What did that bastard say about me? How did you get this tape?" He waved the envelope, thrusting the gun into her stomach.

The attack knocked the breath from her, forcing her to draw back. Still, she held on to her cold smile. "Play the tape and find out what he said, and just remember, that isn't the only copy. Anything happens to me, and a copy of that tape will be delivered to the police."

Carter drew the gun back in preparation to slam it into her face. "You meddler," he said menacingly. "You'll be sorry."

"Don't hurt the woman." Abe Tuttle's command stopped Carter's hand.

Turning to the open cabin door, what Miranda saw was more effective than the blow Carter had been ready to deliver.

Tom, his hands pinned tightly behind his back, stumbled into the room. Tuttle followed, a long-barreled pistol poking mercilessly into Tom's ribs. "Lookee what I found, Sheriff, hiding in the woods."

Abe Tuttle was alive and more menacing than she remembered—and Tom was his prisoner.

"I was wonderin' where you went, Tuttle," Carter said, relief plain on his face. "They got evidence on me. A tape." He shook the envelope, letting the cassette fall to the floor. "They bugged Fremont's phone when he musta been talkin' about the money he gave us."

Miranda connected with Tom's quick glance. She'd done a good job convincing Carter the tape was real, but she had no idea what to do to help Tom.

"What else is on that tape?" Tuttle's jaw tightened, pulling his lips thin and hard. He jabbed Tom in the back with the barrel, and for the first time Miranda saw the red stain dripping down Tom's ribs.

"You're hurt." She was at his side before Tuttle's rough hand grasped the waistband of her pants. He threw her to the floor.

"So, you don't like to see your lover bleed, do you?" He placed the barrel into the bloodstained shirt and pushed.

Tom bent double with pain but suppressed the cry. Fighting against the agony, he stood straight again, giving Miranda a tiny smile.

"What else is on that tape?" Tuttle held the barrel in Tom's shirt. "Spill it, or you can watch ole Tom's blood really flow."

"Ah, just the one conversation." She fought her panic, fought her desire to scream and attack. She had to think fast and straight.

"With who?"

"We don't know. It's just Fremont's voice that we were able to identify." Lie upon lie. She felt herself sinking into deception. How much longer could she continue without tripping over her own falsehoods?

"Fremont and who?" Tuttle demanded, prodding Tom enough to make him gasp.

"We couldn't identify the voice. A man." She slowly pulled herself to her feet, her eyes never leaving Tuttle's flat blue gaze. "I thought you were dead."

Tuttle laughed. "Not by a long shot. I told 'em it wouldn't work, that you wouldn't give yourself up. But it was worth a try, anyway." He laughed again, low and cruel. "Fremont talk about anyone but Carter here?"

Tuttle was leading somewhere, but Miranda couldn't be certain where. What should she say?

"Fremont said that Carter was responsible for Fred Elton's death." Her heart froze at Tuttle's pleased expression.

"So, there's a tape that puts the rap on Carter." He looked at the sheriff and chuckled. "You got yourself worked into a tight spot, ole boy." His laughter was mean, vicious. "I never dreamed when I decided to get even with Tom that I'd have such a chance to even the score with a lot of other folks. Especially not my own third cousin, ole Uley Carter."

Before Carter could react, Tuttle kicked the cassette across the room. "There's no one here to tie me to Carter and his crimes." He grinned malevolently. "Except the sheriff hisself."

The cock of the pistol was the most frightening sound Miranda had ever heard. Tuttle's grin was vicious. He pointed the barrel at Uley Carter's bulging neck. "Me and the sheriff gonna take a little walk. Put me somethin' on to eat. And don't try nothin' foolish, 'cause I remember the last time you were gettin' ready to do somethin' nice for me. I still owe you for that."

His last words made her skin crawl with repulsion. She couldn't let him walk Carter into the woods and execute him. Her frantic thought froze as Tom slowly fell against the wall and slid to the floor. The blood soaking down his pants made her heart thump with fear.

Before Tuttle could stop her, she rushed to him, ripping his shirt away. The bullet hole in his ribs was small, but there was no way to tell how much damage had been done.

She looked up at the grinning Tuttle. "Fix your own damn meal. I've got something else to do."

Tuttle's laughter was cutting and mean. "Bandage him up real good, honey, so he can watch what I do to you when I get back." He laughed as he signaled Carter outside.

"Tuttle, you won't get away with this." Carter's voice was more reasonable than Miranda expected. He had pulled himself together. "We're partners in this. You can't get away with killing me."

Tuttle's laugh was a jeer. "The way I see it, you're a loose end. You set Trimmer up, sending him out to try and kidnap the woman. If you're dead, you can take all the blame."

"You can't kill a lawman!" Carter grew shrill.

"Lawman?" Tuttle roared. "You ain't never been a lawman. You the sheriff, but you ain't no lawman. It's going to give me great pleasure to kill you, then them—" he swung a mad grin at Tom and Miranda "—and make it look like you were all involved. The little lady's got a past history with men who like dynamite, and when I blow this cabin apart, she'll get the blame and there won't be enough of any of you left to use for evidence." His laughter was low, intense.

Revulsion for Tuttle boiled inside Miranda. She kept her mouth shut and her hands busy tearing Tom's shirt into strips. The bleeding had almost stopped, but he was in a daze, slumped against the wall. She tried to lift him, but his sudden grip on her arm was bitingly painful.

His strength startled her, and she examined his face. The pain was real, but he opened his eyes wide. He was alert, not dazed. Slumped against the wall, he was waiting, hoping that Tuttle would assume he was too seriously injured to be a threat.

She knew instinctively that she had to keep Tuttle talking. "You blew up the Tabuga that night?" She threw her question at Tuttle.

"Yeah, it was a perfect setup," Tuttle bragged. "It couldn't fail. If you were blown off the bridge, everyone would believe you were guilty. Since you survived, they found the dynamite I planted."

"Who thought of that plan? You're too stupid to think of something like that on your own."

Tom's fingers dug into her knee, trying to hold her back. She ignored him. "You're nothing but a half-witted lout!" Each word was clear and distinct.

"Damn you." His blue eyes were narrowed. His hand slashed out at her, knocking her to the floor. "Before you die, you're going to take that back," he vowed.

"You make me sick." She shifted to her knees and slowly stood, never letting her green gaze falter. "Worse than that, Tuttle, you're too stupid to scare me."

Tom shifted beside her, and Miranda gave him a warning kick on the leg. She knew exactly what she was doing.

"You lost your wife because you couldn't take care of her. You aren't even a man," she challenged him.

He lunged at her, rage distorting his blunt features.

Tom's well-placed kick caught him in the kneecap. With a sideways twist Miranda evaded him and brought the flat of her palm against his jaw. Swearing with the unexpected pain, Tuttle stumbled and fell, his gun flying across the room.

Miranda dived after it, ignoring Carter's rush from her right side. With another effective kick Tom knocked the fat sheriff off balance and sent him sprawling. His gun slithered across the cabin and slipped to a stop at the refrigerator.

Tuttle's gun was closer and Miranda reached for it. The cold metal of the gun pressed against her fingers. Grabbing the handle, she rolled, pointing it first at Tuttle and then Carter.

She rose shakily to her feet, backing sideways to Tom's side so that he was behind her. Then she allowed a smile of victory.

"Get on the phone," she ordered Carter as she picked up his gun, "and call an ambulance."

Carter hesitated until he saw Miranda cock the gun.

"Don't think I won't," she warned. "Both of you would have murdered us without any compunction."

Her matter-of-fact tone was convincing. Carter picked up the phone.

"There ain't no ambulance, only Doc Wilkes." Carter grinned.

Miranda cast a quick look at Tom. The wound had re-opened, and blood was once again seeping onto the floor. "Call him," she said.

Carter obliged, his pudgy finger dialing the number with maddening slowness. "Doc, this is Sheriff Carter. Tom's been shot up here at your cabin. You'd better come see about him."

There was a brief pause. "Yeah." His expression shifted subtly, and then he hung up. "Doc's on his way."

"You two sit against the wall," Miranda ordered.

She could sense Tom weakening beside her. His eyes were open, but the alert edge was slipping away. She could only hope that Doc would get there, and soon.

Chapter Sixteen

Miranda settled against the wall beside Tom. With her forearms resting on her knees, she could support the gun and give the muscles in her back a rest. She could also keep an eye on Tom.

"Quite the little gunslinger, aren't you?" Tom teased in a soft whisper. The pain had steadied, and his concern was for her, not himself. She'd borne up under the strain and pressure better than most men he'd worked with. Her deliciously feminine body contained a fierce spirit, very much like the river she loved.

Miranda answered him with a smile. "I've discovered several new talents since I met you," she answered. Steadying the gun with one hand, she brushed his cheek with the other. He was too warm.

She saw Tuttle and Carter take in her gesture. They were waiting for an opportunity. They were strong men, and they could easily overpower her if she dropped her defenses for only a moment.

Tuttle tensed, and she shifted the gun to him. "I may not be able to shoot you both, but I will get one of you." She eyed them. "And you don't know which one I'll pick." Her heart was racing beneath her steady voice.

"Who's behind all of this?" Tom asked. He started to sit up more, but slumped back against the wall. The pain was too intense whenever he moved even slightly.

Miranda reached back to check the compress on Tom's wound. Blood soaked the bandage and stained her hand. Quickly she applied more pressure.

Tom brushed her hand away. "Don't show any weakness," he whispered, forcing himself straighter against the wall. Grim determination etched furrows in his forehead, and tiny lines of white spread from the corners of his mouth. "Who's running the show, boys?" he asked. "I want to know."

"Maybe we should let it go for now," Miranda said softly. Tom was near shock, and the revelation that his brother was deeply involved would not do him any good.

"I was working for Fremont," Carter said.

Stalling, Miranda got up and collected more towels from a cabinet. Throwing them at Carter, she ordered him to tear them into strips for additional bandages.

Carter held the soft cotton in his hands, never moving a muscle.

"Don't look like Tom's gonna make it for Doc to patch up." Tuttle shifted forward.

"Shut up!" Miranda ordered. "Or I'll shoot you in the leg. Maybe both of them."

The growl erupted from Tuttle's throat, tearing out of his grim lips. "When Doc..." He stopped, shifting his flat blue eyes to Miranda quickly.

Her heart pounding, Miranda motioned him back to his place on the floor. They were like wild animals, cornered and dangerous.

She checked Tom's wound again. The bleeding had stopped, but any movement or stress might reopen it.

"What did Fremont have to gain?" she quietly asked Carter. It was one of several things she couldn't figure out.

"He had a stake in some property up north of Clark Presley's. The land was deeded to him by Willa Edderly." Carter snorted. "She thought she was leaving it for a wildlife preserve. Fremont woulda been a rich man. All of us woulda."

"Why did you kill him?"

"I didn't," Carter answered, his small eyes wide with shock. "You don't think I killed him, do you? Not on your life. Not me."

"Tuttle?"

The man shook his bearded head. "Me, either. I never been near Washington."

Miranda recalled Cheryl's confession that Doc had been to see Fremont just before he was found dead.

The shrill of the telephone made her jump. Tuttle started forward, and she froze him with the barrel of the gun. "Don't try it," she warned. "Now get the phone."

Tuttle picked up the receiver as if it would bite. "Yeah," he said gruffly. "She's here." He dropped the receiver. "For you." He looked at Miranda.

"Who is it?"

"Russ Sherwood, or something like that."

Miranda edged over to the phone, careful to keep Tuttle and Carter in sight. "How did you get this number?" she asked.

"Doc Wilkes gave it to me," Russ answered. "Listen, Miranda, I had to call you. You're in a lot of danger. I found some papers in Fremont's office."

"I know," she answered. "The payoff records."

"That and something else. It's the past—"

"Save it, Russ. I know about Tom's connection to Fremont, and it doesn't mean a thing. I also know that you're an investor in Clearwater Development. I don't think your newspaper is going to be too pleased about that."

"Miranda, you have to listen."

The roar of a big motor vibrated in the distance. Doc had arrived at last.

"Got to go, Russ." She replaced the receiver before he had a chance to say anything else. Now the most grueling part of her ordeal awaited. She had to convince Doc to take care of his brother, even though she knew that Doc was the mastermind behind the whole plot. As long as she feigned innocence, she might be able to save Tom's life.

"I guess you'd better move away from the door, over against the kitchen wall," she directed Carter and Tuttle. She was taking no chances.

Carter got up, stretching long and yawning, as if he'd awakened from the best sleep. "I was tired of sittin' on that hard floor." He grinned at Miranda. "Old bones, you know."

"You got enough fat to keep your bones from achin'."

Tuttle's abrasive tone bounced right off Carter. Uley grinned and moved to the wall where Miranda directed them.

The motor grew louder until the familiar blue truck wheeled into the yard, plumes of summer dust riding out behind it like ghost vehicles.

"Tom! Miranda!" Doc's voice was so similar to Tom's that Miranda felt her stomach lurch. She had to play it cool. Really cool.

"In here!" She took a breath. "Please hurry, Doc. Tom's been shot. There's no time to waste."

Doc barely glanced at Tuttle and Carter. He went straight to his brother and examined the wound. "Looks like the bullet is lodged just beneath the ribs, but it'll take an X-ray to be certain." He eyed the gun in Miranda's hand. "Who shot him?"

"Tuttle." Her voice registered flat anger. "The blood. I tried to stop it, but every time he moves, it starts again."

She kept the gun on Tuttle and Carter, and they watched her and Doc, with a certain eagerness. "What took you so long getting here?" Miranda asked Doc as he opened his black bag and started removing supplies.

"Cheryl had an emergency with the company. One of the men was struck by a falling tree. I was out on the site when I got the call to come up here. The guy was bleeding pretty bad, and it looked for a while like he might lose his leg."

"There seems to be an awful lot of accidents around Tabuga Springs." Miranda watched him carefully as he treated Tom's wounds.

"Folks around here live closer to nature than city people," Doc said. "Working the land, especially the rugged terrain in this area, can be dangerous."

"Real dangerous," Tuttle said, laughing.

Doc rocked back on his heels and eyed the two men who were sitting on the floor once again. "What's going on here?" He looked from Tom to Miranda. "No, don't tell me. Let's get Tom to the clinic where I can clean out that wound."

Doc reached into the bag and pulled out a syringe and a bottle of medicine. He quickly filled the syringe with a clear fluid.

"What's that?" Miranda asked, an edge to her voice.

"A little something for the pain. Tom's not as tough as he thinks he is. When we move him, he's going to be hurting."

"I don't think he should have that," Miranda said. "No. No shots."

Weak but still able to smile, Tom motioned her over to him. "It's okay," he whispered, "I'm not afraid of shots."

"It isn't that, it's..." She looked at Doc, and then at Tuttle and Carter.

"Miranda, Tom needs this," Doc said softly. "I know you're worried about him, but this will help. And then I'll help you straighten out whatever mess this is."

"Give the shot to Tuttle first."

"What?" Doc looked at her with a worried frown.

"Listen, I know you're in this up to your eyeballs. I found your books. I don't know if you're desperate enough to hurt your brother or not, but I'm not willing to risk it."

"Miranda!" Tom tried to rise up on his elbows, but he dropped back against the wall. "What are you saying?"

"I wanted to tell you, but there wasn't time. I've had my suspicions all along. Yesterday I sneaked into Doc's clinic and went through his books. He's in a lot of trouble. Ask him."

Tom looked at his brother. "Is it true, Doc?"

Still holding the syringe, Doc stood. "Not exactly." He shifted his weight slowly from one foot to another. A tiny drop of clear fluid dripped from the needle.

"Doc!" Tom finally managed to push himself up the wall. "Why didn't you tell me you were in debt? I would have helped."

"I didn't tell you about the debts because I was tired of coming to you, Tom." He smiled, then shook his head. "I wanted to do it myself. That's why I was so excited about the development company. It looked like the perfect way to bring in enough cash to pay off my debts. Besides—" he looked at Miranda "—the debts aren't that bad, really."

"I saw them," Miranda countered. "You're losing everything. Cheryl showed them to me because she was so upset."

"Where were the books?" Doc's voice was too soft, too injured.

"In the library." Miranda couldn't believe he'd given up so easily. He didn't even try to deny it.

"So you believe I've double-crossed you for money?" Doc asked his brother.

"I'm not certain what I believe," Tom said honestly. "We need to sit down and talk this out."

Doc lifted the syringe. "All of this talk doesn't negate Tom's need for this painkiller."

"No!" Miranda insisted. She swung the gun at Doc. "I mean it. Two men are dead and I'm not risking Tom."

"She can't watch all three of us," Tuttle said loudly.

"No, but I can certainly kill one of you." She swung the gun back at him.

"How deep are you in this?" Tom asked softly. His gaze was locked on his brother's.

Doc smiled. "We've gotten pretty close these last few years. How deep do you think I'm capable?"

Miranda watched the terrible moment between the brothers from the corner of her eye. Tuttle and Carter moved closer together, and Tuttle started to rise to his feet.

"Sit down." She carefully pulled the trigger. The bullet tore into the wooden floor beside Tuttle. "I'll shoot you. And I'm a damn good shot."

"What about Fremont?" Tom asked his brother.

"I knew about the money you paid him to get me out of the draft. I've known for a long time."

Tears welled in Miranda's eyes, and she brushed them away with the back of her hand.

She saw the motion out of the corner of her eyes. Reacting on instinct, she brought the gun down and ducked, but the weight of a heavy body crashed her into the wall. Sheriff Uley Carter's full weight nearly crushed her.

She felt the gun slip from her fingers. Twisting as hard as she could, she dropped to one knee in an effort to dodge Carter and recover the gun. But Carter's crushing weight followed her, pinning her to the floor.

"What the hell?" The cry was almost in her ear, and she felt Carter jerk upward. He rolled off her, scrambling to his knees with an amazed expression on his face.

"What the hell, Doc?"

Doc stood over him, the empty syringe in his hand. Carter looked down at his arm and rubbed the spot where the needle had entered. Without changing expression, he tumbled to his side in a boneless heap.

MIRANDA RETRIEVED the gun and backed against the wall. With her free hand she helped Tom struggle to his feet.

"Doc!" Tom looked at his brother with sorrow. "How could you?"

Amazement shifted onto Doc's face. "He isn't dead! Did you think I'd kill him? With the same medication I was about to give you?"

Miranda bent over Carter's body and felt a strong pulse in his neck. "He isn't dead!"

"You really thought . . ." Doc looked at both of them with anger, then defeat. "You thought I'd actually give Tom something that would hurt him?" he asked softly.

"You're in so deep," Miranda finally answered when Tom did not. "We know you're desperate, but I called you to help Tom because I knew you would do the right thing. Deep inside, I knew you couldn't hurt your brother, it's just that..." She pointed the gun at Tuttle. "Can you give him one of those shots, too?"

Doc eyed the other man with speculation. "That might not be a bad idea. Keep the gun on him and don't hesitate to shoot him in the leg if he gives any trouble."

"Wait a minute. Somebody's coming down the drive," Miranda cautioned.

"Who is it?" Doc asked, busy with the medicines.

"I think it's Cheryl." Miranda felt her hopes rise. The redhead would be an ally, and one she could sorely use. She still didn't trust Doc completely. "Yeah, that's her car."

Doc shook his head. "She should have waited in town."

Miranda went to the cabin doorway and began to wave. "Hey! We're in here."

The redhead bolted out of the car and ran up to the porch. "How's Doc?"

"We're all okay. Come on in, just watch out for Tuttle." When they were both inside, Miranda nodded to the telephone. "Maybe we should go ahead and call the authorities. Someone on a federal level since Carter is so deeply involved."

Looking at Tom's bloody clothes and the unconscious Carter, Cheryl went to the receiver. "That sounds like a really sensible suggestion. Then maybe someone could tell me what's going on here." She rattled the switch hook and asked for an operator. In a clear voice she asked for the FBI.

"If ever in my life I needed a drink, it's now," Doc said with a twisted smile on his face. He went and stood by Cheryl as she dialed the phone. "The irony has not escaped me," he said softly. She turned slightly away from him.

When she was finished, she looked at Miranda, completely ignoring Doc. "What's going on?"

"It's a long story," Miranda said. "It would be better if we waited until the authorities come." She felt her emotions rising as she looked at the two of them. Doc's love was so plain to see.

Tuttle sprang to his feet. "Traitor!" he yelled, advancing toward Doc and Cheryl. "You'd better do something and make it quick."

Miranda pulled the trigger, squeezing off a bullet that tore at the door frame beside Tuttle's head. He instinctively dropped back.

"I'll kill you. This time there won't be any doubt," she warned him.

Before the big man could protest, Doc stabbed the needle into his arm. He, too, was on the floor in a matter of seconds.

"You can relax now, Miranda," Doc said softly. "Both you and Tom have had a rough time." He looked at his brother. "And you shouldn't be standing."

"How long will it take those agents to get here?" Cheryl asked Tom. Doc was staring at her, but she wouldn't return his look.

Tom shifted his weight before he answered. "I'd guess the FBI has air and ground units all over Laurel County. Someone should be here soon." He looked at Doc. "It isn't much time, but I'd appreciate hearing this story from you. I never would have believed you would go to such lengths."

"I don't think you have much to worry about." Doc looked at Tom.

"And Fremont?" Tom asked. He pushed off the wall so he was standing without support. "Did you order him killed?"

"Cheryl said you were with him the night he died," Miranda threw in.

Doc's gaze shifted to the slender redhead, where it remained for a full minute. To Miranda's surprise there was no anger in the look, only sadness.

Cheryl slipped beside Miranda, her arm giving Miranda's weary shoulders a hug of support. "I'll take the gun now. You look like you're about to drop. I know what to do," she added as she gently removed the weapon from Miranda's exhausted grip.

Watching the interaction between the women, Doc sighed. "I was with Fremont, at Cheryl's suggestion. She thought I might be able to talk him into approving the dam system. Remember, Tom, she's a third of the partnership, too."

"That's right, Doc. We're all in this together, aren't we?" She brought the barrel of the gun up so that all three of them were pinned in her sights.

"Cheryl?" Miranda couldn't believe what she saw. She looked at Tom and saw a new understanding, and a deep relief, sweep over his features.

"Well, Doc, the cards are finally on the table," Tom said. "And I'm telling you, I like this hand a lot better than I thought I would."

"Don't get too sure of yourself," Cheryl warned. "Nothing has changed, at least not for you. You two—" she swung the barrel back and forth rapidly between Tom and Miranda "—were destined to die in this cabin. Doc, well, he was going to be a handy scapegoat, but he can die here, too. It isn't as tidy, but we can make it work." She looked at Doc without any emotion at all. "Drag Tuttle and Carter out of here. I should leave them, too, but they've been useful in the past."

"Who are you?" Doc asked her softly. "How could I be so wrong about you? I honestly loved you."

"More's the pity," Cheryl said coolly. "Love is the most dangerous emotion of all."

"I've learned that," Doc said, "but what I don't understand is why. We had a good company. We were earning money. Sure, I borrowed against the clinic to build a new one—at your insistence. But I'm not in financial trouble. You had fake books set up to show Miranda, didn't you?"

"It doesn't matter now." Cheryl shook her head. "The dams are going to be built." She glared at Miranda. "How does that suit you, Miranda Conner? The Tabuga will be dammed, and I'll become a wealthy woman."

"You could have become wealthy without hurting so many people," Tom said softly. "Why are you doing this?"

"You don't have a clue, do you?" Cheryl asked bitterly. "But she does. Old scores are the best ones to even up, aren't they, Miranda?"

"What are you talking about? I've never seen you before in my life until I came up here for this WDC project."

"Such a short memory." A mean smile pulled at the corners of her mouth. "But I'll bet you remember this person." She walked backward, still keeping the gun steadily aimed at them. When she reached the door, she pushed it open.

A tall, muscular man with long dark hair stepped into the room. His gaze fell on Miranda, and held hers. "Hello," he said slowly, "don't tell me you've forgotten me? After all we shared. After all those years I spent in prison!" He stepped toward her as if he wanted to strike her, but he stopped short.

"Gregory." Miranda felt the word escape her lips, but she didn't truly believe it. She suddenly knew who the man outside her apartment had been. She recognized the vaguely familiar voice in the phone calls.

"How long has it been?" he asked.

When she started to answer, he interrupted. "No! Let me tell you how long it's been. There was the arrest. Then the trial, which was dragged out over four months. But you know that, don't you? You know it because you testified against me. Right?"

"Gregory, I . . ."

He slashed his hand through the air, silencing her.

Beside her, Miranda felt Tom begin to tense. She had to stop him from doing anything rash. Gregory was a strong man, and she could tell by looking at him that he was capable of just about anything.

"Then there was the prison sentence." Gregory paced the length of the cabin, then returned to stand in front of her. "Do you know that the punishment for being convicted of attempting to sabotage the government is harsher than capital murder, in most cases? Good thing that Senator Fremont took an interest in my case." He smiled at Cheryl. "Lucky thing my wife made sure he was paid to take an interest in me."

Miranda could see the barely controlled rage rising in the man who stood before her. "I never meant to hurt you. I only did what I had to do, Gregory. It was wrong to bomb that building..."

"And we would have gotten away with it if you hadn't ratted on us."

"I never meant to hurt you," she repeated calmly. "I was in love with you. It almost killed me."

"Oh, did it? You seemed to talk very freely as I recall. I almost thought perhaps you'd been paid."

"That's not true!" Miranda started forward. As she did, Doc jumped at Cheryl. With the quickness of a cat, she backed out of his reach and brought the gun down on the side of his head.

"Doc!" Miranda started toward him, but Gregory's hand on her arm stopped her.

"Leave him," he commanded.

"He's not hurt," Cheryl said as she watched Doc slowly sit up, a dazed expression on his face. "But if he tries that again, he's going to be dead."

"You'd better get out of here while you still can," Tom said suddenly. "I wasn't kidding about those agents. The county is crawling with them."

"I never made the call." Cheryl smiled at her own cleverness. "I never really dialed. The whole thing was a fake. We're all alone, and no one knows where any of you are. No one at all." She nudged Doc with her foot. "Now drag Carter and Tuttle out of here, like I told you before." She switched her glance to Gregory. "We'll kill them and blow up the cabin."

"Why are you doing this, Cheryl?" Miranda asked suddenly. "I understand Gregory's anger. Even though it isn't justified, his anger comes from a mutual past. Why are you involved?"

Gregory didn't give her a chance to answer. He burst in with a long, ugly laugh. "Oh, I wasn't the only one who did prison time, Miranda. Did you think it was only me? No, there were three others. Accomplices. One of them was Cheryl's brother."

"Remember the tall, skinny guy with red hair? He used to play the guitar and sing."

A vague memory touched Miranda. There had been such a boy. He was so quiet and shy. She'd never known he was involved in the bombing. He'd turned up on the river late in the summer and disappeared shortly before the bombing took place. He'd loved the song "Bad Moon Rising." She knew then that Cheryl had set the leg trap in an effort to maim or kill her. "His name was Bobby, but he didn't stay around for the bombing. He left. He was fine."

"He went to scout out the area. Oh, he was involved in a minimal kind of way. But the price he paid wasn't minimal!" Cheryl's voice rose. "Only Bobby wasn't able to handle prison, once you sent him there. He was just a kid, and he was a prime target for a lot of those older guys. He hung himself with his own bedsheet."

"I'm sorry." Miranda was stunned. The image of the redheaded youth and his plaintive voice came back to her, echoing off the rocks of the Tabuga. "He loved the river so. I remember that."

"And I loved him!" Cheryl moved closer. "And I vowed that one day you'd pay. When I met Gregory on one of my jail visits to Bobby, we became friends."

"And now we're partners," Gregory said, smiling.

"That's right." Cheryl looked at Doc.

The impact of Cheryl's words made Doc turn away. "You went to a lot of trouble for a little revenge," Doc said, his gaze lingering out the cabin window.

"Not only revenge." Gregory smiled. "Once you and Tom are dead, Cheryl becomes the sole owner of the development company. And with Ms. Conner's stunt of trying to pull a scam with those fish, the WDC is the laughing stock of Congress. The murders of Elton and Fremont have virtually assured us that the dam project will pass without a bit of trouble. We're going to be a very, very rich couple."

"There was a time when money didn't matter to you, Gregory," Miranda said softly. "Have you really left so much of yourself behind?"

"You bet! I left a great deal of myself in that prison, and now I have to make up for all that lost time."

"All these years I've felt terrible about what happened." She took two steps toward him. "I never thought you were a bad person at all, just misguided. I thought that you believed so deeply in preserving the planet that you were willing to commit a radical act. I was wrong about everything, though, wasn't I?"

"You ratted on your friends, and they went to prison while you went off to college. That's not exactly fair," Cheryl accused.

"And Gordon Simms?" Tom asked suddenly. "How did he get involved in this?"

"Gordon has testified at several congressional hearings. I think he's what's known as a professional witness, one with a price. See, he's given false testimony before. We knew a combination of pay and blackmail would work very effectively on him. We found him first, and then Cheryl planted the idea of the raft trip with Tom." Gregory grinned. "It was a simple matter to intercept the cash donation and insert our little list of demands. Gordon really had you going with that fake attack business. He deserves an Oscar."

"He was working for you all the time." Miranda was amazed. The biologist had seemed so sincerely interested in the river. "What about the darters?"

"You'll love this!" Gregory's face lit up. "They're real! That's what makes it all so interesting. I found them at the end of spring when Cheryl and I were camping. I had a friend of a friend of a friend run the test—extinct species. You had the key the entire time."

"Cynthia and Russ were just a ruse to hide Gordon Simms and Fred Elton, weren't they?" Miranda asked. She remembered Russ's call. He'd been trying to tell her something about the past. Well, now she knew what it was.

"Yes, you and Simms were the key players," Gregory said. "I knew you couldn't resist. I've thought about this for years."

"And you killed Elton and Fremont." Tom pointed at Gregory. "Fred found out about Simms, and Fremont got too greedy, right?"

"Almost!" Gregory laughed. "Fremont got cold feet when he began to suspect how far we'd go. He was distressed by Fred Elton's murder, and he never believed you or Miranda did it. He was getting too warm, and even as deeply as he was involved, he would have blown the whistle on us."

"You've thought it out pretty well, haven't you?" Doc asked.

"We've spent a lot of time planning this. We've spent years when I had nothing but time," Gregory said.

"Gregory, could I have a word with you? Alone?" Miranda asked suddenly.

"No!" Cheryl answered. "It's a trick."

Miranda shrugged her shoulders. "How dangerous could an unarmed woman be?" Behind her back she reached down to squeeze Tom's hand before she continued. "There was a time, Gregory, when we were able to talk. I'm only asking for a few moments now."

"Don't listen to her," Cheryl demanded. "It's some trick she's trying to pull."

"What do you want, Miranda?" he asked.

"I want a chance to explain, to try and make you see that what I did wasn't meant to hurt you. I wanted to be...part of the bombing. I wanted to believe that it would make life better. But I couldn't. I still don't."

Looking at the man that Gregory Henson had become, she could still see a remnant of the charismatic youth who'd led a troupe of semiadults on a river adventure.

"Gregory, I'm appealing to the man who loved the Tabuga River as much as I did. Don't you remember the nights we camped out and the sound of the river? We believed we could make a difference. Or at least I believed it."

Gregory shot an uncomfortable look at Cheryl. "Come outside for a moment," he said as he took Miranda's arm.

"Greg!" Cheryl waved the gun at him. Her control was fast disappearing. "We've gone too far to turn back now. We've waited too long for this!" Her voice rose higher. "Two men are dead! We can't back out now."

"I only want to talk with her a moment," Gregory said softly. He went to Cheryl and touched her face. "Nothing has changed. Don't worry. Nothing has changed."

Gripping his injured side, Tom hurled himself from the wall with as much velocity as he could manage. He knocked Miranda to the side as he barreled headlong, pushing Gregory on top of Cheryl.

The discharge of the weapon was muffled by Gregory's body. He grunted softly as the bullet tore into his chest.

Tom rolled sideways to the floor, his hands pressing his side where a new flow of blood had begun. Gregory's weight pushed Cheryl backward, and she tripped over a chair. She sprawled on the floor with Gregory on top of her.

There was a sound of footsteps on the porch, and the cabin door flew open. "Everybody hold it!"

Miranda looked up, expecting to see FBI agents. Instead, Clark Presley and his son, Jason, stood in the doorway, hunting rifles aimed at everyone.

"Well, it looks like Tom's gone and gotten himself shot," Clark said as he stepped into the room, weapon still pointed. "Give him a hand, Jason."

Cheryl's high-pitched wail echoed off the cabin walls. "Oh my God, Gregory's hurt! Somebody help me. He's hurt."

Miranda bent over the still body of Gregory Henson. There was no pulse at his neck, and she could see the blood from the chest wound spreading over Cheryl's clothes. Beneath the body Cheryl Summers screamed over and over again.

"Cheryl." Doc went to her. With Jason Presley's help, they moved the body away. "I'm going to give you something to help you relax," Doc said, speaking to her as gently as if she were a child. He withdrew another syringe from his medical bag and administered the sedative. "Now relax," he said, leading her to a chair where Gregory's body was obscured.

"Tom?" Miranda pressed her hand to the wound. He'd lost so much blood. She touched his pale face with her fingers, then her lips.

"I'm fine," he said, nodding toward the phone. "Make that call to the FBI."

She placed the call, giving a brief but succinct summation of the events. Tom had been correct in his assumptions that units were nearby. She was assured that help would soon be there. Then she turned to Doc. He was sitting beside Cheryl, gently holding her hand as she gazed blankly at a wall. "Are you going to be okay?" Miranda put her hand on his shoulder.

"In time," he said. His eyes which looked so much like Tom's, held pain. "In time."

"We have a lot to learn about each other," she whispered, kissing him softly on the cheek. "I'm so sorry this has happened."

"I loved her so much," Doc answered. "I don't understand. Would you mind leaving us alone for a few moments?"

Tom motioned Miranda over to his side. "Let's take a little walk, shall we? Clark and Jason can sit on the porch and guard Tuttle and Carter, should they come around."

"We'll listen for them," Clark agreed. "It's going to give me great pleasure to turn them over to the feds. I'd say they'll get a minimum of twenty years each."

"The charges are serious, especially for Carter," Tom said as he put his arm around Miranda's shoulders. "Now if you two will excuse me and Miranda."

Miranda eyed the wound in his side. "Maybe we shouldn't."

"Let's go," he insisted, nodding at Doc and Cheryl.

Stepping into the fresh air outside the cabin was one of the best things Miranda had ever experienced, especially with Tom at her side. The woods beckoned them, and they walked slowly until they were alone.

"I guess I owe Doc an apology," Tom said.

"Me, too. I was really sure he was at the bottom of everything."

"This will be hard on him. He really loved Cheryl, and the fact that I suspected him—well, we've got a lot of work."

Miranda picked up Tom's hand and held it as she faced him. "I think Doc will understand how we came to suspect him. I mean, the setup was pretty good."

"Yes, it was pretty slick. So what are you going to do? I mean, what's the next step?"

"I think a hearing on the Tabuga will be the first order of business. We'll have to prove that Gordon lied about the darter. We both know that it does exist." She gave a wide grin. "We have a strong case to stop the dam."

"And after that?"

"How about a long, leisurely camping trip on the wild and free Tabuga River?"

"Maybe we could search for the elusive albino buck, or some mermaids?"

"Sounds good to me." She stood on tiptoe and kissed his cheek. "Anything we do together sounds good to me."

Tom's expression changed to one of concern.

"What?" she asked.

"I don't think I can do that." He shook his head. "No, I'm sorry, I can't."

"Why not?" She searched his eyes. Was he feeling much worse?

"I've made a new rule in my life. I don't go camping with women who aren't related to me by marriage, especially not ones who ride down Pennsylvania Avenue on white horses. So, unless you agree to marry me, we'll have to shelve the camping trip."

"That's not exactly the proposal I dreamed of, but since it's coming from a wounded man, I feel obligated to accept."

"Obligated?"

"My heart would never forgive me if I refused."

Summer Reading
At Its Best

In July, Harlequin and Silhouette bring readers the Big Summer
Read Program. Heat up your summer with these four exciting
new novels by top Harlequin and Silhouette authors.

SOMEWHERE IN TIME by Barbara Bretton
YESTERDAY COMES TOMORROW by Rebecca Flanders
A DAY IN APRIL by Mary Lynn Baxter
LOVE CHILD by Patricia Coughlin

From time travel to fame and fortune, this program offers
something for everyone.

Available at your favorite retail outlet.

BSR

Harlequin Intrigue®

COMING NEXT MONTH

#187 SARABANDE by Madelyn Sanders
After spending her first night in Sandor Szelazeny's
spooky house in North Carolina, Bruce MacLaren
sensed that something was very wrong. But she
didn't heed the warning. And when Sandor spoke
of a curse he'd inherited from Transylvanian
ancestors, nothing daunted Bruce more than the
prospect of exploring that dark mystery. But the
alternative was worse. For Bruce knew with chilling
certainty that love for Sandor had put her life
in peril.

#188 BAYOU MOON by Rebecca York
Louisiana's bayous bred mystery and danger.
Investigating a drowning in Savannah Bayou,
Tess Beaumont was knee-deep in both of them—
and on a collision course with the victim's brother.
Vance Gautreau was a hard-bitten, dangerous man
with a demanding mind and a savage heart. Tess
was a stranger to a society that lived by its own
rules—and died by them. And in the bayou, she
learned, passion was deadlier than hate.

® **Harlequin**®

JANELLE TAYLOR

Valley of Fire

HARLEQUIN IS PROUD TO PRESENT *VALLEY OF FIRE* **BY JANELLE TAYLOR—AUTHOR OF TWENTY-TWO BOOKS, INCLUDING SIX** *NEW YORK TIMES* **BESTSELLERS**

VALLEY OF FIRE—the warm and passionate story of Kathy Alexander, a famous romance author, and Steven Winngate, entrepreneur and owner of the magazine that intended to expose the real Kathy "Brandy" Alexander to her fans.

Don't miss VALLEY OF FIRE, available in May.